April — 2008

DEADLY BONES

Su Katy —

As A lover of
mysteries, I
hope you love
this one —

Bovir

A JAKE WANDERMAN MYSTERY

DEADLY BONES

BORIS RISKIN

FIVE STAR
A part of Gale, Cengage Learning

GALE
CENGAGE Learning™

Detroit • New York • San Francisco • New Haven, Conn • Waterville, Maine • London

Set in 11 pt. Plantin.
Printed on permanent paper.

LIBRARY OF CONGRESS CATALOGING-IN-PUBLICATION DATA

Riskin, Boris.
    Deadly bones : a Jake Wanderman mystery / Boris Riskin. —
1st ed.
        p. cm.
    ISBN-13: 978-1-59414-715-9 (hardcover : alk. paper)
    ISBN-10: 1-59414-715-9 (hardcover: alk. paper)
    1. Retired teachers—Fiction. 2. Murder—Investigation—Fiction. 3. Theft of relics—Fiction. I. Title.
PS3618.I73D43 2008
813'.6—dc22   2008032113

First Edition. First Printing: November 2008.
Published in 2008 in conjunction with Tekno Books and Ed Gorman.

Printed in the United States of America
1 2 3 4 5 6 7 12 11 10 09 08

DEDICATION

This work is dedicated to my wife, Kiki. Her talent as an artist and her human spirit remain unsurpassed by anyone else I have ever known. I have no doubt that without her, my life would have been dull and uninteresting. She made it fun and exciting.

It is also dedicated to my loving family: Faith, my daughter; my son, Harold and his wife, Caren; my grandchildren: Aaron, Russell, Alex, Joshua and Bradley; and my sweet great-granddaughter, Hannah (at last a girl in the family).

I am most grateful for their love, support and enthusiasm for my work.

DEDICATION

ACKNOWLEDGMENTS

There are many who helped me by giving me their time, knowledge and advice.

Foremost are those dedicated writers who form the Ashawagh Hall Writers Workshop, led by the indomitable and brilliant Maryjane Meaker, also known to thousands of Young Adult readers as M.E. Kerr. Their astute comments and analysis of my work greatly contributed to the manuscript's actually being written, as well as how it was written. They provided me with advice and encouragement, sorely needed by every writer in the world.

Expert advice on medical matters came from my brother-in-law, Dr. Joseph Greenberg. Sergeant Vincent Posillipo of the Suffolk County Homicide Division, provided me with knowledge of the workings of a large Homicide Department. Thomas Fabiano, the Chief of Police of Sag Harbor, took the time to give me details of the workings of a village police department. Leonard Stein took me on a personal tour of Jerusalem and showed me sights I would not have seen on my own. Innumerable friends gave me valuable insights and much encouragement: Dr. Estelle Gellman, Gloria Beckerman, Stacey Donovan, Sandy Husick. I hope others whom I've neglected to mention will forgive me.

PROLOGUE

Cormac Blather was upset. He'd just gotten an e-mail from Jerusalem advising him that the IAA, the Israel Antiquities Authority, was questioning several artifacts that were on the world market. What distressed Cormac was that he had just sold one of those artifacts to his best client, a man in the top twenty of Forbes 400 *richest.*

He stared out the window of his antique shop on Main Street in Sag Harbor. He'd sold Bryson Mergenthaler a limestone burial box or ossuary. They were used to contain the bones of the dead in Jewish burial ceremonies thousands of years ago.

The sender of the e-mail was a dealer and friend for many years. He'd bought the ossuary from him, knowing it was a forgery. He'd agreed to invest in it because it was an unusual opportunity. The box itself had been checked out and determined to be from the time of the First Temple. What was needed was something to indicate it had held the bones of someone important. His friend had come up with James, the brother of Jesus. Drawings had been added to the box, along with other markings. In addition to the engraver's efforts, documents had to be forged, experts persuaded to help authenticate it. These procedures entailed the outlay of more than a hundred thousand dollars, shared by Cormac and his dealer friend.

Perhaps it was the amount of his investment that had spurred Cormac to sell it to Mergenthaler. Or perhaps it was his pleasure to see this powerful man deceived. Whatever the reason, and he suspected his ego was involved as well, if this client had somehow learned that anything he had purchased from Cormac was a fake, that would be

9

very bad news indeed. Mergenthaler had a fearsome reputation in the business world. He was a dangerous man.

Cormac kept moving around the shop, unable to keep still. He felt somewhat like the chickadees he used to watch as a child from his bedroom window in the borough of Bromley, not far from the part of London where his father worked in a furniture store. Confidence, not nervousness, was more his style.

His antique business covered a wide spectrum, from Louis XIV furniture to Tiffany glass to Renaissance paintings to statuary from Tutankhamen's tomb. It is true that along the way he may have handled some items whose origin could not be strictly accounted for. This had begun with his access to looted Nazi art and had more or less continued ever since. But his clients were understanding. They recognized that some things could only be attained in a certain manner and they were quite willing to abide by the unstated but recognized rules, the most important one being keep your mouth shut.

Years before, when he conducted business in London, he'd let greed overcome his intelligence. And now he might have done it again. Too irresistible. But stupid, stupid, stupid, he told himself. Most of what he'd sold Mergenthaler had been genuine. But then he had slipped in a fake Tintoretto and a more modern Picasso without a problem.

The sudden ring of the telephone startled him.

"Mr. Blather?"

"Yes."

"This is Landis Kalem, Mr. Mergenthaler's secretary."

"Yes?"

"Mr. Mergenthaler would like you to come to his home this evening at seven p.m."

Blather felt a ringing in his ears. "Tonight?"

"Yes. This evening. Seven p.m. Is that satisfactory?"

"Of course. I shall be there."

"Good." The phone clicked.

Now what? What was there to do? He could try claiming that he had been a victim himself. Had no idea anything was fraudulent. Offer to repay. It hadn't worked in London. But it might work here. After all, there was no publicity. No stories in the media. No one had been caught for forging masterpieces or faking antiquities.

Not yet, anyway. He realized now how very important that was. It was one loophole he had to close immediately. He had to make contact with his current forger of paintings. First, have him cease working on the latest forgery, a cubist work in the style of Braque. Then get him to understand that he had better keep his mouth shut or the consequences would be dire. Better yet. He would give the man money to leave town. And as quickly as possible, meaning right now. He was sure he could convince him, although the forger was a rather peculiar individual, given to odd behavior. Cormac had visited him once and found him painting in the nude. But what artist was without eccentricities?

As far as his man in Jerusalem was concerned, he was nothing, if not prudent, and would do all in his power to quash any investigation.

He picked up the phone to call the artist and put the phone down. Better to do this in person. He thought about locking up right away, then decided against it. He would wait until later. He would see the painter first, and proceed to Mergenthaler. That way he would have an opportunity to dine. He didn't function well on an empty stomach.

Customers coming in made the time pass more easily. Several hours later he was preparing to leave when the door opened and a man entered. Cormac had installed a bell on the door that jingled when it was opened. He thought it was a nice old-fashioned touch. It was dusk and he hadn't yet turned on the lights so it was difficult to make out what the person looked like.

The man approached him. He wore a cap pulled down and a scarf that covered the lower half of his face. "Good evening, Mr. Blather."

The man's voice was muffled by the scarf but he seemed to have an accent that Cormac couldn't quite place. There was something

11

familiar about him. "Yes?" he said.

The man pulled the scarf down so that his face was exposed.

"What are you doing here?" Cormac said. "I thought—"

"I came to do something I should have done a long time ago," the man said, and his hand came out of his pocket with a rapid movement.

Cormac felt something sting him in the chest. First, surprise. Then he felt an enormous pain and realized he'd been stabbed. There was another thrust, then another, and another. He opened his mouth to say something, but no sound emerged. He crumpled to the floor and was still, the pain gradually diminishing. He didn't understand why this man had attacked him. Why? he thought. I hardly know him.

He had no more time to think because in another moment he was dead.

The killer went to the door and turned the sign hanging there to show that the store was closed. He locked the door, then dragged the body so that it was out of sight. There was a trail of blood on the floor. He didn't worry about footprints because he'd worn plastic booties over his shoes. Next he went to Cormac's small office and switched on the desk lamp. He had no need to be concerned about fingerprints either because he had taken the precaution of wearing disposable gloves. The coat he wore would be disposed of as well. He ignored the file cabinets and the drawers of the desk. He looked at what was on top of the desk but did not find what he was looking for. He went back to the shop and took a small flashlight out of his pocket. He sent the beam over the walls. He still did not find the object of his search. He went back to the office and threw the light on the walls near the desk. "Ah," he muttered. "I should have looked here first." He took a painting off the wall. It was not more than eight inches square. He held it under the light so he could look at it. The painting was a miniature version of Sandro Botticelli's Birth of Venus where the nude Venus is standing on a shell, emerging from the pale blue sea from which she was born. It was a masterful piece of work. Even in that light he could see the incredible detail and beauty of the original. Only the signature was not that of Botticelli.

He turned off the lamp and left the store, holding the painting flat against his body with one hand to keep it as hidden from view as possible.

The bell jingled when he closed the door but no one was there to hear it.

CHAPTER 1

It was Sunday morning, for so many years my favorite time of the week: WMNR playing beautiful music, in this case, Mahler's Symphony #2, conducted by Bernstein; scrambled eggs and bacon; the *New York Times* spread out on the floor around me; a mug of black coffee in my hand.

When the phone rang I waited for my wife, Rosalind, to pick it up the way she always did. She liked to answer the phone. I didn't. Then it hit me. Rosalind wasn't going to answer the phone.

As usual, lines from Shakespeare popped into my head. They'd been there before. I couldn't get them out:

> *Cry woe, destruction, ruin and decay;*
> *The worst is death, and death will have his day.*

"Good morning," I said.

"Did you hear the news?" my father said, and didn't wait for me to answer. "Cormac Blather's dead. Looks like he was murdered."

"When did this happen?" I grabbed the remote and switched on the TV to Channel 12, our local station. They were talking about the weather.

"I'm not sure but I can't believe it, sonny. Killed in his own shop by a person or persons unknown." My dad had a tendency to speak in sound bites. He knew Cormac well because Dad and his girlfriend, Zeena, had become quite involved in the stolen Fabergé eggs situation.

"That's terrible news," I said.

"Death, be not proud," he said.

It would have been a weird comment from anyone else, but I knew what he meant. He was referring to Rosalind. He'd loved her like a daughter. He'd been terribly upset about her sudden death. He and Zeena had come out at that time to stay with me. But they had their own lives to live back in the city, and when the *shiva,* the seven days of mourning, was over, they went home.

"Who do you think killed him?" he asked. "Do you think it might have been one of the Russians?"

"I don't have any idea. But I doubt it was the Russians. They got everything they wanted. At least the big shots did."

"Exactly. But what about Solofsky? He could be the type to hold a grudge."

Jascha Solofsky was a mobster who had lost out on his share of the stolen Fabergé eggs. "True. But my guess is he's too busy watching his back in jail to bother getting involved in something that could possibly give him more trouble."

"I'm not so sure. He's a guy who could want revenge even from a jail cell. If I were you I'd be very careful."

"I will."

"How do you feel otherwise?"

"I'm upset, of course. I liked Blather."

"I know you did. Me, too."

He wished me well and I sent my love to Zeena.

After we'd hung up I thought about my father's suggestion that Solofsky might have killed Cormac to get even. In that case I'd be on his list, too. Even though it was possible I didn't buy it. What I did think was that Cormac's past might have caught up with him from another source. Long ago he'd been involved with art looted by the Nazis. And he'd once, in an unexpected moment of candor, told me a story of how years back in London, an artist had produced forgeries for him.

Murder is rare in the Hamptons. There'd been a few that were drug related. They got a couple of lines in the "Police Blotter" section of the local papers. The only case that got real headlines was when a mega-rich dude named Ammon got himself murdered by his wife's lover, their electrician no less, a guy named Pelosi. That had all the right ingredients: moneyed class versus the working class, plus adultery and greed.

Cormac's murder would grab the media's attention because he was the father of the famous Toby Welch. That had come out during his involvement with those stolen Fabergé eggs. His role in that had not been exemplary but no charges were ever leveled against him since the eggs had been returned intact to the Armory Museum in the Kremlin from which they'd been taken.

I watched TV for a while. They showed the front of the shop with police tape at the door. They interviewed the Chief who had nothing much to say. The reporter gave some background on Cormac, but hadn't done her homework and only reported that he was the owner of an antique shop. She even got his name wrong.

CHAPTER 2

I called Toby. She and Rosalind had been close friends, and I'd come to like and respect her.

"I'm really sorry," I said. "In spite of everything, I admired your father. He was an unusual guy."

"It's so awful, Jake," she said. "Even though they knew who it was, I had to identify the body."

"That must have been rough. If you'd called me I would've gone with you."

"I never thought. I went with my P.A. She's good, but nothing like Rosalind. Rosalind was the best assistant I ever had." She began to sob. "Oh, Jake. It's so horrible. First Rosalind and now my father. It's too much to bear."

Her sobs caused my eyes to fill. "I know," I said. "Would it help if I came over for a while?"

"Would you? That would be so nice. I'd very much appreciate it."

She had a formal way of speaking that I used to find annoying and off-putting, but now it only amused me. She couldn't help herself. That was just who she was: competent, efficient, everything in the right place, even her words.

Toby's house was in the Georgica section of East Hampton which inevitably meant it had a gate and an intercom. I announced myself and went up the long driveway to the house. Her residence was not outlandish in the modern McMansion sense. Large, of course, but not ostentatious, the architecture, the landscaping, perfect in every detail.

Before I had a chance to ring the bell the front door opened. Standing there was Carlos, who with his wife Anita took care of most her needs. He was short, stocky with dark brown skin. When he spoke it was with a heavy Hispanic accent. He was from Ecuador, his wife, Anita, from Colombia. We'd met once before, in the middle of the Fabergé eggs deal when I'd come into the house and found them all bound and gagged. "She there," he said, raising his arm and pointing.

"In the kitchen?" I asked, recognizing the direction in which he'd pointed.

He nodded.

Toby's kitchen had often been on TV. She'd made a point of using it for her demonstrations. It had sea-foam colored cabinets, butterscotch walls, stainless steel appliances, refrigerated drawers, and an oversized work island.

I found Toby alone in that huge room, her elbows on the countertop, chin in her hands. As I expected, she was immaculately groomed, perfect makeup, dirty-blonde hair artfully unkempt. Her eyes followed me as I entered, but the rest of her body remained still. She looked at me but didn't say a word.

"What're you doing?" I asked.

"Nothing. Trying to get my head together. I like being in the kitchen. I'm most comfortable here."

She was sitting on a barstool. I pulled one over and sat next to her. "It's tough being an orphan," I said.

"Omigod," she said. "I never even realized that."

"It seems impossible now, but you'll adjust." I took one of her hands in mine. "Knowing you, I'd be willing to bet you'll adjust better than most."

She took her hand away. "Oh sure. Superwoman, right? That's what I'm supposed to be. There is nothing I cannot handle. Nothing I cannot deal with. Well, let me tell you something. I am not Superwoman. I cannot handle this. I do not want to handle this. I want to cry and be miserable."

"Go ahead. Probably be good for you."

"Don't think I haven't. I was up all night." She stood and began pacing.

Toby was six feet tall, an imposing presence. In spite of her looks and her reputation, I saw a vulnerability I'd never noticed before. You couldn't say it was a frailty, nothing about Toby could ever be frail. But somehow she seemed to shrink a little in size.

"Did they tell you anything?" I asked. "Like how he was killed? And do they have any idea who did it?"

"He was murdered. That's all I know. They wouldn't tell me anything else. At least for now. They said they were keeping all that kind of information to themselves. And they asked *me* if I had any ideas. If I knew anyone who might have a reason to do such a thing."

"And do you?"

"Of course not. What kind of question is that? Why would anyone want to murder my father? What could he have done to deserve being killed?"

"That's just what the cops would like to know."

"They did say that it didn't look as if anything was stolen. Although they couldn't really tell because they didn't know what was in his inventory. They asked me if I had any knowledge in that regard, and of course I had no idea what he had. I don't think I was even in his shop more than a few times."

"So they wouldn't know if one or two items were taken," I said. "Maybe he had something really valuable. Is that possible?"

"Anything is possible. But why would they kill him? Why not just steal it?"

"He might have known the thief. Maybe they got into an argument."

"I suppose that's a possibility." She went to the sink, came back with a sponge and a paper towel. She carefully rubbed the sponge over something on the Delft tile countertop, then wiped the spot with the towel. "I'm not sure if I should mention this but—" she paused.

"Something you didn't tell the police?"

"You knew my father, so it won't be much of a surprise to you. I had the feeling he was getting up to his old tricks again."

"Stolen art? Forged art?"

"I'm not sure. I don't know what it was, but I noticed a change in him. For a long time after he moved in with me he was listless. He went back to work but he didn't seem to have an interest in it anymore. It was like he had no real reason to leave the house. And then it changed. He seemed to get back his old spirit. He moved his shop to Sag Harbor. He left here and went back to live in his own house. He had a spring in his step, a light in his eyes. When we had our weekly dinner together I asked him what happened. He said it was nothing specific. He guessed it had just taken time to get over all the bad things. I wanted to believe him."

"But now you're not so sure?"

"Perhaps he was doing something questionable. I don't know."

"Did he ever tell you how he got started selling forgeries?"

"No. He never spoke to me about that."

"He told this to me once when we were hanging out. You know, when he was hiding from the Russians. An artist had contacted him offering to do paintings on demand, claimed he could copy anyone. This happened a long time ago when he was in London. The artist was apparently desperate for money."

"I never heard this before," Toby said, frowning.

"I'm sorry. It was stupid of me. I should have realized you'd find it upsetting."

"No. Go on. I want to hear it."

"You're sure?"

She nodded.

"Okay. When your father saw how good the copies were he decided to try selling one. It sold easily and for a good price. So he went back and asked the guy for more. Each time he paid a token. For a lark he took one of the paintings to Christie's and they valued it at thirty thousand dollars."

"I can guess the rest," she said. "My father was hooked."

"Exactly. But here's the kicker. Your father didn't know that one time the artist had made two copies of the same work, a small landscape by Pisarro. One he sold to Cormac, the other he tried to sell on his own. He was caught. He named your father as his dealer. Your dad was smart enough to keep no written records and to always pay in cash. In that sense he was safe from the police, but not, unfortunately, from the papers. His name was mentioned. It cost him a lot of money. And more."

"What do you mean by *more?*"

"I can still hear him chuckling when he told me this: '*Apparently the repayment of money wasn't enough for everyone. I found myself in a room, my arm in a cast and my jaw wired. A nurse said there was a phone call. The client who sent the bruiser who did the deed was calling. "I told him to rough you up a bit, old chap, not to put you in hospital. Sorry about that." '* "

Toby smiled. "That sounds like my father."

I couldn't help wondering what Cormac had left out of his story, but didn't mention that. "Think you should tell the cops anything?"

"What should I tell them? That I was suspicious of my own father? That my father was possibly doing something illicit? Would that help solve his murder?"

22

I shrugged. "I don't know. Maybe yes, maybe no."

"I'm not going to tarnish his reputation on a maybe."

"Okay, so what *are* you going to do?"

"Nothing. Let them do their jobs. They're the experts. At least, I hope they are."

"Sounds like a good idea."

"I've got another idea," she said. "How would you like a cup of coffee? I have some freshly made scones."

"Did you make them?"

"Don't be silly. Anita is a fabulous cook. Better than I ever could be. Just don't tell anyone."

CHAPTER 3

"Jake Wanderman?" the voice on the phone asked. It was the following morning.

"You got it."

"Oh, good." It was a male voice, totally unfamiliar.

"Who is this?" I asked.

"It's Rabbi Benvenuti."

I had never heard his voice on the phone before. It sounded different from the one I'd heard from the *bima*, which is what a pulpit is in a church. "Hello, Rabbi. This is a surprise. What can I do for you?"

"First, I want to tell you how sorry I am about the passing of your wife. I'm sure it must be devastating for you."

"Thanks, Rabbi. I appreciate that, even though you expressed that thought before at the funeral service."

"That was six months ago, Jake. I'm sure you're still feeling the loss."

"Yes. Yes, I am. I'm still feeling it."

"Of course. It's normal. It takes a long time to recover from the loss of a loved one."

I knew he was being nice but men of the cloth were traditionally long-winded. I'd had enough. "Why are you calling, Rabbi? Something I can do for you?"

He didn't hesitate. "Exactly, Jake. I need your help."

"What kind of help could you need from me?"

"We all know about your involvement with the stolen Fab-

24

eggs and how you were instrumental in solving that case. It got a ton of publicity out here. For a guy who was a teacher you did a great job."

I'd been lucky to get out of that caper alive. "Sure," I said. "That and a token'll get me a ride on the subway. Oh, I forgot. No more tokens. I guess I ought to say a Metro Card."

"In case you don't know it, you became famous, Jake. The local papers were calling you the Sam Spade of Sag Harbor."

"I think I hold my liquor better than he did."

"Seriously, something's come up and I feel you're the one person I know who can help me. You've got a special way of dealing with people. I can tell that."

"That's kind of you. What's this about?"

"I don't want to talk about it on the phone. Can you come to my office in the synagogue?"

"I suppose. When?"

"What's good for you?"

I looked at my watch. "Eleven okay? About an hour from now?"

"Eleven is fine. See you then."

I hung up and tried to imagine what he could possibly want from me. After two seconds of thinking about it I gave up. Might as well wait and find out.

There were dozens of condolence cards and letters piled on the dining room table. I had left them there as a reminder to me to acknowledge them. So far I hadn't been able to do it. Since I had an hour this would be a good time to start.

I drank the rest of my coffee and listened to Mahler instead.

I took Long Beach Road which runs along Noyac Bay to Ferry Road, then over the bridge into Sag Harbor village. I could get to the synagogue one of two ways: 114 to Elizabeth Street, very narrow and hard to turn into, or 114 to Division Street, beyond the Goat Alley Gallery and Expresso, the good

Italian take-out. Either way required twists and turns. I decided on Elizabeth Street where I had to make a sharp left onto Atlantic Avenue, a grand name for a street that was two blocks long. I parked in the lot adjacent to the synagogue. There were no other cars but that didn't surprise me. I had heard that the rabbi didn't have a car. He didn't need one because he rented a house within walking distance.

The side door was open. Even though it was daytime, the room I entered was in semidarkness, the windows covered by draperies. No lights were on. I waited for someone to acknowledge me but there was not a sound. It was eerily silent. It suddenly reminded me of the time in the middle of the Fabergé eggs business when I'd walked into Toby Welch's house, similarly quiet, and found everyone tied up and a dead body upstairs.

"Hello?" I called, a bit apprehensive.

A door opened from a room on the side and light spilled out. "Jake? Is that you?" The rabbi's head appeared. "I'm in here."

I muttered, "Thank God," and proceeded to his office.

It was a small carpeted room, just large enough to accommodate his desk, a chair in front of the desk, and some file cabinets. There were frames on the walls containing diplomas, photographs, and a painting that looked like a Chagall.

He shook my hand. He had the soft hands of a scholar and a wide friendly smile. His eyes were the kind that looked at you without examining you. They were brown, as was his hair, suit, tie, and oxford shoes. Seemed to be straight but he wasn't married, so who knew?

Rabbi Jon Benvenuti had been the rabbi of Temple Adas Israel in Sag Harbor for only three years. His name seemed abnormal but the explanation was simple. He was descended from Italian Jews. Being the rabbi of this synagogue was abnormal in other ways though. Unlike traditional houses of worship, it did not operate on a year-round basis. Because it was located in a resort area, the congregation all but vanished in the winter, forcing it to close for several months. The consequences of this were many but one of the most important was that because it was essentially a part-time temple it could only pay its rabbi accordingly. This made the finding of a rabbi not an easy task. Luckily for the congregation, they had been blessed. This guy was good: caring, empathetic, knowledgeable, and his sermons hardly ever put me to sleep.

His desk was cluttered with file folders. He gestured at them. "I've got work all the time. Not only from here but from my school in Jerusalem, as well."

"Must keep you pretty busy."

"I do counseling, too," he said. "As a rabbi, it's part of my job. I majored in social studies and became an LCSW before I became a rabbi so I have some experience in that area."

"What made you drop the social work?"

He shrugged and smiled. "Would you object if I said I'd been 'called'?"

"Why would I object? To each his own."

"Actually it's the counseling that's the cause of the problem. The reason I contacted you."

I waited for him to continue.

"I'll get right to it. Here's what happened. A member of the congregation was having marital problems. She asked if I would counsel her and her husband. She thought it would be better to see me than a professional marriage counselor because she had a lot of confidence in me.

"I agreed and we began therapy sessions. It was immediately obvious to me that their marriage was in trouble. He was domineering. Everything had to be his way. He gave her no respect whatsoever. I tried my best to help them but after a while I could see that my efforts were in vain." He paused and sighed.

"So then what?" I asked.

"I told them they ought to see a professional. That I was not able to help them. I told them I knew of one who had been very successful in helping other couples. He had a great record. They agreed to see him."

"But obviously that wasn't the end of it."

He gave me a wan smile. "That was the beginning of the end. They went to this man, who, by the way, I've known for more than ten years, with never a problem."

"But not this time?"

He motioned with his hand. "To make a long story short, the wife and the marriage counselor fell in love. She left her husband and moved in with the counselor. And ever since I've been getting abusive letters and phone calls in the middle of the night. The letters aren't signed. And the voice is disguised, but I'm sure it's the husband. Sometimes he even threatens me."

"What does he say?"

"*You're a bum. How can you call yourself a man of God? You don't deserve to live.* That kind of thing."

"He says he's going to kill you?"

"No. Not really. He just goes on about what a terrible person I am. I'm sure he wouldn't physically harm me."

"What makes you so sure?"

"Well, I just don't think so. He's an artist."

I had to smile. "Artists can't hurt someone?"

"Of course they can. But I'm talking about this one particular man. He's just not the type."

"If you say so. Now what if it turns out he's not the one you think it is?"

"Who else could it be?"

"Anyone else you might have counseled?"

He gave me a puzzled look.

"That was supposed to be funny," I said.

"It's not."

"I know. I have a tendency to make inappropriate remarks. Rosalind was always on me about that." At the mention of her name my eyes suddenly filled. I pressed my lips together, bent forward and covered my face with my hand. This kind of thing happened a lot. It was always unexpected and impossible to prevent. "I'm sorry," I said. "Give me a minute."

"Of course."

After a few moments, I took out a handkerchief and wiped my eyes. "I'm okay now. So what's this artist's name?"

He hesitated. "I don't think I ought to reveal that information. At least not yet. Not until I know you're definitely going to help me."

"Fair enough. But let me say, I'm not really sure what it is you want. I don't see what I can do for you."

"I'm not sure myself. I thought maybe you could talk to him. Sound him out. These letters and phone calls are very upsetting. It's gotten so I don't get any sleep. I keep waiting for the phone to ring. I thought about having an unlisted number but it wouldn't be right. People have to be able to get in touch with me."

"They could contact you through the synagogue. Leave a message."

He shook his head. "Not my style."

"I can understand that. What about the police?"

"What would they do for me? I have no proof. Also, if I went to them the story might get out. You know how bad that would be?"

I nodded, imagining the river of wild gossip slithering through the small-town atmosphere of Sag Harbor and the rest of the East End.

"I thought if you could find out that he is definitely the one doing this, then I would have some leverage. If he's the one, and I'm sure it's him, then you could tell him that if he doesn't cut it out I'll go to the police. Although I still don't think I would. The publicity would be bad. Believe it or not I'm more concerned about how bad it would be for the board and the congregation than for me."

What he said made a lot of sense. It would not be good for the temple and the rabbi to be the subject of gossip. We'd had it years before when a local rabbi had been accused of having affairs with members of his congregation. It had led to his being forced to resign. But in the aftermath were jokes and remarks that leached out into the entire community. I know it made me uncomfortable, like it's okay for me to rag on my bro' but not okay for you.

I was still pretty skeptical about the entire affair. I hadn't the slightest idea of how I could do what he wanted. I guessed it would require ingenuity and self-confidence, both of which I was now sorely lacking. When Rosalind died, without so much as a final smile or word, we'd only been back together a short while after having been separated for a few months. Twenty years of marriage and then, *bang*. Since then, I'd been not much better than a robot masquerading as a human being.

"I'll tell you what, Rabbi. Let me think about it. I'll see if I can come up with any ideas. I'd really like to help, but I have to tell you, honestly, I doubt I'll be able to." I stood up.

He came around the desk and grasped my hand. He was trying to smile but it wasn't working. "Thanks for coming, Jake. I appreciate it. If you don't feel you want to do anything, I'll understand. I don't want you to feel obligated. But I have to emphasize that I'm not kidding when I say I'm getting desperate. And that I need your help."

I went out of his office, feeling uncomfortable about what he had just said. He was putting pressure on me. I guessed that had been his intention.

Before leaving the building I paused to look at the sanctuary, what little I could see of it in the poor light. This was what had drawn me here originally. The synagogue itself was the oldest surviving one on Long Island. It had been built in 1898. The altar with the Lions of Judah flanking the Tablets of the Law had been hand carved by one of the founders and was still in place. The wooden pews, sacred scrolls, grill work were all intact. There were long Gothic windows filled with stained glass. Light filtered through them even now. When the chandeliers were on and the candles were lit for Shabbat services the old place gleamed and shone like a jewel.

Rosalind had dragged me there against my will. I had no interest in religion. But I had to admit that the beauty of the surroundings made for a spirituality that got to me after a while, so much so that I almost enjoyed going. Two years ago I even decided to fast on Yom Kippur, the holiest of holy days.

"Are you sure you want to do this?" Rosalind asked me.

"If you can do it, so can I."

"It's not a contest."

"To me, it is," I said.

With that memory clinging to me, I went outside, got back into my car and drove home.

CHAPTER 4

I couldn't help being aware I was having a bad time. My brain wasn't functioning. Neither was my body. I'd stopped doing the exercises I'd been doing most of my life. Yoga, karate, sit-ups, push-ups, and Waitankung, the Tai-Chi and yoga-like movements I'd learned in Thailand when Rosalind and I had spent a month there. We'd done a lot of traveling. In addition to Thailand we'd been through most of Europe and had once made it to Israel.

I hadn't touched the heavy bag or the speed bag in the basement. I hadn't played tennis, or been on my bike. The only exercise I got was my daily walk on Long Beach. It was October so I was usually the only one there. I didn't care about the weather, in fact, didn't even notice the weather. But I did listen to the sound of the waves. There was something mournful in their sound as they broke and washed up on the sand that made it easy for me to feel sorry for myself. I thought about what had happened over and over again.

We'd gone out for dinner and a movie, but there'd been a long line for the movie so we skipped it and had a hamburger at Rowdy Hall. I always had mine with sautéed onions and she always had hers with Swiss cheese. We both liked them rare. We came home and I followed her into the house. Without warning, she slid to the floor. I bent over her to see what was the matter. Her eyes were open. I looked into them saw they were blank. I blew into her mouth but there was no response. I didn't know what else to do. I felt as if I were sinking into a huge black pit. I picked up the phone and dialed 911 knowing all the time it was no use.

They conducted an autopsy. It was the law. It was determined she had had a brain hemorrhage, possibly caused by an embolism. Her father had died of the same thing so it was probably genetic. But knowing what killed her didn't help. She was gone and I had nowhere to go.

Again, Shakespeare popped into my head: *O God! That one might read the book of fate . . .* And at the same time I remembered a fight Rosie and I once had. She was angry about my not doing anything since I'd retired except to follow her around the supermarket, and her saying if I quoted Shakespeare one more time she'd strangle me.

But Shakespeare was in my blood, like a substitute for a deity. He had more answers that I could believe in, that was for sure. He understood the human condition as no man before or since. I often thought he might well have been the underlying inspiration for my becoming a high school English teacher.

It's odd that I came to feel this way because when *I* was in high school, and I was first ordered to read Shakespeare, I couldn't stand him. I didn't know what the fuss was about. His language was strange to my All-American ears, and difficult to understand. At the movies I saw Marlon Brando trying to be Mark Antony and it was all I could do to keep from laughing out loud at how ridiculous he sounded.

But something happened when I grew older. It was a lot like the attitude we had as children towards our parents. Somebody once said it: at eighteen we thought they were pathetic fools. At twenty-one we were amazed at how much they had learned in only three years.

I tried to give some thought to the rabbi's situation but got nowhere. I had Rosalind on my mind. I had Cormac Blather to think about. I put on a jacket, got back into the car and drove to the beach at the end of Ocean Road in Bridgehampton. I was surprised to see more than half a dozen cars already there. I got out and looked around. There were people on the beach, some of them with dogs chasing sticks, a couple of guys throwing a football, some even picnicking on take-out heros. It took me a few seconds before I realized why they were there. It was a beautiful day, one of the perfect ones we sometimes get in October in the Hamptons. There was a gentle breeze, the air was mild and sweet, the sky was a soft blue with a few white clouds, the sun was warm. It had been a long time since I'd noticed the beauty of nature.

I strolled along the water's edge trying to think about the rabbi and his problem. Could I do what he wanted, talk to this man? That was the first question. And if I did talk to him, could I find out if he was the one responsible for the phone calls and the letters? That was the second question. Suddenly there were lots of other questions crowding my brain but I shut them out and tried to concentrate on the first two. I could certainly talk to him once I found out who he was and where he was. That was simple enough. But how would I approach him? That was much more complicated. That would require a strategy, one I didn't have. Yet.

As I walked I realized my heart was pumping more adrenaline than I'd had in my body for a long time. Maybe the rabbi had done me a favor. By calling and asking for help, he'd given me something I'd been missing ever since Rosalind died. A goal. A reason to get out of bed in the morning other than to go through the motions of what amounted to a facsimile of living.

I continued trudging through the soft sand near the water. I had gone a long way, leaving the other people far behind me. The sand was littered with broken shells, bits of seaweed, odd pieces of driftwood. Now that I was alone, I was once again aware of the waves crashing on the shore. The sound was power-ful, exhilarating, like the cymbals and pounding bass drums in Sibelius. They weren't mournful at all.

I turned and headed back thinking, what did I have to lose? Why not give it a shot?

CHAPTER 5

When I got back from the beach I called the rabbi.

"That's so great, Jake. I can't thank you enough."

"Let me do something before you thank me. What's the guy's name and where is he?"

"His name is Chase McCleod."

"With that name he's an M.O.T.?"

"What's an M.O.T.?"

"Where did you grow up, Rabbi? Member of the Tribe."

"I never heard that before. But I grew up in Cleveland, so what do I know? Anyhow, that's not his real name. His real name is William Terbaum. When he realized he wanted to be an artist he decided to change it. He felt that Chase McCleod had more spice to it."

"Can't fault him for that."

"He lives over in Springs." He gave me the address and phone number.

"Okay," I said. "I'll check him out and let you know."

"I hope you can do something, Jake," Rabbi Benvenuti said. "It will be a great benefit to all of us. And, of course, I'll pay you for your time."

"Consider this *pro bono*, Rabbi. I don't feel that I should take money from you."

"Expenses, then. If you have any expenses."

"I'll let you know."

Luckily, I didn't need his money. My pension and our investments over the years had given me a comfortable existence. It was almost 1:30. My stomach told me I'd better have something to eat before I did anything else.

I cut two slices of sourdough bread, spread them with butter, shook on garlic powder and Goya's Adobo, added a layer of ham and Swiss and put the result under the broiler. When the cheese bubbled, I ate the slices piping hot, drank some sparkling water, which used to be called seltzer in Brooklyn, and in fifteen minutes was on the road.

Springs had always been a blue-collar kind of area, but also one that included artists. Jackson Pollock had lived here in the fifties and lots of fellow artists like DeKooning had followed. There were still working class people around but properties that had been worth seventy thousand dollars were now rising to a million. The signs of affluence were everywhere: wood shingles replacing asphalt, extensive landscaping with Leyland cypresses to keep out curious eyes, in-ground pool installations, Jaguars, Mercedes, and Land Rovers.

I took 114 to Stephen Hand's Path, then Cedar to North Main Street and on to Springs Fireplace Road. I guessed he was a couple of miles north of that intersection. He was not that far but even with a map it was a hassle to find his place. If he was in Springs it was in a section I'd never seen before. I finally located it on an unmarked road. The house was conventional, a two story Cape Cod with a small front yard enclosed with a white picket fence. The grass was slightly overgrown but the place seemed tidy enough. Considering that the man's wife had recently run off with another guy, it looked like he was holding himself together, at least on the outside.

I parked on the street, walked up to the front door and rang the bell. I waited for someone to open the door but nothing happened. There was a beat-up old Saab in the driveway so I guessed someone was home. I pushed the bell again.

"Who's that?"

The voice startled me. I didn't see anyone. Then I realized it came from an intercom attached to the side of the doorframe. There was a camera above it, pointing at me. An unusual artist, I thought.

I hadn't decided on a strategy. It was too late for one now. "My name's Jake Wanderman. Are you Chase McCleod?"

"Go away."

"Mr. McCleod? It's important I speak to you."

"Not to me it isn't. I don't know you. Go away."

"Listen, it's really important. I'm not selling anything."

"I don't care. I don't want to talk to anybody."

"Mr. McCleod, I'm going to show you something." I took out the leather case with the badge clipped on it and held it up to the camera. "Can you see this?"

"Looks like a badge." His voice had become subdued.

"That's what it is. Now, can we talk?"

"Okay, okay. Come around the side of the house. There's a building in the back. My studio. I'm in there."

The badge looked official. I didn't see any reason to tell him it wasn't. I'd seen it in a novelty shop and bought it on a whim. I also had business cards printed that proclaimed the name of the company Rosalind and I had decided on, *W. Shakespeare Co.* with my name and *Private Investigations* under it. That was right after the successful conclusion of the Fabergé eggs case. Rosalind and I had thought it would be a great idea for me to become a PI. When I actually looked into it the idea quickly soured. In order to get a license in the state of New York, I would first have to go to school, then take a rigorous exam. That was the easy part. I had no doubt I would pass the exam. But after that, I would have to work as an employee of a private agency or a government agency for three years. I could not see that happening. Since I was already in possession of the business cards and the badge, I hadn't seen any reason to throw them away even though Rosalind said I ought to. "Why do you want to keep them?" she asked. I didn't know. Because I'd paid for them? No, I knew that wasn't it. Something else. Maybe a secret wish that they were real?

There was a smaller building set back about twenty yards behind the main house. One wall was fitted with glass panels, obviously the studio. I went to open the door but it was locked.

"Hold your horses. I'll be right with you," I heard.

A few minutes went by, and the door opened.

He was a skinny runt by anyone's standards. Couldn't have been more than five feet five and a hundred and twenty pounds even with a jug of wine in each hand.

"Okay, c'mon in," he said. He wore a paint-smeared T-shirt and jeans and no shoes or socks.

It was a working artist's studio. Lots of light from those big windows. And the smell: a combination of paint, turpentine, linseed oil, and anything else he might have used. There were paint splatters on the floor, the tables, the walls, in addition to what was on McCleod himself. Primary colors and secondary colors. He didn't miss one. A table had open cans and tubes of paint on it. I thought I had interrupted him in the middle of work but when I turned to look at what he was working on I couldn't see anything. There was a canvas on an easel but it was covered with a cloth. There were stacks of paintings leaning against the walls, all turned so that I could only see the backs of the canvases.

"You don't like anyone to see what you're painting?" I said.

"Only dealers. Someone who's going to pay me for what I do."

"I'm not a dealer but I like art. I go to a lot of openings. I don't remember seeing your work. Do you show locally?"

He gave me a suspicious look. He had one of those narrow

faces with a long pointed nose and deep-set raccoon eyes. "I'm not interested in discussing my work with amateurs. You want to tell me what's on your mind? What's a cop want with me, anyhow?"

"I'm not exactly a cop, Mr. McCleod. I'm more like a private investigator."

"So what's with the badge?"

"It's a private investigator's badge. Not official."

"Then I don't have to talk to you. You got in here under false pretenses."

"I didn't say I was a policeman."

"No, but you inferred it."

"No, *you* inferred it. I only implied it."

"What's the difference? I don't have to talk to you. So get the hell out of here."

"Just a minute, Mr. McCleod. I think you'll reconsider when I tell you why I'm here."

"I don't think so."

"Ever hear of Rabbi Benvenuti?"

He had been in the process of gesturing at me to get out of his studio. The name stopped him. His mouth opened in surprise to reveal startlingly white teeth with one in the middle of the lower set missing.

"Gotcha," I said.

"What does he have to do with anything?"

"How about those phone calls? How about those letters?" I realized I'd made a dumb mistake in not having looked at the letters before I came here. Knowing exactly what was in them would have been helpful. Hopefully, I could bluff it out.

"I don't know what you're talking about."

His tone of voice and body language told me all I needed to know. He was scared and that put me in charge. It also helped that I was a foot taller, had fifty pounds on him, and could take him out easily with one good punch.

"I think you know exactly what I'm talking about. Do you mind if I sit down?"

Without waiting for an answer I sat on a paint splattered chair. I hoped the paint was dry.

He jammed his hands into the pockets of his jeans and didn't reply.

"From what I understand, your wife left you and you're pissed. You blame the rabbi. He was only trying to help."

"Some help," he said.

"He's not Jesus Christ. He can't perform miracles."

"What's that supposed to mean?"

"I can only go by what I see. And what I see tells me that if I were your wife I'd have left you, too."

"You have no right to say that. You don't know what the fuck you're talking about. I love my wife. And she loved me. It was that son of a bitch marriage counselor. He put the moves on her."

"Maybe he did. But nobody forced her, right? And, as I said, the rabbi was only trying to help."

"You can't do anything about it. There's no proof."

I smiled. "If you think that, you're dumber than I thought. If I take those letters to the police, I'd be willing to bet you left your fingerprints all over them. Not only that, but the phone records'll show that you made the phone calls. I'm pretty sure you didn't make the calls from a public phone. Not in the middle of the night."

The look on his face told me my guesses were bull's-eyes.

He went and got a chair for himself. "Okay. You're right. I couldn't help myself. I was so mad, I didn't know what to do. It was easy to blame the rabbi. He was close by and he'd been the one we went to in the first place."

"Look, the rabbi is a forgiving guy. That's his business. You're lucky it wasn't me. I'd have you thrown in the can. All he wants is for you to stop. If you do, he's willing to forgive and forget."

"He'll do that?"

"That's what he said."

"Then sure. Sure. I promise. I won't bother him again."

I gave him a long hard look to show him I meant business. "I can count on that?"

"Absolutely. I give you my word."

He stuck out his dirty hand. I had no recourse but to shake it. "Okay, Mr. Chase McCleod. I'll take your word." I stood up to go. "I asked you before but didn't get an answer. Do you show locally?"

"Are you kidding? I've shown a lot. I even won a prize one year at the Guild Hall members' show. And I show my work in the Lipper gallery over on Newtown Lane."

"I guess I just missed it. You must make out pretty well."

He gave me a disgusted look. "If my name was Lichtenstein maybe, or Red Grooms. Not many artists survive without teaching, framing, doing portraits of somebody's kid. It comes down to the critics. They make you or break you. I had a show in New York once and this critic, this son of a bitch, called my work *derivative*. Can you believe that? Me? Derivative? If he said I couldn't paint, I wouldn't've cared. But *derivative?* If there's one thing I'm not and never have been, it's derivative." He shook his head. "He killed me, that prick. August Hydecrown is the fuck's name. I'd like to strangle him with my bare hands."

"But you wouldn't actually do that, would you? If you could?"

"Nah, but I would like to kick his ass."

"Maybe you'll luck out and get the chance. I can't say it's been a pleasure meeting you, but I wish you good luck in your artistic endeavors. And, by the way, I like that name. Chase McCleod. Has a nice ring to it."

I got back in the car. I felt pretty good. You might even say smug and self-satisfied. It had been so easy. I'd done a good job. And I was sure Terbaum-McCleod wasn't about to do anymore anonymous anything, not when he knew I had the goods on him.

I gave the rabbi the news from my cell.

CHAPTER 6

Landis Kalem slouched low behind the wheel and observed the man as he came out of McCleod's studio. The man was solidly built, fit, about six feet in height and looked to be in his fifties. He could be a cop, of course, but there was no way to know. He watched as he got into his car and used a cell phone to make a call. A short while later, the man drove away, but not before Landis jotted down the color and make of the car and the license plate number. He didn't know what use he might make of that information but he was a believer in knowing as much as possible about whatever subject he was interested in.

The current subject of his interest was Chase McCleod, erstwhile artist and consummate forger. He'd done his homework on McCleod, once known as William Terbaum. He was born in Cleveland, left after high school with a scholarship to the Art Student's League in New York. Had some talent, was represented over the years by several galleries but had never hit it big in the art market. Supported himself by teaching, doing portraits, and selling an occasional painting.

Landis hadn't been able to learn how Blather and McCleod had gotten together but since he knew Mr. Cormac Blather's history as well as he knew his own, it was clear forgery had to be involved.

When he'd traced Blather to the Hamptons it became imperative to persuade Mr. Mergenthaler to buy a house there to add to his other residences and his yacht.

"Your biggest competitors have homes in the Hamptons," he'd said to Mergenthaler. "These days it's a must to be there for at least part of the summer season."

"Maybe you're right," Mergenthaler said. "Find me something suitable."

He'd gone out with several brokers and eventually located a substantial home in North Haven near Sag Harbor. It was on a promontory with a magnificent view of Noyac Bay. A steal at nine million. Three years later it had doubled in value.

After they had moved in and were established he told Mergenthaler about a man in the area who was well known for having a superb collection of art and art objects for sale at quite reasonable prices. Mergenthaler was a well-known collector but what was not well known was that he never paid what the market called for. He loved nothing better than a good bargain.

Mergenthaler said he'd go to Blather's shop. After Landis introduced them, he looked at almost everything and bought a small 19th century marine painting by James Edward Buttersworth. After some bargaining, he paid sixty thousand for it. "It's pretty," he said. "I like this kind of thing. It'll look good near my desk."

When they left he told Landis that Blather had nice things but not much of the caliber he was looking for. "But I'd say the painting was worth double what I paid so my time wasn't wasted."

Landis made sure to call Blather and tell him that Mergenthaler was pleased but that he was in the market for higher caliber art. And Blather had responded, as Landis knew he would. He brought in one of Edward Steichen's very rare landscapes, a William Merritt Chase, Mary Cassatt, Kandinsky, Emile Bernard, and offered them to Mergenthaler at prices well below what they'd previously got at auction. Landis knew what Blather was doing. He'd begun with the lower tier of painters and the unusual landscape by Steichen, best known as a photographer, to demonstrate to Mergenthaler that he was knowledgeable about the art market. He was saving the big names, the Picassos, Modiglianis, and so on, for later, after he had won Mergenthaler's trust.

And that was exactly what happened. A Degas charcoal and pastel on paper was found of a woman in her bath *"sa toilette,"* with a signature and provenance. Mergenthaler was not a fool. He had it looked over and appraised. It had last sold at auction for four hundred fifty-nine thousand dollars. He paid three hundred seventy-five thousand.

Landis was impressed. He was sure it was a forgery but apparently the forger was very, very good. Whenever he had free time he staked out the shop in the hope of seeing someone deliver a canvas. After days and weeks and countless hours of hanging around Blather's place on Main Street in Sag Harbor at all hours of the day and night, his patience was rewarded.

That night the shop was closed but Blather remained inside. Not unusual. Blather often stayed after hours. A man—small and skinny—got out of a car and carried a large object covered in brown paper into the shop. It was obviously a framed painting judging by its size and the way it was held. The person stayed inside about ten minutes and when he left, Landis had followed him. That was how he'd found Chase McCleod.

He now took out the pay-on-demand cell phone he'd paid cash for in Macy's, which made it untraceable to him. When McCleod answered, he said, "Did you hear what happened to Cormac Blather?"

"No. Who's this?"

"He's dead. It's on the news."

"Why are you telling me this? What does it have to do with me?"

"You don't know me, Mr. McCleod. But I know you. I know

all about you."

"So what? There's not that much to know. Who is this?"

"I want to talk to you about something that may be beneficial to both of us."

"Why should I talk to you? You won't even tell me who you are."

"My name is Landis Kalem. I work for Bryson Mergenthaler. I'm quite sure you know that name."

"I don't know what you're talking about," McCleod said, and hung up.

Landis redialed. "I know about your relationship with Cormac Blather so don't hang up on me again. You wouldn't want the police involved, would you?"

"What do you want?"

"I'll explain everything when I see you."

"When will that be?"

"Right now."

Landis snapped the phone closed and crossed the street to the studio. He knocked on the door.

McCleod opened it, making a sour face. "Why didn't you say you were outside?"

Landis shrugged. "Not important. What is important is that you hear what I have to say."

"When did Blather die? What happened?"

"You can find out on TV or the radio. I'm not here to talk about him."

"Okay, I'm listening," McCleod said. "Have a seat." He wiped his hands on his jeans. His skin looked gray and his eyes seemed to be looking everywhere but at Landis.

Landis glanced at the dirty-looking chair, the rags, the paint-splattered floor. "This won't take long. I know you were doing forgeries for Blather."

McCleod began to protest but Landis cut him off.

"Don't bother denying it. I know Blather's history. Selling forgeries was a major part of it. And I also know you've been delivering paintings to him when his shop was closed. They're very good, by the way."

"You better believe it."

"But Blather is dead. So you have no way of selling your work. That's where I come in."

"What can *you* do?"

"I will continue to sell them to Mergenthaler."

"How you gonna do that?"

"It's not your concern. I'll manage it. You'll make more with me than you did with Blather. I can promise you that."

"I was getting three thousand a painting and a cut of the sale price."

"I'm not here to bargain with you. What were you working on when Blather left this world?"

"A Klee."

"Good. Let me know when it's done."

"I'm not so sure about this. How do I know you're on the up and up?"

"Look at it this way," Landis said. "I have the ability to get you into a lot of trouble. But I'm not going to do that. Instead, I'm going to let you keep doing what you've been doing so well. And make money."

McCleod picked up a rag and wiped his hands with it. "How do I get in touch with you?"

"You don't. I'll be in touch with you." Landis turned to go. "By the way, who was that man who left before I got here?"

"What man?"

"Don't be coy with me, McCleod. I saw him leave just a few minutes ago."

"It's got nothing to do with art. It's a private matter."

"He wasn't from the police, was he?"

"I told you, it's none of your business. So quit asking me about it. But he wasn't a cop."

"What was he here about? I need to know. Private matters can get in the way, too."

"All right, all right. It had to do with my rabbi. I was mad at him because I thought he helped break up my marriage. This guy came over to tell me to stop bothering him."

"And did you agree?"

"What else could I do?"

"Good. That was smart. And that's it? You're sure there's nothing else?"

"You don't stop, do you? That's all there is."

"What's this man's name?"

"Wanderman. I don't know anything about him except he works for the rabbi. Told me he was a private dick."

"Very good," Landis said. "I appreciate your telling me. It shows we can trust each other."

He was about to leave when McCleod said, "Hey, you know, I think I do know you. I might have seen you before at Blather's store on Main Street."

"It's possible. I was there many times with Mr. Mergenthaler, but I never saw you."

"I always stayed out of sight. But I just now remembered your voice. And I think I also saw you one night . . ." He was about to say something more, but stopped.

"Oh? When was that?"

McCleod shook his head. "No, no. I was mixing you up with somebody else."

"All right then," Landis said. "I'll be in touch."

When he was outside, he paused for a moment thinking about what McCleod had said about seeing him one night and then saying it was a mistake. Could he have seen him that last time?

Boris Riskin

He'd been sure no one was in the vicinity when he'd left. He didn't trust McCleod and now he had to wonder.

CHAPTER 7

Vincent J. Mazzini was the Chief of Police of Sag Harbor. He was a no bullshit kind of guy. After our first encounter relating to the Fabergé eggs, not a pleasant one, we ended up becoming good friends.

Even though Toby hadn't asked me to I thought I'd try and have a chat with him and see what I could find out about Cormac's murder. My dealing with the rabbi's artist had gone well, so I felt okay about doing this.

I had to admit I was curious. More than curious. I'd gotten very close to Cormac and his being murdered was something I just couldn't accept. Cormac's antique shop on Main Street was still marked with yellow crime-scene tape. It was gruesome to think of his being killed there. I wanted to know something, at least learn how he'd been murdered. So far they'd stuck with their policy of keeping everything under wraps.

I decided not to phone and not to drop in at the station. I knew Vince liked to have lunch sometimes at Estia's on the turnpike so the next day I drove by there between the hours of twelve and two hoping to spot his car. No luck.

Be calm, I told myself. Be like Iago, *How poor are they that have not patience!* I wasn't anything like that crafty devil. He needed time and patience for his schemes to come to fruition. That kind of waiting was definitely not in my nature. I tended to respond more with my gut than my head. But in regard to the Chief I had the feeling that if I wanted information, ap-

51

proaching him casually was the best way to get it.

So I hung on and did the same drive by the next day. Still no luck. One more shot, I decided, and that's it. When he wasn't there again the following day, I said the hell with this and drove directly to the station.

The old police station was closed because they were building a new one. They had set up a temporary office over by Marine Park on Bay Street. The wharf was only a few yards away and sailboats were still tied up at the docks, the die-hard sailors hanging on waiting until the savage winds of winter finally drove them off.

The building substituting for the police station didn't have so much as a sign. It resembled a trailer in a mobile home development. It had wooden steps and a ramp for the disabled attached to the side of it. I noticed with satisfaction that the Chief's Crown Victoria was parked right in front.

I went in and found a cramped entryway with a high counter and a woman behind it. She wore civilian clothes. I told her my name and asked for the Chief.

She went back, knocked on a closed door and disappeared behind it. In a little while she reappeared and said the Chief would be with me in a few minutes.

It was not a waiting room. There was no place to sit. I stared at a map of Sag Harbor on the wall behind me. The village was divided into sections by a red marker, each section designated with a number. I assumed these were the areas covered by the local police. There were not many. I hadn't realized before how small Sag Harbor actually was.

The door to his office opened and out came Vince. He was a sturdy-looking guy with olive skin, a long nose, and an air of authority. The uniform contributed to that: a military-styled white shirt, with epaulets, and a gold shield pinned to it. There were some other badges, too. He gave me a friendly smile and motioned me to follow him back into his office.

We shook hands. "Condolences on the loss of your wife, Mr. Wanderman."

"What's with the Mister Wanderman?"

"Sorry, Jake."

"That's better. And thanks."

He sat down behind his desk and leaned back in his chair. He knew I was there to pump him but he played it cool, waiting for me to speak first. Maybe that's why he'd called me Mister, to put up a wall.

"Listen, Chief. This guy who was murdered . . . you know we were friends."

"Yeah. I know."

"And his daughter and my wife were very close friends."

He didn't say anything.

"We were talking the other day, his daughter and me." I'd been an English teacher but deliberately broke the rules sometimes when I didn't want to sound elitist. "Naturally, she's very upset."

"Of course."

"She asked me if I could find out what's going on. Nobody'll tell her anything."

"What does she want to know?"

"Who killed her father, for one thing."

He gave me one of those looks that suggested I was brain dead. "Don't you think that's what we're trying to find out?"

"You know what I mean. They won't even tell her how he died."

"I don't have anything to do with that. Suffolk County's in charge of the investigation. We help. We have a man working with them at all times. But they make all the decisions."

"How come?"

"We're a small outfit here. No facilities. Suffolk has it all, the coroner, the forensic people, fingerprint experts, photographers, and most important, lots of detectives to assign to a case. I have one detective, that's it."

"So how's the investigation going?"

"We're digging into everything. I can tell you that."

"That's a big help. You know how he was killed, don't you?"

He nodded.

"Can you tell me?"

"I'm afraid not. I can't tell you that or anything else, for that matter. This is serious stuff. We're not at liberty to give out information to civilians."

The remark about "civilians" hurt. But he was right. I was a civilian. I guess I didn't want to be.

"Come on, Vince. I'm not asking for such a big deal. And you know I'll keep it confidential."

He shook his head. "Can't do it."

"Okay, Vince. I'll tell her what you said. I'll try and get her to understand she's only the daughter and not entitled to know anything. Sorry I bothered you."

He had a picture frame on his desk with a photo of his wife and two daughters. He leaned forward and touched the side of the frame. "I'd like to help you out, Jake. But I can't do it. For right now they want to keep everything buttoned up. That's just the way it is."

"Okay, Chief. I don't see it as such a big deal but if that's the way it's got to be, I'll have to live with it." I stood and held out my hand. "Thanks for your time."

"Not at all. Good to see you again, Jake. Why don't you stop by sometime? We'll have lunch. We can talk football."

"Will do," I said. We shook hands one more time and that was that.

CHAPTER 8

Landis Kalem walked into the room that had been converted into an opulent office. It was almost time for the detective to show up. He'd suggested to his employer that he had no obligation to talk to the police, but unsurprisingly, his suggestion had been disregarded.

He looked out at the magnificent view of Noyac Bay and remembered that when he'd first begun working for Bryson Mergenthaler everything they did and everywhere they went was exciting. The house in the Hamptons, the Park Avenue duplex in New York, the townhouse in London, the apartment in Paris, the two-hundred-fifty-foot yacht. Some of these residences had been sold and replaced more than once over the years as well as the Mercedes limousine, Bell Ranger helicopter, Gulfstream jet, and the yacht. Bryson Mergenthaler was not a man to sit still or remain content with anything, including his wives.

Exception: Landis.

He'd kept Landis as his secretary and personal assistant since he'd snatched him up from Agem Industries back in 1987. How exciting that had been! Bryson had acquired the company in one of his famous corporate takeovers, and shortly afterward walked into Landis's office and sat down with the air of someone who owned the place. Of course he did own it.

"Do you know who I am?" he asked.

Landis sat upright. He was twenty-six, had been at Agem for

three years and thought he was moving up, but now this.

"You're Bryson Mergenthaler. And I have a feeling I'm about to be fired."

Mergenthaler smiled. "You think I have the time or the inclination to go about firing people? I have people who do that. No, I have something else in mind." He paused, waiting for it to register. "How would you like to come work for me?"

Landis was young but not naïve. "Doing what?"

Mergenthaler's eyes appeared to be half-closed, and made him look half asleep. They used to be called "bedroom eyes." Lots of women had been attracted by those eyes as well as his deep pockets. He examined Landis for a long moment before he spoke. "How much are you making here?"

Landis was quite sure Mergenthaler knew exactly what his salary was. "Fifty-five thousand a year."

"Any extras? Expense account? Stock options? Bonuses?"

"I got a thousand-dollar Christmas bonus last year."

"I'll give you a hundred fifty thousand dollars per, an expense account, the opportunity to get in on stock options. I don't believe in bonuses but I reward people who do good work for me. Do you still want to know what the job is?"

"More so than before."

Mergenthaler laughed loudly. "I knew I had the right guy. I had you checked out when I was looking over the company. My instincts are never wrong." He got to his feet. "You'll be my personal secretary, assistant, right-hand man, whatever you want to call it. I need a young, smart guy with a lot of energy. A guy I can trust. I think you're that person. What do you say?"

Landis came around the desk and held out his hand. "I'm your man," he said.

And so he had been for the next twenty years. Along the way he'd been promised an opportunity to move up, possibly run one of the many companies and properties Bryson Mergenthaler had acquired. But whenever he asked, he was always told to be patient, that he couldn't be spared just then, that he was too valuable where he was at that particular moment.

His salary had increased to four hundred thousand, his personal assets had grown considerably. He owned a duplex on East 83rd with a magnificent view, had a Z3 in the garage. He was worth three million, not including the apartment. But it wasn't good enough anymore. He was tired of being a subordinate, had been tired of it for a long time. He was the one who'd been doing the real work, who'd actually been running the show. Now he had the chance to prove to himself, if not Mergenthaler, who was really in charge.

Mergenthaler came in. He had just celebrated his sixty-second birthday. Since Landis had begun working for him he'd added a few pounds. His hair was still his own, just a touch of gray at the temples. There was a bit of fat softening his jaw line, but everything else about him was still diamond-hard. He had a gym in each of his residences and worked out with a trainer.

"Where's that son of a bitch? We told him two o'clock, didn't we?"

Landis looked at his watch. "It's not quite two yet."

"Wouldn't hurt the guy to be a few minutes early." He went behind the desk and sat in the high-backed chair that could also recline and massage. "You think I shouldn't be talking to this guy."

"Actually, I never said you *shouldn't* talk to him. I said that you had no obligation to do so. But I've changed my mind. After thinking it through again, I think it's a good idea to let him ask his questions. That way, you will have been shown to be cooperative, and since you are certainly not a suspect in the murder, it will all be over and done with."

"What makes you think I'm not a suspect?"

"It would be absurd. There's no possible motive. All you ever did was buy some paintings and antiques from the man. You may have overpaid for some of them, but that's hardly a motive for murder."

Mergenthaler leaned back in his chair and put his feet on the desk. "I'm so pleased that you're still able to amuse me, Landis. You have such an interesting way of putting things."

Landis had never been gifted with a sense of humor. "How do you mean?"

"Out of the blue you tell me that I overpaid? You never intimated anything like that before."

"It was hardly my place. I'm not an art expert."

"You certainly aren't. Not only have I *not* overpaid, I've gotten a few stupendous bargains. That's why I began doing business with him in the first place. You vetted him so you should know. We both knew his reputation was not strictly kosher."

"Of course. I suppose I shouldn't have said anything."

At that moment they heard the faraway sound of the door chime and they both held off speaking. They waited. There would be no sound of footsteps because all the floors were thickly carpeted. Mario knocked on the door even though it was open. "You have visitors, sir."

"More than one?"

"Two, sir."

"Okay, Mario, bring them up," Mergenthaler said.

Mario went away and in a little while came back with a man and a woman. The man wore a police uniform, the woman, a jacket and slacks.

"Come in, please," Mergenthaler said. "Have a seat. Landis, get them some chairs, would you?"

There were already two chairs facing the desk. Landis gestured at them. The woman sat but the man in uniform went to the desk and extended his hand. "I'm Vincent Mazzini, Chief of Police of Sag Harbor. I want to thank you for agreeing to see us."

Mergenthaler shook his hand. "Pleased to meet you, Chief. Vincent, you said? Is it all right if I call you that?"

"Sure. And I want to point out that this will be an informal meeting. We will not be recording either with tape or video, just taking some notes, if that's all right with you."

"No problem." Mergenthaler gestured toward Landis. "This is my assistant, Landis Kalem. You don't mind if he sits in, do you?"

"Not at all," Chief Mazzini said. "Glad to have him. This is Detective Sienna Nolan. She's the lead detective on Mr. Blather's murder. Of course you know that's why we're here."

"Nobody said anything specific to me when the call was made to set up this appointment. But I gathered as much. I assume you went through his records and found that he and I did a little business together."

"I wouldn't say it was a *little* business, Mr. Mergenthaler. Looks like you bought a lot of stuff from him."

"Stuff," Mergenthaler smiled. "That's good. Yes, I did buy a lot of stuff from him. So what is it you'd like to know? How much I paid? It's no doubt in his records."

"So it is, Mr. Mergenthaler. But I'll let Detective Nolan ask the questions. Go ahead, Detective."

Detective Sienna Nolan, a compact woman with reddish-brown hair cut short, had already taken a small notebook out of her pocket. She appeared to be in her middle thirties, wore no makeup but had the kind of skin that didn't need any. Her features were regular, nothing outstanding, until you saw her eyes. They were a dark shade of green and all but glowed with intensity. She opened the notebook and looked at the page as if she were studying it. "How long have you known Mr. Blather?"

Mergenthaler didn't answer. He looked over at Landis.

59

Landis said, "Mr. Mergenthaler met Mr. Blather eight years ago, in the month of December."

"And when did you first start doing business with him?"

"At that time. Mr. Mergenthaler had heard that Blather had a particularly beautiful Degas drawing. He was especially interested in Degas then and so he got in touch with Blather and bought the drawing. And that was the beginning of their relationship."

"Landis is good at dates and history," said Mergenthaler. "He's got an amazing memory."

Detective Nolan's expression was blank, apparently so that the person being interviewed would not know what affect the answers were having. What she couldn't hide was the powerful gaze from her eyes. She wrote something in her notebook. "How did you learn that Mr. Blather had the drawing?"

"We had feelers out. I'd contacted a lot of dealers and they knew I was in the market for Degas drawings. Someone told me but I don't remember who it was. Does it matter?"

"What was your impression of Mr. Blather?"

"How do you mean? Did I like him?"

"Something like that. Did you find him easy to do business with?"

"He was very pleasant. And easy to deal with. He wasn't a haggler. He usually quoted a fair price and stuck to it."

"So you found him honorable in his dealings with you?"

"Absolutely. Never had a problem."

"I suppose you know he had somewhat of a shady past."

Mergenthaler looked at Landis as if asking him to respond.

Landis said, "I looked into his background before Mr. Mergenthaler did any business with him. It's our standard practice. I found a number of allegations. Lots of rumors. But he was never arrested for anything. After reviewing all the facts, Mr. Mergenthaler saw no reason not to do business with him."

"What was the nature of your phone call to him on the day he died?"

"Phone call?" Mergenthaler raised his eyebrows. "I'm not aware of a phone call."

Detective Nolan looked down at her notebook. "There was a call made from this residence to his shop on Main Street at 2:37 p.m. that day."

"Do you know anything about this, Landis?" Mergenthaler asked.

"Let me think," Landis said. He was annoyed with himself for not realizing in advance that the police would have a record of all the phone calls to the shop.

"It was only a few days ago," she said, her tone of voice suggesting that a man with his impressive memory should have no trouble recalling it.

"Oh yes," Landis said. "Of course. I wanted to ask him if he could locate some good netsukes. I've recently become interested in collecting them. This was strictly personal. It had nothing to do with Mr. Mergenthaler. You know what netsukes are, Detective Nolan?"

"Yes. I know what they are."

"I don't," said the Chief. "What are they?"

"Japanese figurines of ivory or wood with a hole through them. They were originally used to hold kimono sashes. There's a worldwide cult of collectors."

Landis bowed his head. "I'm impressed, Detective."

She ignored his comment. "So the phone call wouldn't have anything to do with the item from Jerusalem?"

"What item was that?"

"Among the list of objects you bought from Mr. Blather was some kind of burial box, also known as an ossuary."

"Why would I be calling him about it?"

"I assumed you were aware of a report that a dealer in Jerusalem was implicated in a ring that faked a number of these objects."

"Really?" Mergenthaler said.

"The story broke not too long ago, a couple of weeks maybe. Certainly not more than a month. You had no knowledge of this?"

"None. This is the first I've heard of it."

Nolan's blank look changed to a wide smile. "Mr. Mergenthaler, you don't really expect me to believe that, do you?"

"I'm not sure what you should believe, Detective. Nor do I much care." He suddenly stood up. "But I do have a lot of work to do, so I'm afraid we have to conclude this interview." He pushed a button on the desk.

Chief Mazzini got to his feet quickly. Detective Nolan slowly followed.

"Thanks for your time, gentlemen," the Chief said. "It's very much appreciated."

Mario appeared in the doorway.

"These people are leaving, Mario. Show them the way out, would you?"

After they left, Mergenthaler said, "That was good, Landis. Netsukes. Where did you get that from? Are you really collecting them? I never took you for a collector."

"I happened to come across something about them in an article about Japan. I had to say something, didn't I? I wasn't about to tell them the real reason."

"They seem to have figured it out, anyhow. Not much we can do about that. Do you think they're going to bother me again?"

"I think it's a distinct possibility," said Landis Kalem.

CHAPTER 9

I was treating myself to *Coq au Vin,* meaning I was in the kitchen getting ready to cook it. The kitchen was my favorite room in the house. No, I take it back. It was a tie between the kitchen and the den. It had been ordinary when we bought the house but Rosalind had transformed it, with a couple of suggestions from me thrown in. The countertops were butcher block. We had a double sink with a Price Pfister faucet that I could pull out and use as a spray. We'd decided to splurge on the stove and refrigerator so we got a Zero King refrigerator and a Viking stove that could cook a roast the size of a horse. The walls were done in wainscoting painted white and filled with pots and pans and strainers and all kinds of kitchen utensils. We had a window put in above the sink and a skylight. It was ridiculous and extravagant but Rosalind had said something to the effect that we only live once. *Why not?* she'd said. She'd been a pretty good cook but was content to let me do most of it, *since you seem to enjoy it so much,* she'd said.

I made *Coq au Vin* no more than two or three times a year because it was a lot of work. Rosalind loved the dish; it was one of her favorites, probably because it was loaded with butter and wine. This was the first time since she died that I'd attempted it. It came about because I had a sudden yearning. That was when I usually cooked it, the juices flowing with the memory of my introduction to it back in Paris when I was a young student there.

I had laid out all the ingredients: shallots, pearl onions, bacon, garlic, mushrooms, flour, brandy, a bottle of Burgundy, a bouquet garni of leek, celery, thyme, and a bay leaf wrapped in cheesecloth. And of course, a three-and-a-half-pound free-range chicken that I'd cut up. I had the water boiling and was about to pour it over the shallots so that I could peel them when I heard a car pull into the driveway and a door slam.

I put the water back on the stove, turned the heat down, and went to the door.

It was a woman flashing an ID at me. She was small, wore jeans and a T-shirt and a serious expression on an attractive face. "Detective Sienna Nolan," she said. "Can I come in?"

"Sure." I led her back into the den, my other favorite room in the house. Rosalind had made it like a library with floor to ceiling bookshelves filled mostly with books, some sculpture and pottery. The chairs were leather and comfortable. There was a 32-inch TV, a decent stereo system, and a glass wall looking out to the garden. Most visitors, especially women, made some comment about the room, but not this one. "What can I do for you?" I asked.

"Answer a couple of questions."

"What about?"

"Cormac Blather."

"You're one of the detectives on the case?"

"I'm the lead detective."

"Have a seat," I said.

"You live alone?" she asked.

"Yes. My wife died a short time ago."

"I'm sorry." She took a plastic bag out of her pocket and handed it to me. "Would you care to tell me anything about this?"

I took it from her. Inside the bag was my Private Investigator card. I'd given one to Cormac right after I'd had them printed.

That was when I was still expecting to become a PI. I was handing them out all over the place, ostensibly to solicit business. I
was also showing off. "What do you want me to say?"

"We found it in Mr. Blather's files. I looked you up. You don't
have a license."

"I know that."

"Then tell me something. Why are you handing out business
cards saying you're a Private Investigator? That's impersonation.
A felony."

"Give me a break. I wasn't impersonating anything. When I
gave it to him I expected to be one."

"What happened?"

"It's a long story."

"I've got time."

"I didn't want to work for somebody else for three years in
order to get a license."

"Okay. You and Blather were quite involved with each other
at one time. Were you still involved?"

"No business, if that's what you mean. Just friends. I had
dinner with him and his daughter a couple of times, that's all. I
assume you know who his daughter is."

"Toby Welch. Superstar. Do you do anything for her?"

"What do you mean, *do anything?*"

She shrugged. "Business, of course."

"No." I was beginning to be annoyed by this woman even
though she had the most startling green eyes I'd ever seen.
"And I don't understand why you're asking me these questions."

"I'm interviewing everyone connected in some way with Mr.
Blather. I'm trying to find out who killed him. That's all. Am I
clear?"

"Clear."

"Let's get back to Blather. You weren't helping him out in his antique business or anything else?"

"No."

"You're sure? You were very connected with him and those stolen Fabergé eggs from Russia."

"I see you've looked into his background. I said, no. That was then, this is now."

"What about Bryson Mergenthaler?"

"What about him?"

"Blather did quite a lot of business with him. Did you have any contact with him?"

"None. As I said, I wasn't working with Cormac. I'm retired. We were just friends."

"What did you do before you retired?"

"I was a teacher. An English teacher. I specialized in Shakespeare."

"Huh," she said. "I never understood what the fuss was about when it came to Shakespeare. Left me cold." She held out her hand for the plastic bag. "When was the last time you saw Blather?"

"I'm not exactly sure. I stopped by his shop to say hello. It might've been a week or so before he was killed."

She took a card out of her wallet. "This is *my* card. If you think of anything that might be useful."

We didn't shake hands. I let her out the door and went back to the kitchen. The water had boiled out of the pot and the pot was getting scorched on the stove. "Shit!" I yelled, turning off the gas.

I ran water over the pot and then filled it to let it soak. I'd have to scrub it with Brillo for a half hour if I wanted to salvage it.

The ruined pot and the downright unpleasant interview took care of any desire to make the *Coq au Vin*. I put all the ingredients away and opened a can of chili.

CHAPTER 10

I was slowly getting back into my groove. I was reading *Will in the World* by Stephen Greenblatt. The writer provides some great descriptions of what life was like in the London of Shakespeare's day. The population was near two hundred thousand, fifteen times larger than any other city in England and Wales. There was a lot of drinking and whoring as well as the constant danger of attacks by thieves and cutthroats. Sewage and garbage everywhere. Epidemics were common. Bubonic plague wiped out tens of thousands of people and caused the extermination of every cat and dog in the mistaken belief they were spreading the plague. Unfortunately, this left the rats, which actually carried the disease, free to multiply.

Another outcome of the plague was the closing of all places of public gatherings except for the churches. This ruling bankrupted the theaters. It got so bad that at one point only two theater groups remained in all of London out of six or more. One of them was the Lord Chamberlain Players, which Shakespeare belonged to. It managed not only to survive but to profit by adding many of the well-known players of the groups that went under. Good luck for Will, who owned a piece of the action.

Exercise was a great help, too, in getting me back into my groove. I did push-ups, crunches, free weights, and the light bag. I began riding my bike again. I'd also resumed yoga and Waitankung. I hadn't gotten to the tennis courts yet but I knew it was only a matter of time.

I was in the middle of a workout when Toby called. A week or so had passed since the nasty experience with Detective Nolan. There'd been no further developments regarding Cormac's murder, at least, as far as I knew. The only thing I'd learned was from Toby. They had finally told her that Cormac had been stabbed.

"I went to see Pokharam," Toby said. "You remember her, don't you?"

How could anyone forget Toby's tarot reader? Toby made no important decisions without consulting her first. She had taken us to see Pokharam when she'd been conflicted about her father's involvement with the stolen Fabergés. This woman was someone from another time, another place. She lived deep in the woods in a yellow house, wore a yellow dress, white gloves, served us tea and watercress sandwiches, and asked in a cultured British voice, *Shall I be Mother?*

"It was very important that I speak to her," Toby said. "I told her about my father and how the police have gotten nowhere."

"I know how much you depend on her. What did she have to say?"

"You'll be quite surprised. She said I should persuade you to investigate his murder. That the police will not be able to do it themselves."

"I thought she was smarter than that."

"With Pokharam it's not a question of intelligence. She doesn't think the way ordinary people do. She exists on a different level."

"I hear you. But in this case, her level is off kilter." I went into the kitchen to get some water.

"I will pay you well to do it."

"That's nice but beside the point. I don't see how I can do anything that's going to help solve your father's murder."

"Why not?"

"Lots of reasons. For a start, I don't have access. That means I don't know what there is to know. I had to practically beg the Chief, who I thought was a friend, to tell me how your father was killed. And I got nowhere." I held the phone with my shoulder and put a glass under the water spout in the refrigerator door.

"It doesn't mean you can't catch up."

"How would I do that?"

"I have a lot of clout. I may be able to do something."

"In a murder investigation? Somehow I doubt it."

"Jake, trust me. I know a lot of powerful people. Governors, United States senators, mayors, county executives. Even the President, although I don't think I'd ask him to get involved. If you're willing to do it, I'll see what I can accomplish."

"Are you kidding? I'd love to do it. I'd give a lot to find out who killed your father. I told you, I had a lot of warm feelings toward that man."

"That's all I need to know," she said.

I drank the glass of water wondering if she could really get it done.

CHAPTER 11

A couple of days later I got a call from Chief Vincent J. Mazzini.

"What's going on?" he said.

"About what?"

"I just heard from the primary investigator on the Blather murder case. She was very upset."

"You talking about Detective Nolan? What was she complaining about? I didn't break down and confess to the murder?"

"Worse than that. She said she'd been told by her sergeant to let you see the records on the case."

"No kidding?"

"Yep, they're going to let you look through the files. That's pretty amazing."

I was smiling, but glad that he didn't know. "So why did she call you? To see if you could do something about it?"

"No comment. I just wanted to know how you managed it."

"I didn't. But I'll give you a clue. You know the old saying, 'It ain't what you know, it's who you know'?"

"I get your drift. What I don't understand is, what's in it for you?"

"Nothing, except the daughter thinks I can help. Who knows? It can't hurt for a pair of fresh eyes to take a look."

"They may give you quite a bit of grief over there. Cops don't like outsiders looking over their shoulders."

"I'll just have to deal with it. Wouldn't it be great if I could help catch whoever did it?"

"I hear you."

"Well, I have a question. What do I do now? Is Nolan going to get in touch with me?"

"Not on your life. She's not going to hand you anything on a silver platter. If you want something, you'll have to chase her."

"I don't know what I did to rub her the wrong way."

"From what I understand it doesn't take much. If you need anything from me, give me a holler. Good luck."

CHAPTER 12

Before I did anything else I called Toby, a mug of coffee in one hand, phone in the other. "How'd you do it?"

"Believe me, it wasn't easy. I had to make quite a number of phone calls and do a lot of pleading. I think I got some extra sympathy because it was my father I was concerned about. That seemed to have turned the tide."

"You got me access only to the records, is that right? Not to anything else?"

"Sorry. That's all I could get."

"Then there may not be much I can do."

"I know you better than you know yourself. I have confidence that if there's any way you can do more you will."

"I'll try my best, Toby."

"I'm counting on it," she said.

I finished the coffee and looked up the homicide division of the police department in the Suffolk County telephone book. I dialed and asked for Detective Sienna Nolan. When she answered I told her who I was.

"Oh, you," she said.

"Right. And you know why I'm calling."

"Look. Let's get something straight. I don't know how you pulled this off and I don't care. I never heard of anybody outside the department who's been allowed to look at a file like this. But if my sergeant says do it, I have to do it. Just remember one thing, you're an observer. Strictly an observer. No hands-on anything. Is that clear?"

"Clear. I am a camera."

"What does that mean?"

"It means that I'll look and observe and not say anything. It's the title of a book by Christopher Isherwood."

"Christopher Isherwood?" There was a pause. I had a feeling she was swallowing hard not to say, *Who the fuck is Christopher Isherwood?* What she did say was, "Okay, you want to be a camera? Fine. Just remember, a camera doesn't talk."

"When can I see the file?"

"Be here tomorrow morning at eight."

CHAPTER 13

The John L. Barry police headquarters in Hauppauge was about an hour's drive from Sag Harbor. It was a massive concrete building surrounded by parking lots so that it gave the impression of being a fortress protected by a moat. I was there at 7:30 a.m. I told the cop at the desk I had an appointment with Detective Sienna Nolan.

He picked up the phone and spoke to someone. "She'll be right down," he said. "I need your driver's license." He took it and did something with it on his computer. "Picture phones not allowed. Do you have one?"

I nodded.

"Hand it over and have a seat," he said. "You get the license and the phone back when you leave."

I sat on a plastic chair for forty-five minutes before Nolan appeared. She wore a plain gray suit with a simple blouse, nothing like those sexy female detectives on *Law and Order* and *CSI*. She didn't appear to be wearing makeup but she looked good anyway.

After entering a code in a locked door, she led me along unmarked corridors needing paint, up a staircase, then more walking, all the while her not saying a word. We finally entered a large office with a scattering of desks, some of them occupied by detectives and some not. The other detectives were men. They looked at me without smiling or speaking. The resentment in the room was palpable. I knew they didn't want me there but

74

the atmosphere was so hostile I wondered if they objected to Nolan as well.

Even though the room had windows and was lit with fluorescent light, I felt as if I were underground and without air.

She called out to a tall man wearing a white shirt and a blue tie, holding a container of coffee. "Sarge, this is the guy."

"Oh, yeah?" He came over and stuck one hand out. "I'm Detective Sergeant Constantine. Always wanted to meet a guy with brass balls."

"Nah," I said, shaking his hand. "They're more like copper."

He gave me a look and walked away.

Detective Nolan pointed at the chair next to her desk. On the desk was a gray manila folder tied with a string. "You have to look at everything here," she said. "Can't take it out of this room." She pushed the folder in my direction. "This is the Case Jacket. Everything that's been covered so far. CC, Incident Report, Death Report, Property Invoice, Evidence Analysis, fingerprints, photographs, autopsy, interviews. Read it and weep."

"Meaning what?"

"Meaning you won't learn anything."

I untied the string and began to look through the files having no idea what I would find. Various teams had gone through the crime scene. There were fingerprint records and photographs of the antique shop, and of the victim. Poor Cormac was lying on the floor. He was on his back, his right arm at his side, his left outstretched. He had fallen next to a table on top of which was a small brass lamp. There was an unreadable expression on his face. It was a strange look, puzzled. Maybe he was thinking, why is this happening to me? Or was he thinking, why did this person kill me? There were a bunch of photographs of the shop that detailed the many kinds of objects in the shop. Interesting but unhelpful.

There were also photographs of the autopsy. These were grue-some and gory and something I could not deal with at that hour of the morning. To tell the truth, I didn't think I could look at them anytime without wanting to vomit. I glanced at them quickly.

The autopsy report noted that he'd been stabbed multiple times. The blade that killed him was three inches long, serrated, and probably from a knife that folded, such as a hunting knife. It also stated that the killer was probably right handed. I guessed they could tell that from the angle of the knife thrusts.

There was a list of his customers, a long list. There were lots of famous people in and around Sag Harbor who had been patrons of Cormac Blather. Alan Alda, Steven Spielberg, Julie Andrews, Ben Gazzara; the writers, Alan Furst and Thomas Harris. Not famous but locally well known were the presidents of the John Jermain Library and the Sag Harbor Historical Society.

There were many other locals whom Rosalind and I had met at the library, or the Whaling Museum, or just picking up the Sunday *Times* at the bagel store. The same-people-at-the-same-hour-every-Sunday kind of thing. And even a few of the men and women I played tennis with.

I wrote down some of the names of people I knew. I thought it might be a good idea to talk to them and pick up something of local gossip about Cormac they might not have told the cop who interviewed them.

Knowing Cormac, I guessed there were deals he had not recorded because they had probably been paid in cash to avoid sales tax on the purchaser's part and income tax on Cormac's part. I would have liked knowing who those people were.

Detective Nolan and her team had spoken to the customer who found the body, a woman who had not been able to tell them anything other than that she had seen his body on the floor and ran out to call for help. They had canvassed the merchants on the block, starting with those on either side of Cormac's shop, and talked to everyone who was out on the street at the time they began the canvass. All negative. Nobody had seen or heard anything.

The team had interviewed many on the list. Toby, of course, and most of the other well-known names. Again negative. It seemed obvious that none of the interviewees had a motive to commit murder. Then I came across the interview with Bryson Mergenthaler. Detective Nolan had conducted that one with my buddy, the Sag Harbor Chief of Police. He'd told me that he liked to stay in touch with what was going on. I guessed he also wanted to meet the guy who was one of the richest men in the world as well as a major art collector.

What I found interesting in the interview was Detective Nolan's reference to the burial box and her implication that it might be a fake. How would she know or even suspect such a thing? She must have done a lot of research on poor old Cormac. She probably found out what Mergenthaler must have known as well, that he was dealing with a man who had a murky past. I would guess he also knew that although Cormac had never been prosecuted he had been accused of having sold forged paintings. What would he do if he learned that the old burial box he had bought for what had to be a lot of money was another one of Cormac's fakes? Would he resort to murder?

My first reaction was, *absolutely not.* After a little more thought, my next feeling was, *not likely.* Another period of thought, and I was saying to myself: *Who knows what one of the most powerful men in the world might do if faced with treachery? He could be capable of anything.*

I made a note about the burial box. My eyes were getting tired. The papers I'd already looked at were piled up on Nolan's desk. My watch told me I'd been reading a couple of hours. My stomach was rumbling as well, letting me know I could use something to eat and drink. I looked for Nolan but she wasn't in the room.

"Anyone know where Detective Nolan is?" I called out.

One of the detectives in the corner muttered, "Probably in the ladies' room, injecting a tampon."

There was a snicker. I didn't respond. For whatever reason, gender, abrasive personality, or both, it was clear Detective Nolan was not universally loved. I rubbed my eyes and went back to the reports.

They had subpoenaed records of all the phone calls in and out for the day of the murder as well as the week before. The names of the callers were listed next to their phone numbers. I couldn't help noticing the name of a person I'd recently spoken to myself, Chase McCleod. He'd called twice, the day before the murder, and the day before that.

What connection could there be between Chase and Cormac? Cormac didn't sell modern paintings so the possibility of something illicit was distinctly possible. That should definitely be looked into. I decided not to mention it right away, my reasoning being that it would look too much like an attention grabber. I didn't want to put Nolan off any more than she already was. I wrote down his name.

When Nolan got back, I told her I'd had enough for one day and asked would it be okay if I could come back another time.

"They said you could look but they didn't say how many times. I'd have to check with the sergeant first."

"That's fine," I said. I was being especially polite. "I'll call later and you can let me know. By the way, would you care to have some lunch? I'm buying."

She gave me the look women give men in crowded subways who get too close. "Thanks, but no thanks," she said, moderating her tone so that even though she might grant that I wasn't one of those creeps, she'd like to be rid of me anyway.

"Aren't you hungry?"

"I rarely eat lunch."

Bullshit, I thought. You just don't want to sit across a table from me while I ask you a million questions.

"Okay," I said. "I get it."

"Get what?"

"Nothing." I wasn't going to give her the satisfaction of begging. "Let me ask you something. What's next on the agenda?"

"You mean, what am I going to do after this?"

"Exactly."

"You saw the list. There are more people to question."

"You mean, you just see everyone on the list?"

"You have a better idea?" she snapped.

"Hey," I said, raising my hands. "I don't have any idea at all. I'm just asking."

She made a face. "Sorry. I'm a little uptight today. I didn't mean to jump all over you like that."

My immediate thought was, *You can jump all over me any time you want.* Then it hit me that I hadn't had that instinctive male reaction in a long time. In fact, not since Rosalind died had I even felt a spark of lust. I hurriedly pushed that out of my mind and said, "Don't worry about it. But why don't we have a cup of coffee or something? We can talk about the case a little more."

"There's really nothing I want to talk about."

I took a deep breath. "Look, Detective Nolan. I know I've only been given a shot at the records, and that's all, but I want you to know one thing. I'm not here to get in your way. I'm not here to criticize or obstruct. Do you follow what I'm saying? All I want is to help." I hoped I wasn't laying the molasses on too thick.

For a long moment she didn't respond. Those startling green eyes now looked me over as if I were a tuna suspended on a hook and she was the buyer for a Japanese sushi bar. She turned her head to look around the room. I followed her look and saw the others busy at their desks, apparently paying no attention to us. She spoke in a low voice not much more than a whisper. "I'll meet you outside in fifteen minutes."

Better a witty fool than a foolish wit.

She put all the files back in the big envelope, dropped it into a drawer of her desk and locked it. I stood up and made sure everyone knew I was leaving. "Thanks a lot, Detective," I said, a little louder than necessary. "I appreciate the time you gave me."

CHAPTER 14

I sat in my car slumped as low as possible hoping nobody from Nolan's unit would walk by and recognize me. It was about twenty minutes before she showed.

"Sorry to keep you waiting. I did it on purpose. I'd just as soon the others didn't know we were going for coffee."

"They hate my guts," I said. "I could see that. I thought you did, too."

"I do, or at least, I did. It's a cop thing. Don't want civilians butting into our affairs. But I get the feeling you're not a bad guy. You don't strike me as a hot dog, anyway. If you did, I wouldn't be here."

"I'm glad," I said. "Where can we go?"

"Follow me."

I followed her red Mitsubishi Eclipse from Yaphank Road to the LIE, otherwise known as the Long Island Expressway, or more often, Crawlway, where we turned west. After many miles we left the LIE at Horseblock Road and arrived at a diner somewhere in Medford, the middle middle of Long Island. Didn't matter. North, South, East, or West, every diner on the Island looks the same. Outside there's an acre of gleaming chrome and cinder blocks of glass guarding the entrance. Inside, ornate chandeliers, vinyl covered booths, and waitresses chewing gum.

I couldn't help wondering if our having lunch a long way from her fellow detectives might have something to do with the sexist comment I'd heard in the squad room. I had a BLT on rye toast and black coffee. I'd never liked sugar in my coffee but at one time used to add milk. Over time I'd come to prefer it *au naturel*. The bacon in my sandwich was overdone and greasy. Nolan had a spinach pie that she attacked as though she hadn't eaten for a month. "Must be good," I said, a bit envious.

"You mean because I'm wolfing it down? No, it's ordinary. That's just the way I eat. I grew up in a large Irish family. All cops, by the way. My brothers were bigger than me and I had to be fast if I wanted to get my share. But I don't deny I have a big appetite."

"How do you keep your svelte figure?"

The *creep* look she had given me before came back. "By having to deal with people like you busting my chops."

I laughed. "Okay. I give up. No personal remarks. Just business."

I went back to my cardboard sandwich and she continued to gobble her lunch at an incredible speed.

When the waitress came to refill our coffee cups, she asked if we wanted dessert.

I shook my head but Nolan's face lit up. "What've you got?"

Without pause our waitress recited the list: three kinds of Danish, a slew of pies—blueberry, apple, lemon meringue, chocolate cream, banana cream. She finished up with rice pudding, and assorted flavors of ice cream.

Nolan decided on blueberry pie topped with a scoop of vanilla. "Just one scoop," she said.

"One scoop," I said. "Commendable. Always good to be calorie conscious."

She gave me a cool smile, displaying nice teeth, straight and white. "Okay. Let's talk."

"You sure you don't want to have your dessert first? I wouldn't want to interfere with your meal."

"You made your point. But know this, if there's one thing I can't stand, it's a wise guy. So if you want to talk business, now's the time."

"You're right," I said. "I apologize." I held out my hand. She made a face but shook it anyway, with a firm grip. "Okay. I'd like to know how you came to ask Bryson Mergenthaler about that ossuary, the burial box. What made you think it might be a fake?"

She gave me a Cheshire cat smile. "Pretty good, wasn't it? I think it hit him right in the nuts. What I shouldn't have done was make that wise-ass remark that caused him to terminate the interview." She leaned forward. "It was just a hunch. For one thing I'd read a story in the *Times* about fake antiques in Jerusalem. And Blather's computer had an e-mail from Jerusalem the day he died. It was in English but didn't make sense so I guessed it was coded. But after I read it a few times I felt like there was a hint in it about some kind of trouble. When I went through Blather's record of sales, I picked up on the ossuary because where else would that have come from if not Jerusalem? I took a chance and it paid off. Mergenthaler's reaction was proof, to me anyway, that something's fishy. That's one avenue I have to explore."

The waitress slid the blueberry pie in front of her. It was a slice of pie large enough to cover the entire plate. The ball of ice cream sat on top melting happily away. Nolan didn't hesitate. She gave her full attention to the food.

I waited for her to pause for breath. "How would you go about that, contact the cops in Jerusalem?"

"Go about what?" she said, putting another forkful into her mouth.

"Finding out if the burial box that Cormac sold to Mergenthaler was a fake."

"Oh yeah, right. That's what I'll do. Try to find out the person to talk to over there. They might have a guy who specializes in that kind of thing."

"I know someone here who might be able to help."

"Who's that?"

"My rabbi. He goes to Jerusalem a lot. He teaches in a school there in the winter when our temple closes down. I could ask him if he knows anyone connected with antique forgeries. I wouldn't be surprised to find they have someone who looks into things like that. I know I've read about fake scrolls that people tried to pass off, supposedly like the Dead Sea Scrolls. Somebody caught them."

"Sure. Ask him. What have we got to lose?"

"I will." I thought it was encouraging that she said, *we*. She swallowed the last of the pie and drained her cup of coffee. "That was good." She began to slide out of the booth. "I have to get going."

"So soon?"

"I have some personal stuff to take care of. The murder case is my number-one priority, but life gets in the way. I can't be a detective twenty-four hours a day, even though that's what they'd like. Let me know how you make out with the rabbi." She reached the end of the booth and stood up. "Thanks for the lunch."

"You're welcome."

I watched her walk away. She had good legs and a nice behind. She moved smoothly, like a long-distance runner. While I finished my coffee I heard her pull out of the parking lot, tires squealing. I decided not to take it personally.

CHAPTER 15

As soon as I got home I called Rabbi Benvenuti. Naturally, I got a recording. Why is it that when you really want to speak to someone you always get an answering machine? I left a message asking him to call me back.

Then I called Toby. I thought she ought to hear what had happened since she'd gone to a lot of trouble to get me into this. And it also occurred to me that she might know Bryson Mergenthaler. She certainly hung out with the rich and famous, so it was a possibility. I didn't know what good that would do even if she did know him, but it was worth exploring.

Another machine. I left her a brief message telling her I'd made the initial contact.

To pass the time I did some stretching, fifteen minutes on the light bag, and twenty minutes of free weights. When there was still no return call from anyone, I changed into my biking gear, grabbed my cell, and headed out for a long ride. I needed the air and the solitude. I used to do a lot of good thinking when I was pedaling around and working up a sweat.

As it turned out, I got the sweat and the fresh air but no thoughts that helped. No return call either. By that time it was five o'clock. An older friend of ours, who enjoyed her liquor, called it *drinkey poo* time. I poured myself a double Luksusowa over rocks, added a slice of lemon, switched on WMNR and listened to the taped programs of the late Karl Haas. While sipping my vodka and listening to *The Moldau,* I thought about

Cormac's murder and my involvement in it. Would I really be able to do anything to help solve the case? Detective Nolan had become somewhat conciliatory but I had no illusions that she was going to let me inside. I was a civilian and it seemed obvious that her sergeant and the other detectives wanted me to stay that way. Why would she fight the system?

Dinner was good, and easy, too. I had leftover lamb shanks in the fridge. All I had to do was whip up some mashed potatoes, make a tomato and onion salad, and pour a glass of Cabernet Sauvignon.

I was asleep shortly afterwards.

The phone woke me. I looked at the glowing numerals on the clock next to my bed. It was 3:15 a.m. I mumbled hello.

"Meestair Wanderman? I hope you are feeling well. Meestair Blather is dead. Is possible you are next if you stick your nose in."

Click.

Now I was awake. Heavy Russian accent. Could my father have been right about Solofsky's wanting revenge? Was the threat real or just someone trying to throw a scare into me? Solofsky could have been told about Blather and gotten the idea to use the murder to take advantage of it. Or it could be the real murderer trying to scare me off the case. But how would he or she know about my being involved?

I didn't have any answers.

It was a good couple of hours before I finally fell asleep again.

The next morning, I tried putting the nastiness of the night behind me and dialed the rabbi. He picked up. After the hellos and how-are-you's, I got to the point. "I imagine you know a lot of people in Jerusalem."

"I do."

"Any official types?"

"You mean, people in government?"

"Exactly."

"As a matter of fact, yes."

"Do they have any kind of an office that deals with checking out antiques? You know, if someone should claim he has the Dead Sea Scrolls, or something like that?"

"They do. Why do you ask?"

"Just curious."

"As a matter of fact, they've made quite a name for themselves exposing fakes. A friend of mine is pretty close to the man in charge of it."

"That's amazing. I hope you don't mind my asking, but how do you come to know such important people?"

"Jerusalem is a big city but in a lot of ways it's a small town. I spend a lot of time over there, and being associated with a school has given me a certain amount of entrée. Another thing is, there are groups of Americans like me who tend to congregate together. Equally, there are groups of Israelis who like Americans and want to know everything about us. It just so happens that a lot of these people are high up in government."

"Fantastic. What's your friend's name? Maybe I can contact him."

"Jake, you really helped me out and I appreciate it. But I'm a little uncertain about this. I think I ought to know why you want it first. Why all the interest?"

"Umm," I hesitated. As usual, I hadn't thought this through. I had no idea what I should say, but felt I should definitely not tell him there was a connection to a murder and a police investigation. If Nolan heard I'd shot off my mouth she'd have my ass in a sling, or worse. So I lied. "I recently read a piece in the *Times* about something that took place in Jerusalem. It rang a bell because I knew you spent a lot of time there."

"Okay, but why do you want to know individual names?"

Rabbi Benvenuti was a cool cat, all right, sounding more like a lawyer than a religioso. "Like I said, curiosity. I like names. It grounds everything, know what I mean?"

"Not really."

"What harm can it do if you give me the name? I'm not going to stalk the guy."

"I'm really sorry about this, Jake. But this man is a good friend. I don't feel free to bandy his name about."

"Forget about it. Not important. What about the name of the outfit? I'm pretty sure it was mentioned in the paper." I hadn't read the story but it was possible.

"I can tell you that. It's called the Antiquities Authority. They do a lot of investigating because there are, unfortunately, a lot of fakers out there."

"Sorry to hear that. Jews taking advantage of other Jews?"

He laughed. "Since when is that news?"

"What was I thinking? Anyway, thanks for the information."

"Why do I have this funny feeling that you're not telling me the whole story here, Jake?"

"I have no idea what you mean, Rabbi. I'm as pure as the driven snow. Or, as Shakespeare might say, *If you can look into the seeds of time, And say which grain will grow and which will not, Speak then to me.*"

I hung up before he could ask me either to explain how that applied to the situation at hand or get me to say anything else that might cause me to reveal more than I should.

Okay, I now thought, on the one hand, I had something to work with. It shouldn't be too hard for Detective Nolan to track them down. On the other hand, did I want Nolan to find it? (*On the one hand, on the other hand,* I sounded like Tevye in *Fiddler on the Roof.*)

And what about the phone call in the middle of the night? Should I mention it to Nolan? I wasn't sure if she'd take it seriously or laugh at me.

The answer was obvious, at least in regard to Jerusalem: get the info, then tell Nolan.

CHAPTER 16

Ha! Google had it, the whole thing. I asked for Antiquities Authority and up it came. The IAA, Israel Antiquities Authority. Only it was all in Hebrew. Then I looked more closely and saw they had an English version. Those Jews, they think of everything. Now I had the whole works, all open to the public, even including the name of the guy who ran it. I didn't need the rabbi's friend, the man he was so protective of, why, I didn't know. The head guy was Shlomo Wittnauer. There was even a *Contact Us* tab. I could write to him myself and see what I could find out. Once again, I shot down that idea. This was Nolan territory. I had to give this information to her and let her do the follow-up.

I got on the phone to give her the good news. Guess what? She wasn't there. One more time I left my number.

God, I was antsy. I didn't know what to do with myself. I wanted action. I *needed action.* I had to do something, anything, but had no idea what to do.

I marched around the house, from the kitchen to the bathroom to the living room to the bedrooms to the basement. Up the stairs and down the stairs. Back and forth. Over and over.

On my last trip near the front door I happened to notice the umbrella stand. I stopped moving and felt my eyes fill. I could feel my mouth twisting as I tried to stop what was happening. Unexpected things, reminders of Rosalind, almost always brought this on.

My body began to tremble. I sat on the small chair near the door. There was an old umbrella in the umbrella stand, not ours, so someone must have left it. A kind of fog seemed to enter my bloodstream and drain all the energy from my body and brain. This too, had happened before.

Rosalind had come across this once rusty lump of iron on one of her expeditions through antique shops and yard sales. "It'll be great," she'd said. "You just get the rust off for me, that's all. I'll do the rest." And she had, painting it with an assortment of tiny petals so that it ended up looking more like a flowering shrub than a holder for umbrellas.

It happened less frequently now, and would probably end someday, I imagined. With time, the scars heal, they say, and one manages to forget. I hoped that wouldn't happen to me. I didn't want the scars to heal.

I waited for the episode to pass, as I knew it would. It was only a matter of allowing it to run its course. Eventually I was able to take a couple of deep breaths and stand up. I was back in the real world.

Now I noticed the notebook I'd taken with me to the police station. I opened it. Immediately, a name jumped out at me. McCleod. Of course. I remembered thinking when I wrote the note there was something fishy about him all along, and now, with those telephone calls to Cormac, there was no doubt in my mind that he and Cormac had been up to something, most definitely not kosher.

I would go and see him. To hell with Sienna Nolan. I couldn't wait around forever for her to come back from her personal stuff, whatever that was. Maybe *she* wasn't a detective twenty-four hours a day, but I sure as hell could make like one!

So off I went to McCleod's house in the Springs. I strode around to the studio without ringing the front door bell and having to submit to his video and intercom. I banged on the door.

"Who's that?"

"Jake Wanderman. Remember me?"

"What do you want?"

"I need to talk to you, my friend."

"I'm not your friend and don't want to be."

"Shut the fuck up and open the door," I said.

There was a long silence. Then I heard a click, as the lock in the door turned and the door opened. He held onto the handle looking exactly the same as before: a runt with malevolent raccoon eyes, paint splattered T-shirt and jeans, and bare feet.

"Don't you ever wear shoes?" I asked.

"I hate shoes."

I brushed past him, into the studio and right to the easel where he'd been working, hoping to see an imitation of a masterpiece. What I saw was a realistic interpretation of a small boat with oars, sitting in a pond. I'm not an art expert but I could tell it wasn't a very good painting. The scene looked real but had no life. I was disappointed, not in the painting, but in not finding a forged Renoir or a forgery of anyone else, for that matter. "I didn't know you did this kind of thing."

"How would you know what I do, anyway?"

I nodded. "Right. I wouldn't. But the fact that you knew Cormac Blather makes me think you paint other kinds of stuff, too. Am I right?"

"Cormac who?"

"Don't give me that shit. You know who he is. I happen to know you called him at his store just before he was killed."

The expression on his face changed so suddenly it was almost funny. One minute he was rambunctious and confrontational, the next, his mouth was open and he'd lost all the color in his skin. That wasn't easy, since his complexion was a pasty gray to begin with.

"Okay," I said. "Now you want to tell me about it?"

"I got to sit down," he said. He walked over to a stool looking as if he was about to throw up.

"Are you going to be sick?" I asked.

"I'm sick already. I got a bleeding ulcer."

"That's too bad, but I still want to know what you and Cormac were up to."

"I got nothing to say."

"Would you rather talk to the cops? I'll just tell them I suspect you were doing forgeries for Cormac and see where they go from there."

He sat, closed his eyes and shook his head slowly from side to side. "Why me? Why do these things always happen to me?"

"I'll give you three guesses. You're devious, dishonest, and you don't want to admit it. Woe is you."

He clutched at his stomach. "I'm feeling really bad."

I believed him. His pallor now had a tinge of green in it and his hands were trembling. I thought he might tumble off the stool. "Can I get you anything?"

He pointed. "Back there. Fridge. Milk."

I found the refrigerator. There was an open quart of milk, small tubs of Yoplait yogurt, bottles of water, cans of Diet Pepsi and Seven-Up. I didn't see any glasses so I just brought him the container of milk.

He tilted it back and swallowed a few gulps. "Thanks, that should help." He took a package of Tums out of his pocket and popped two into his mouth.

"You get these attacks a lot?"

"On and off. I learned to deal with it. Beats an operation."

"I'm sorry about your ulcer but I need to know what you and Cormac were up to."

"Just because I called him, that don't prove anything."

"Let me save you the trouble of lying, okay? I'm positive you were doing forgeries for him. You know how I know? Because what you were doing for him was nothing new. When he lived in England a long time ago he found a talented guy like you. Guess what he did? Got the guy to produce original paintings . . . Picassos, Renoirs, Degas, and so on. The artist went to jail but Cormac didn't. Do you want to wind up the same way?"

"How do you know this stuff?"

"Because I was a close friend of his."

He massaged his stomach. "Can we keep the cops out of this?"

"I can't promise."

"If the cops find out I'm a dead duck."

"I said I'll try to keep it confidential."

He sighed. "What do you want to know?"

"The whole deal. You were doing forgeries for him, right?"

He nodded.

"What kind?"

"All kinds. Mostly Impressionists. The real old ones are tricky because it takes a lot of work finding old canvas, matching the paint, a lot of technical stuff. With the moderns you eliminate all that shit."

"What were you calling him about?"

"I just finished one. A Mary Cassatt. Beautiful job, if I do say so myself. I wanted to know when I could bring it over. I needed the money."

"What was he paying you?"

"A thousand bucks up front and a percentage of what he sold it for."

"Not a bad deal. So you were doing okay. Why'd you call him twice?"

"To confirm. I was supposed to deliver the painting on

Saturday, just after closing time."

"The day he was murdered?"

"Right."

"But you didn't deliver it, did you? There was no new canvas anywhere. He wouldn't've had time to put it away."

"I didn't deliver it because he was dead when I got there."

"What time was that?"

"I'm not sure. Six, six-thirty, maybe."

"Tell me what happened."

He was still holding the container of milk. He had another gulp of it. "This conversation ain't helping my stomach any."

"Fuck your stomach."

"Okay, okay. I wrapped the canvas in brown paper and taped it good. Then I put it in my car and drove over there. I took one-fourteen and drove over to Madison Street so I could come into Main Street on the other side across from Cormac. I parked in front of Sylvester's because that's where I always park when I go to him. It was already getting dark. You know, this time of year it gets dark early. The streetlights were on but the stores were closed. There were no cars parked the way they always are and nobody on the sidewalks. Sag Harbor is really pretty when no one's around.

"I took out the canvas and was about to cross when I saw a guy come out of his store. I waited for him to walk away, which he did. I didn't see where he went so he might have walked down that alley where there's parking in the back. You know, behind the stores."

"I know. Go on."

"I crossed the street, opened the door and saw Blather on the floor. I was sure he was dead, I don't know why. He just looked dead, somehow. But I took a step closer to make sure. As soon as I saw the blood I was certain. Then I got out of there as fast as I could."

"So you saw the guy who killed Cormac? You saw the murderer? What did he look like?"

"It was already dark. I wasn't paying attention. I have no idea what he looked like."

"Was he tall, short, fat, skinny? How was he dressed?"

"He was medium. Not tall, not short. He wasn't fat. He was wearing dark clothes, that's all I remember. He might have had a hat on, I'm not sure."

"What kind of hat?"

"I only said that because I don't remember the color of his hair, maybe it was black, but it could've been brown, or it could have been covered up by a cap. It wasn't blond, I can tell you that. I would've noticed blond."

"Um," I said. I was trying to think. How important was this information? It established the time of death, told us the killer was a man. The description wasn't much help, but it was better than nothing.

McCleod said, "I told you everything I know. Please don't tell the cops it was me that told you. What good would it do? They'd bust me for sure and it wouldn't help find the murderer, would it?"

"I'll do my best to keep you out of it. But it won't be easy."

He gulped down some more of the milk. "God, I feel rotten."

"That's funny," I said. "I feel pretty good."

CHAPTER 17

Landis Kalem opened his eyes. He glanced at the clock on the night table. 4:03 a.m. He wondered why he was awake. In the city it wouldn't have surprised him because he was a light sleeper and city noises were plentiful, but here night sound was unusual. Yet something had disturbed his sleep. A sound of some kind. Alien, unfamiliar.

He listened for another moment, trying to hear if whatever it was might be repeated. He had no fear that it could be an intruder. His employer's house in North Haven was, as were all Mergenthaler's residences, equipped with a security system that had every bell and whistle. If Landis were tempted to leave his room at night and wander down a hall, alarms would go off. This was not something he liked but had to endure.

His bedroom was located in the servants' area of the house, far from where his employer slept. Mergenthaler rewarded him financially but always made sure that no matter how much time they spent together, and no matter how much he might know about the man's private life, their relationship remained what it had been from the beginning: employer and employee. Putting him with the other servants was a way of reinforcing that distinction.

He may have been put in the servants' area of the residence and at a distance from his employer, but he was given the kind of room few servants ever slept in. It was, in fact, a suite, consisting of a sitting room, a bedroom, and a bathroom containing a

Jacuzzi and a shower that produced steam. Bryson Mergenthaler was a great believer in the carrot and the stick. Because of
that belief the bed Landis slept in was a French Art Nouveau
piece with a matching nightstand. The dresser was from the
French Regence period, made of carved walnut with a marble
top. On the bed frame was a Dux mattress that cost five
thousand dollars. The pillows were down, and the sheets were
600-count cotton. The paintings and prints on the walls were
from Mergenthaler's collection.

Landis stared up at the ceiling in the darkness, and realized
how far he had come from his childhood. Years of never having
enough of anything, a father who'd gone to prison and a mother
who had turned to alcohol to get through the days. She'd
eventually been put into a facility for the mentally ill. His father
had not been able to bear the disgrace of prison and had hanged
himself with a bedsheet. Landis had been placed with a foster
family who were decent enough but preferred their own children
to him. At sixteen he'd told them he was leaving. The foster
parents had tried to persuade him to stay but he knew they
were only interested in continuing to receive the monthly
stipend. He took his few belongings and had been on his own
ever since.

There were two doors to his suite, one directly into the
bedroom and one that opened into the sitting room. There it
was . . . something. He couldn't identify it but it was there.
Some kind of sound that filtered through the door nearest to
him. Mergenthaler's office was just down the hall, one room
past the staircase that led down to the main floor. Was Mergenthaler in his office at four o'clock in the morning? It was
unlikely but not impossible. It had happened before. The man
had a mind that only stopped thinking and scheming when he
was asleep. But his sleeping habits were erratic. It was probably
for that reason he had had the alarm system set in zones so that

he could shut off any area of the house he wished from a master panel in his bedroom.

Landis got out of bed and opened the bedroom door. He looked both ways but saw nothing unusual. Then he heard it again. The sound was clearer. Of one thing he was sure. Someone was in the office. He saw a sliver of light coming out from under the door. He started down the hall toward the sound, then stopped, went back and got an umbrella out of his closet. It wasn't much of a weapon but if a burglar had somehow gotten into the house, it would help. Once more he moved down the corridor and waited for the alarm to go off. When it didn't he felt more convinced that it was Mergenthaler in the office and that he had perhaps disabled the entire alarm system by mistake.

The sound he had heard was repeated once more and now he thought it was a drawer being slid open, and carefully, so as to make as little noise as possible. But why was his employer being so careful not to make any noise? Consideration for others was not a hallmark of Bryson Mergenthaler's character. Indeed, when he did occasionally show some thoughtfulness for another, it was usually hailed as an event that ought to rightfully propel him toward sainthood.

Landis had to decide whether to discreetly tap or to just open the door. He knew that if he opened the door without knocking he would see exactly what his employer was up to. And he had to admit to himself that he was more than curious to know what it was. But to do so without knocking might bring down torrents of wrath. He had seen some of that anger directed at others in Mergenthaler's employ but up to now had never had that sort of fury directed at him.

He hesitated. He turned his head so that one ear was closer to the door, straining to hear something. But now there was nothing, no sound of any kind.

Prudence overcame his curiosity. What good would it do to surprise his employer? Certainly there was nothing he could learn that would give Landis an advantage in this situation or in any other. For that matter, if he came upon something embarrassing, it would put him in an awkward position because then Mergenthaler would forever be uncomfortable at someone having knowledge about him that he had no way of controlling.

Having made the decision, he rapped the door lightly with the knuckles of his right hand. There was still no sound and no response. As he raised his hand again the door slowly began to open. He moved forward to enter the room and saw that it was now in darkness. "Mr. Mergenthaler?" He was suddenly lifted off his feet. An arm went around his throat, closing off the air to his lungs. He pulled as hard as he could to try and dislodge the arm but was unable to. The umbrella fell out of his hand. He tried kicking back but his bare feet made no impression on the attacker.

The pressure on his throat increased. He could feel his airway being cut off. An accented voice whispered: "Do you want to live?" The arm relaxed enough for him to breathe.

The whisperer said: "Don't talk. Just nod your head and do what I say."

Landis nodded. He didn't think he could talk anyway. It felt as if his larynx had been cracked.

"Stand still and don't turn around."

The arm came away from his throat and he was back on his feet. Landis had no intention of refusing to comply with the instructions that he should not move. He somehow knew that if he disobeyed it would mean certain death.

He stood and waited, hands at his side, wondering what was going to happen next. In spite of what he could recognize as a situation fraught with uncertainty, he wasn't afraid.

Suddenly there was a split-second flash of light, then everything was black.

CHAPTER 18

Landis came to with Mario standing over him, a worried look on his face. That was no indication of anything because Mario's face always had an expression of worry.

Mario was wringing his hands. "Are you all right, Mr. Kalem? I heard something and saw that your door was open. I looked in but you weren't there, so I went down the hall and found you."

"I don't know." He moved his head slowly from side to side. A jolt of pain shot through his skull and down his right side. "No," he said. He found it difficult to talk. "Maybe . . . a doctor."

"I must tell the master first."

Landis hated Mario calling Mergenthaler "master." The connotation, of course, was *master and slave.* He had tried getting Mario to stop doing it although he liked Mario addressing *him* as Mister Kalem. The truth was he wanted Mario to think of *him* as the master and Mario the slave.

Mario had been brought into the house as a majordomo of sorts from the yacht, where he had begun as a cabin boy at the age of sixteen. They'd taken him aboard in Sicily four years before when the cabin boy they'd had abandoned them. He'd immediately pleased everyone with his work ethic and demeanor. Notice was eventually brought to Mergenthaler. He told Landis to keep an eye on the boy. Landis found it easy to do. The boy had a magnificent ass. It didn't take him long to recognize that the boy was a jewel, in more ways than one.

"All right," Landis said. "But . . . quick . . . please . . ."

Mario left and in a few minutes was back, Mergenthaler with him.

"What happened?" Mergenthaler asked.

Landis tried to tell him what happened but his throat was too sore to say much.

"How did he get in? The alarm system is supposed to be impregnable."

Landis contained himself from sarcasm and just shook his head to indicate agreement.

"How do you feel?"

He found it easier to speak. "I was in a lot of pain a few minutes ago, but it seems to be getting better."

"We have to find out what he was doing here. Are you able to stand up?"

"I'll try."

Mario got him to his feet and he sat in a chair. He felt a little dizzy, but the pain in his throat was definitely receding, and for that he was grateful. "Give me a few minutes."

"What do you think he was after?" Mergenthaler said. "Nothing looks disarranged. Maybe he didn't find what he was looking for."

"I thought I heard him going through the desk."

"Those drawers were locked." Mergenthaler shook his head. "What the hell good are locks and alarms when someone can so easily bypass them?"

"Locks and alarms work up to a point," Landis said. "But there's always someone with the expertise to defeat them."

"Sometimes, Landis, your comments are painfully obvious. I'll forgive you, however, because it only happens occasionally, and you've been hurt." Mergenthaler went over to the far side of the room where there was a cabinet with glass doors. He grunted. "We don't have to look anymore. These locks didn't work, either. I know what the bastard came for."

As soon as he said it, Landis also knew.

"Call nine-one-one," Mergenthaler said.

Chapter 19

When I left McCleod, having gotten all the information about his connection with Cormac as well as the fact that he had probably seen the murderer, I was feeling pretty cocky. I thought I'd handled him like a pro. Now all I had to do was call Detective Nolan, tell her what I'd learned, and wait for her to pay me a compliment. Yeah, right!

Then I remembered my promise to McCleod to keep his name out of it as far as the police were concerned. How would I be able to do that? As usual, I'd opened my mouth only to find my foot in it. Hell! I didn't like the idea of going back on my word but I didn't see that I had a choice. If I were hoping to get Detective Nolan to let me in I would have to give her this stuff from McCleod. I could at least plead with her not to prosecute him on forgery charges since he was helping out with the murder. That might help both him and my moral standing.

Suddenly I felt confused by my choices. Which was right, which was wrong? My stomach growled at me, too. I decided to have something to eat, then sleep on it and see how I felt in the morning.

I slept erratically, getting up to pee a couple of times, but when I was finally up and had my coffee, brewed in my French Bodum coffee press, I knew what I had to do. I went straight to the secretary desk in the den. That desk had belonged to Rosalind's parents. They were redoing their house once and were going to donate it to the Salvation Army. The finish was a dark mahogany and badly scratched. But the lines of the piece were lovely, the hardware old curlicued metal, and the interior a gem of cubbyholes and drawers. We said we would take it. They laughed at us, of course. Silly kids wanting a piece of junk. At the time we were in a small apartment in Brooklyn. We spread newspapers on the living room floor, put the piece there and began to strip the finish. A messy job. It took us weeks, working on it at night, after working all day. When we got down to the original wood, we found beautiful grained oak underneath the gunk. We felt vindicated and were especially happy when her parents said they didn't recognize it.

I had my electronic Rolodex in the desk along with a pile of papers and my notebook. I'd neglected to enter Nolan's number at Police Headquarters but I knew I had written it down. I managed to locate it on a scrap of paper. It was only a little after eight but I called anyway.

For a change, she was there. "I got good information about Jerusalem," I began. I'd decided to first tell her what I'd learned about the Antiquities Authority in Jerusalem and then blow her mind with the stuff about McCleod. But I didn't get a chance because she interrupted me.

"I don't think those folks in Jerusalem are going to be any help," she said. "At least not now."

"Why not?"

"We don't have anything to show them. The ossuary was stolen last night."

I was standing in front of the desk with the cordless phone to my ear and suddenly felt that I had to sit down. "From Mergenthaler? How could that happen? Didn't he have it locked up along with the rest of his art collection?"

"They called nine-one-one at five this morning. Someone broke in, attacked the secretary and almost broke his neck. I went there the minute I heard. Only just got back a little while ago."

"Are you thinking what I'm thinking?" I said.

"Probably not."

I disregarded her sarcasm. "I'm thinking that maybe Mergenthaler arranged the whole thing. He heard what you said about it possibly being fake. He could've guessed you would look into that, maybe get an expert to examine it. But if it's stolen the heat is off him. Now nobody can say whether it's authentic or not."

"It's possible. But more important is trying to figure out what can be done about it either way. A real burglary or a fake one. At this point all we can do is investigate it as a real one and see what we come up with."

"How do you do that?"

"We look for physical evidence, fingerprints, footprints, tire marks that might help identify the car he was using. But if this guy could bypass their alarm system it's not likely he's going to leave us anything."

"Unless he had help with the alarm system."

"I'll keep it in mind. The other thing we do is reach out to the NYPD and the FBI. They have people who specialize in stolen art. We ask them to alert us if they hear anything."

"I just had another thought," I said. "Maybe it wasn't Mergenthaler who stole it. Maybe it was the guy in Jerusalem, the one Cormac got it from. He has the same motivation. If it's out of sight, it can't be examined and nobody can pin anything on him."

"You're full of theories," she said.

"Better than being full of something else. So what happens next?"

"I'm going to follow up on the burglary and continue to interview people."

"How about if I help with the interviews?"

"I don't know about that," she said.

"Why?"

"Let me think about it."

"What's there to think about?"

"I'll get back to you," she said, stonewalling me again.

That night I had my usual trouble falling asleep. I stared into blackness for a long time. Flipped on the radio hoping music would help. All it did was bring Rosalind back. We'd both loved night music putting us to sleep. I thought about the time she'd had her hair done to see how she'd look with a frizzy perm. It didn't suit her and we laughed about it. I didn't laugh lying there in bed remembering. I didn't even smile. Instead, I felt tears come into my eyes. I let them come. I knew eventually they would stop.

CHAPTER 20

Nolan had left me with nothing to do but stick my thumb in the usual place. I wondered if Shakespeare had anything spellbinding to say about that. There were more than thirty books on my shelves having to do with Shakespeare, his work and his life. Quite a few dated back to my college days, and were falling apart, having been annotated over and over again. Some of the newer ones I'd only read parts of, not being happy with the content. I knew Shakespeare had had a lot to say about asses, but the donkey kind, not the human. I was trying to remember something that would apply to my situation. Which was? Helpless? Suspended in air like a slab of meat on a hook? Ugh.

I needed to be patient. *How poor are they that have not patience,* said Iago. *What wound did ever heal but by degrees.* He was right, but it didn't help me because I was in no mood to sit and do nothing. I'd gotten a good bit of information from McCleod on my own. What else could I do?

I was staring at the bookshelves when the phone rang. It was an annoying ring, like a chirping bird. I'd bought a new cordless phone a while back with a choice of ring tones but I'd never gotten around to selecting one I liked.

It was my father. "I'm checking up on you, sonny. What's new?"

I was always hesitant to give information to my father because of his tendency to immediately try to take charge, tell me what I should or shouldn't do. To suggest to him that he might be a control freak (as I'd once attempted) would not only be a waste of time but would inevitably bring forth a torrent of guilt-inducing remarks such as, "How could you say that to the one person in the world who loves you more than himself?"

This time frustration got the better of me. "You won't believe it," I said. "I'm absolutely fed up."

"About what?"

It blew out of me, everything: Toby, Mergenthaler, McCleod, Detective Nolan, the whole shebang. The only thing I didn't tell him about was the late night phone call.

"So she won't let you do anything, this lady detective?"

"Exactly. Toby got me into the case, but the cops don't like the whole idea. They don't want any part of me."

"Did you say the box that was stolen came from Jerusalem?"

"Yeah. What about it?"

"I know a cop from the NYPD."

"So what? I think the NYPD has more than ten thousand cops."

"There you go again. Mr. Smart Mouth. Why don't you wait to hear what I have to say?"

I sighed. "Shoot."

My father was a Mister-know-it-all. He also had the kind of nature that had caused him to go through five wives and count-less women. It was a source of amazement to me that his cur-rent half-a-century-younger girlfriend Zeena was still with him. I wasn't sure if my father was mellowing or if Zeena truly loved him as she once told me she did. They'd been engaged for a year, which in itself was some kind of a record.

"I'm not an idiot. I know there are thousands of cops in the city. I happen to know one who's now in Jerusalem."

"What's he doing there?"

"He's what's called a liaison. The commissioner sent him

there after nine-eleven to work with the local cops on terrorism. He's smart as a whip. Speaks fluent Hebrew. And he's a good buddy of mine."

"Now that is interesting," I said. I held the phone to my ear with my shoulder and straightened a few books. "He might be able to help."

"I think he might help a lot."

"Can you get in touch with him?"

"Sure. I have his e-mail address. I even have his phone number."

I sat in one of the leather chairs. "I'm not sure I want to know, but how is it that you are so buddy-buddy with a cop?"

"He's very religious. Orthodox. He wears *tzitses* and lays *tefillin* every morning. The whole works."

Tzitses is a short garment that orthodox Jews wear underneath their clothing. It has fringes that hang out. *Tefillin* are phylacteries or two strips of leather with a little black leather box attached to each. The boxes contain tiny parchments inscribed in Hebrew, passages from Exodus and Deuteronomy. In an ancient ritual for morning prayers they are wrapped around the head and forearms. It's referred to as laying *tefillin*. Of course there was an adolescent joke about laying *tefillin*. Does she have a sister?

"But you're not orthodox," I said.

My father's voice became solemn. "At certain times in my life I became very religious."

"Is that a fact?"

"You know a bit about my life, sonny. But not the whole story."

"I believe you." I knew what was coming next. A yarn, a tale. Never to know if real or imagined. I couldn't stay in the chair. I got up and began pacing back and forth.

"Let's just say I was doing a deal involving imports and exports," he said. "And some of the items were not officially supposed to be imported and exported, if you get my drift."

"I think I get it."

"Anyhow, Herbie was the cop in charge of the investigation. A really nice man. A *mensch*. We talked a lot. He invited me to his shul. An old synagogue in the heart of Borough Park. I went there and I prayed. Prayer is a wonderful invention."

"It is for some people."

"You wouldn't believe how it helped. A lot of praying. And also a generous endowment to their building fund."

"So you became friends?"

"It was a funny thing. We just hit it off. There was a chemistry. Even though he's in his forties, he doesn't treat me like I'm old. We're friends on an equal basis, man-to-man. Zeena and I met his wife, his kids. He's got five of them, three boys and two girls. We've been to his home for dinner."

Zeena's career as a systems analyst continued as well as her part-time performance art, and my father, at seventy-eight, was still making new friends and cutting deals. True, the marriage my father had insisted on had not yet come to pass—I didn't know why—but maybe that was a good thing. "I'm glad you've got this friend. He might be just the guy I need." I was still in nonstop mode while on the phone, marching from the living room to the den and back again. "Let me think how to do this. Suppose you e-mail him. Introduce me. Tell him your son is going to write to him. I just have to figure out what to say."

"What's there to figure out? Simply ask him what you want to ask him."

"Could you just do what I ask without the instructions?"

"Touchy, touchy. Okay. I'll do it."

"And don't give him any details. Just say your son wants to get in touch with him."

"I hear you. I don't need to be told twice."

"I love you, too, Dad."

Chapter 21

Landis was in turmoil. The burglary had changed everything. He didn't know who'd broken in or why, but he reasoned it had to be connected to the people who'd sold the ossuary to Blather. But why they'd stolen it was another matter. And what else did they have in mind? He didn't like that it brought the police back in. You never knew what they might turn up.

He decided he could not go ahead with his plans for McCleod. The artist was an unknown factor and unknown facts were unpredictable. One way to eliminate the unpredictability factor was to eliminate the cause of it. Thinking about McCleod brought back what he'd said about the man Landis had seen leaving the studio. The name Wanderman hadn't meant anything to him at the time but thinking about the ramifications of the burglary had dredged up a memory. His research on Blather had uncovered the matter of the stolen Fabergé eggs and of this man's involvement. Wanderman was close to Blather which would explain his being at McCleod's. The story McCleod had come up with about a rabbi was probably a fiction, although he had been able to determine that McCleod was indeed a member of the congregation of the local synagogue. What was more likely was that Wanderman was investigating Blather's murder. He thought about following him to see what he was up to but decided now was not the time for that. McCleod came first. Once he'd taken care of McCleod he'd look into this man Wanderman.

He remembered what McCleod had said about seeing him one night on Main Street. That may have been the night of the murder. Perhaps he had noticed something that made him suspect it was Landis he'd seen, which would explain why he'd suddenly stopped talking. Altogether it was much too dangerous to wait. He couldn't take the chance and allow McCleod to live any longer. His only regret was that he would have to forgo the pleasant idea he'd had of fleecing Mergenthaler with more forgeries.

Now it became a matter of choosing the right time. He would go at night when visibility was low. He knew there was a surveillance camera so he'd wear the plastic booties, disposable gloves, a cap and muffler and oversize coat similar to the ones he'd picked up before at the Ladies' Village Improvement Society's resale shop in East Hampton. He'd gotten rid of everything before and he'd do the same again.

In spite of it being risky he'd kept the knife because he'd gone to so much trouble to acquire it. He'd always known that when he found Blather he would kill him. So he'd spent some time thinking about how he would do it. It soon was obvious that a knife was the best choice. It was easy to carry, could fit into a pocket, and was not necessarily a weapon. He knew he wanted a knife with a blade that stayed in the handle until it was needed. But he was not about to go into a store and buy one. It was simpler and safer to find one on the Internet. He came across a company called Sportsman's Guide. He rented a post office box and had them send a catalog, knowing he could pay for the knife with a money order.

The knife he'd picked out was a beauty, made by Beretta, the gun maker. It was lightweight, just 56 grams, with a hollow ground, high-alloy, high-carbon stainless steel blade that held its edge. It could be had standard or serrated; he'd decided on serrated. He liked the image of the serrated edge slicing through

Blather's fat body to get at the veins, the muscles, the arteries. He had imagined the blood flowing out of the wounds as if they were open faucets.

When he first got the knife he would stand in front of the full-length mirror, taking the knife out of his pocket, pressing the knurled thumbscrew, and watching the blade spring into place with a satisfying click. He'd thrust the knife forward and imagine the surprised look on Blather's face as it entered his body. It had happened almost exactly as he'd imagined it.

Now it was time to use the knife again.

Mergenthaler was meeting someone for dinner in a few days. That would be when he'd do it. He usually spent those free evenings with Mario drinking good wine and enjoying the pleasures that Mario provided but this was obviously much more important. He would have to invent a story to explain his not being there for him.

The night came soon enough and he prepared to leave the house. Earlier in the day he'd made sure to put the coat, hat, and muffler in the car, insuring that Mario would not see them when he left. He waited a half hour after Mergenthaler had gone, then left without saying goodnight. It was better if Mario didn't know what time he'd left.

He drove to McCleod's neighborhood, careful to observe speed limits and stop signs. He parked at the end of the street and walked silently to the house. The light was on in the studio. He rang the bell. The security light came on and the camera too, of course, but he didn't look up, in fact, he leaned forward so that the bill of his cap obscured his face.

"Who's that?" McCleod asked.

"It's me. Kalem. We need to talk."

"What about? Why didn't you call first?"

"Something important has come up. I need to talk to you."

"Shit," McCleod said.

The door opened. McCleod stood there with a paint brush in one hand and a rag in the other. As usual his clothes were spattered with paint. "What's so important? I'm working hard trying to finish the Klee."

Landis stepped inside and shut the door behind him, then put one hand in the pocket where the knife was. "That's what I want to talk to you about. Can I see it?"

"That's what you came over for? To look at my goddamned painting?"

"No, but while I'm here I'd like to see it."

"I don't show my work until it's finished." He turned away. Landis pulled the knife from his pocket, pressed the spring that unloaded the blade and heard it click into place. He tried to drive the knife into McCleod's back just below the shoulder blade but he had misjudged the distance so the knife only went partly in.

McCleod yelled something and turned around. He saw Landis holding the knife. "What the hell are you doing?" he said. He turned and began to run toward the other part of the studio.

Landis lunged and managed to shove the knife into McCleod's side. McCleod howled in pain. He stopped running and reached for the knife. Landis stepped towards him, pulled the knife out and tried to shove the knife into McCleod's abdomen.

The artist reached out. His fingernails dug into Landis's wrist and the back of his hand but it did not prevent Landis from plunging the blade into his stomach.

McCleod twisted and jerked his body, crying out at the same time. "Goddamn you fuck goddamn you."

The artist tried to hit out at Landis but his strength had gone with the blood now pouring from the wounds. He slumped and crumpled to the floor. He lay there sideways, one leg caught under him as if he were still trying to run away. Blood trickled from the corner of his mouth. He was murmuring something

117

unintelligible. Landis bent down to hear and get a closer look. The artist's eyes were still open, but they weren't seeing anything. His mouth remained open but the sounds had stopped.

"I suppose I should say this hurts me more than it hurts you," Landis said. "But I'd be lying." He thrust the knife in one more time.

McCleod's eyes closed.

He leaned close to his victim's face to listen for any sign of breath. He heard nothing. The man's chest didn't move either. He wiped the blade on the artist's pants, then went to the sink, rinsed the blade under the faucet and wiped it with a paper towel. He snapped it closed and put it into his pants pocket. Quickly he looked for the wire that ran from the surveillance camera to the tape, found the box holding the tape and removed it.

He left, leaving the lights on.

Before he got into his car, he removed the plastic from his hands and shoes and put them into a supermarket bag. The cap and muffler went into another bag and the coat into a trash bag. He drove to the medical center off Pantigo Road where he knew there was a Dumpster. He pushed the coat as far down in the Dumpster as he could. Next he drove to the back of the IGA where there was another Dumpster. There he disposed of the cap and muffler. On Route 114 he stopped where the woods were close to the road. He walked into the woods and buried the supermarket bag under a pile of leaves and branches. Further along the road he stopped once more to go into the woods. He pulled the surveillance film out of the case and cut it into pieces. Then he scattered the scraps in the woods and tossed the canister as far as he could.

Driving the rest of the way home he thought it was still early enough to have some wine with Mario.

CHAPTER 22

Herbert Warshavsky. Good old-fashioned name. Not usual for an NYPD cop but not terribly unusual. The Irish had always been dominant in the police department and they might have been the first to form their own group within the group, the Emerald Society. But the Jews had the Shomrin Society, the Italians, the Columbia Association. There was a Hispanic Society. For Scandinavians, the Viking Association. Germans, the Steuben League. And how about the Gay Officers Association?

I sent him an e-mail:

Hi Herb,
    My name is Jake Wanderman. I'm Harold's son. I asked him to contact you to tell you that I was going to write.
    This is what it's about.

I stopped writing. I'd been about to lay out the whole story for him, beginning with the ossuary, the possibility of its being fake, the murder and the rest of it, when I realized that e-mail can be read by all kinds of people. Who knew who might be monitoring this guy's mail? It could be Israelis. It could be CIA, FBI, any number of initials you could think of. I didn't think it would be such a good idea to let the world in on this stuff.

So all I did finally was to tell him I was Harold's son and would he mind answering a few questions. My feeling was that if we made contact, I'd figure out a way to ask for his help, although I wasn't exactly sure what that would be.

I sent it off, called Toby and left another message, then went into the kitchen and looked in the Zero King freezer for something interesting. I wasn't hungry but I needed something to occupy my time. I'd always found cooking a great escape as well as a way to be involved in something creative. The process required concentration, which was good, and since I usually cooked with wine, a bit of wine tasting as well. And at the end of the deal, unless there was a royal screw-up, I usually got something enjoyable to eat.

I thought about this New York cop in Jerusalem and remembered when Rosalind and I were there. We'd walked through the old city, with its little stalls selling all kinds of goods and food. We went to all the churches and the Gardens of Gethsemane. We followed the Stations of the Cross. And of course we went to Yad Vashem, the memorial to the Holocaust that tore us up and brought tears.

In the freezer I found split chicken breasts, pork chops, shrimp, Italian hot sausage, and a top round London broil. And loads of frozen vegetables. I liked having them because fresh ones didn't last and I never knew what I might feel like eating from one day to the next. I also came across three plastic containers filled with unidentifiable contents. I knew they were leftovers, but not much good to me now because I'd been too dumb to label them. I wasn't in the mood to find out what they were but I left them there anyway in case I might decide to check them out some time in the future. Deep down I knew I'd end up tossing them but a part of me prevented me from doing it right away. It might have been my grandmother's influence. I'd lived with her for a few years after my mother died. I had to finish everything on my plate. When I left something uneaten she'd say, "Jakey. Think of the starving children in Albania. They'd love to have what you want to throw away."

With all of that variety in the freezer, nothing grabbed me. The kitchen was not going to be a source of salvation.

When the phone rang again I was glad to answer it. It was Toby. "You called me? Do you have some news?"

"No."

"What are you up to then?"

It would have been nice to dump all my frustrations on her but I didn't feel I could or should. "Not a damn thing."

"How would you like to come over here for a drink and something to eat?"

"What a great offer," I said. "But I hope you don't mind if I leave my Superman outfit home."

On my way over I wondered what had brought this invitation about. She and Rosalind had been very close, but I was never in their scenario. It was strictly a girl thing. And other than spending a lot of time with her because of her father's involvement with the Fabergé eggs, there'd never been any social stuff between us.

Anita, one half of her housekeeper team, let me in with a smile. She spoke English much better than Carlos, her husband. "Mees Welch ees in the garden room."

I'd never been in that room but Rosalind had told me how amazing it was. "Where's that?"

"I show you."

I knew the house was large but I was still surprised by how many rooms and hallways we had to negotiate to get to the garden room. I could see why Rosalind had loved it. I felt as if I'd stepped into a forest. There were dozens of plants of all sizes, some standing tall in tubs, others in low pots on the floor. More trailed down from above. A variety of colors: yellow, white, and pink daisies bloomed, blue and purple flowers I thought might have been orchids. Tiny lights twinkled in the ceiling and combined with the light coming in through the walls of glass.

The air was fragrant with the scent of flowers and greenery.

Toby came toward me with a smile. She wore a loose-fitting dress in a pale burgundy color that seemed to make her skin glow. It didn't hurt that her hair swirled softly while framing her face.

"Beautiful room," I said. "But you know that."

"Yes, isn't it? Outside of the kitchen, it's my favorite place in the house. I always come in here when I'm stressed out, and it usually helps. I hope you won't mind if I tell you that Rosalind and I had a lot of long talks in here."

"I don't mind." The mention of Rosalind's name caused a tremor inside me but I managed to overcome it.

We held hands, kissed cheeks, and settled in with drinks in front of a low table containing a bowl of cashews and a small plate of crudités.

"Is that why you invited me over here?" I said. "Because you're stressed?"

She sipped from her wine glass, taking her time before answering, as if she were trying to decide how much she wanted to say. "No, it isn't. It's true that I'm upset about a lot of things. My father, business, other considerations that I'd just as soon not get into." She looked at me. "But I think what I wanted was to be with someone I could trust for a change."

"I'm glad you feel that way. I know I said it before, but I'll repeat myself. You can count on me for anything."

"Anything?" she said, smiling.

For a moment, the way she said *anything* struck me as having a sexual innuendo. Then I thought, that's ridiculous. The last thing someone like Toby might be interested in would be an *alter kocker* like me. I probably had twenty years on her. No, on second thought, probably not more than fifteen.

"That's right," I went on. "Whatever you need or want, if I can do it I will."

"That's very sweet. Why don't you start by telling me how things are going with the investigation?"

"I can do that. But I better swallow some more of this vodka to ease the misery."

"It's that bad?"

I nodded, gulped some vodka, then proceeded to fill her in on everything, including the NYPD cop my father knew.

"A New York cop in Jerusalem? Do you think he might be of any help?"

"I don't know. It's possible. I sent him an e-mail and I'm waiting to see if I get a response."

"Would it do any good for you to go over there?"

"You mean, to Jerusalem? Now?"

"Yes. You wouldn't have to do e-mail. You could speak to him directly."

"I'll have to think about that," I said.

"Of course, I would pay all expenses."

"Let's not rush into anything, okay? I said I'll have to think about it."

"You sound annoyed."

"I don't like it when I feel like I'm being pushed."

"That wasn't my intention at all, Jake. I was trying to be helpful."

"Sorry. I know that. I guess my frustration is rearing its ugly head."

She stood up, tall and regal. She was at least my height. Once again I couldn't help being aware of what an imposing presence she was. "Why don't we have something to eat? That ought to make you feel better."

We ate in the dining room. The lighting was subdued, enhanced by candles on the table. Anita served us a simple meal of arugula and beet salad, sautéed catfish, asparagus and wild rice, and a lemon sorbet for dessert. We drank a delicate

California Chardonnay, and topped off the meal with espresso.

During dinner we talked about everything else: movies, food, local doings, the rising prices of real estate in the Hamptons and what to do about affordable housing. Toby was actually concerned about where people of moderate income were going to live if the price of land and housing kept shooting into the stratosphere.

When we were done, I stretched and stood up. "That was a fine dinner," I said.

"Anita is good, isn't she?" Toby said.

"So good, anytime you want to re-invite me, I'll come running." I held out my hand and took hers. "I'll head home now. But I want to thank you. I feel a lot better about things than I did before I came here."

"I'm glad."

She walked me to the door. Just before I left I leaned over to peck a goodnight kiss. Instead, she pulled my lips to hers and kissed me fully and expertly.

"I just felt like doing that," she said. "You don't mind, do you?"

I hoped I didn't look as stupid as I felt. "No, no," I said. "Thanks a lot."

I zipped out the door as if I'd been pushed.

CHAPTER 23

The doorbell rang early next morning. I answered it in my pajamas. There stood Detective Sienna Nolan, trim, pant-suited, touch of lipstick, no other makeup, holding a paper bag. "Had your coffee yet?" she said.

"I haven't even brushed my teeth."

"What are you waiting for?"

She went by me, a whiff of her perfume skittering up my nose. "Nice," I said. "Chanel Number Five?"

"Number Six. I live dangerously."

She'd one-upped me again but I stayed cool. "Make yourself comfortable. I'll be back in a minute."

I pulled on a pair of jeans, tucked in a shirt, and found her in the den sipping from a 7-Eleven container of coffee. She pointed at another container and something wrapped in wax paper on the table in front of her. "Bagel and coffee for you." I unwrapped the bagel and took off the top of the container to make sure the coffee was black.

She noticed. "I remembered how you take your coffee. From the diner."

"Very good. Now tell me, to what do I owe this honor and privilege?"

"I just felt the need for your company," she said.

"Could we cut out the bullshit?"

"The truth is I need your help."

"How come?"

"All of a sudden people are getting killed. We've had four homicides in the past week. Every detective is working two shifts. I've got nobody."

I drank some coffee to give me time to react. "Go on."

"That's it. In addition to the murder case, there's the complication of the burglary. And the fakery possibility. All of that needs to be followed up. And there are still a dozen or more people left to speak to. I don't expect anything from it but good detective work means you dot every i and cross every t."

"So what do you want me to do?"

"Some of the interviews. You come with me to a couple to observe and learn how to do it. You're smart. I think you'll catch on pretty fast."

"And this is with department approval?"

She shook her head. "Not a chance. It's strictly between us. If they find out, I'll get a swift boot in the ass."

"Maybe worse."

"It's possible. But I'm willing to take the chance. What do you say?"

"Sure," I said. "And I'll tell you who we should talk to first. McCleod." I filled her in on what he'd told me about his doing forgeries for Cormac and having seen the murderer.

"Hey. That's important. Why didn't you tell me this before?"

"I tried, but you cut me off."

"Okay." She stood up. "Let's do it right now."

We decided to use two cars in case she had to leave in a hurry. There was no fast route. We took 114 to Cedar Street, then on to Three Mile Harbor Road, until we found the turnoff to McCleod's street. We parked in the driveway and I led her around the back to his studio. I was about to explain about his security system when I saw that the door to his studio was not fully closed.

"That's funny," I said. "He's security conscious. I don't think he'd leave the door open."

"Maybe he wanted fresh air."

"You don't know McCleod. Fresh isn't in his vocabulary."

Abruptly, she was all business. "Stand back," she said, drawing a gun from a holster on her belt. "Don't move from where you are. I'll call you if I need you." She held the gun in a ready position and went slowly to the side of the door. She listened for a moment then called out, "McCleod. Are you in there?"

There was no answer.

"McCleod? Can you hear me?"

Still no answer.

She pushed the door with her foot to make it swing fully open. Then, lowering the gun so that it pointed forward, she stepped quickly through the door. I saw her turn her head to the left and to the right. Then she moved out of sight. I went through the door after her and saw her on one knee leaning over McCleod, her hand on his wrist. He lay sprawled on the floor, faceup. There was blood on his face and his shirt. I went closer and saw a pool of darker blood on the floor next to him. I couldn't help noticing the color of the blood on the floor was the same color as Nolan's hair.

"He's been stabbed," she said. "But he's still alive." She got on her cell and called 911. "We need an ambulance in a hurry. The victim is bleeding badly." She turned to me. "What's the address?"

My mind went blank. "Christ. I don't remember. Wait a minute. Let me think."

"Hurry."

I'd originally gotten the address from the rabbi and written it down, but I'd forgotten it once I knew how to get there. It came back. "Country Lane. Number four fifty-four."

Nolan tried stopping the flow with towels but couldn't do much. An ambulance arrived within five minutes. It was lucky for McCleod it did, because he had lost a lot of blood. The medics did what they had to do, got him into the ambulance and were on their way, siren screaming, all within ten minutes.

While we waited she cautiously went through the studio looking for the knife, but didn't find it. "Let's go outside. Maybe the guy ditched it there."

We both looked all around the property without success.

Nolan had called the Crime Lab immediately after the ambulance call. The guys with the white coats along with the photographer got there shortly after McCleod had been removed from the scene. Nolan had tried to keep the ambulance people from touching anything they didn't need to touch but she felt the crime scene was compromised anyway.

We went outside to allow forensics to do their thing. "Nothing to do but go with the flow," she said. "Saving the guy's life comes first."

Two local cops showed up and rolled out yellow tape all over the place. Nolan told them to do another search on the property for the knife. She looked closely at the front door to see if it had been jimmied open but there were no marks. "McCleod let him in so he must have known the guy."

"We don't know that it was a guy," I said.

"You told me he saw the murderer and that it was a man. Don't you think this perp is the same one who did Blather?"

"All signs point to it but that doesn't make it a fact. Theoretically, it could have been anyone who hated McCleod enough to want to kill him."

"Yeah, yeah. Technically, you're right. But one gets you ten it's the same guy."

"Probably," I said.

"Definitely."

"Okay. You win. What now?"

"We'll wait and see if we get any prints. I doubt it but we can hope. In the meantime, let's head over to the hospital to see how McCleod is doing. If he comes to we might be able to question him."

"From your mouth," I said.

"Right."

We began walking to our cars when she stopped. "Wait a minute," she said. "He had a surveillance camera, right? Maybe there's film in it. We might see the guy who did it."

She called over a young female techie wearing a gold ring in her nose. She looked at the girl's ID tag and said, "Hi Ruthie, I'm Detective Nolan. You know anything about surveillance cameras?"

Ruthie smiled. "Everything."

"Good. The victim had one. The camera's outside the front door. Could you find the recorder that has the film?"

"Shouldn't be too hard," Ruthie said.

We watched her go outside to look at the camera, then come back in. She evidently saw something I didn't, because she went over to the corner of the room and bent down to the baseboard where there was a box attached to the wall. She opened it and took out a canister, then held it up for us to see. "Here it is."

Nolan took it from her and opened it. The tone of her voice was bitter. "Shit. It's empty. Either the perp took it with him or McCleod never bothered to use film in the first place."

"That would be my guess," I said. "He probably just wanted to make sure no one could walk in on him when he was working on a forgery."

We drove back down Three Mile Harbor Road. She was in her Mitsubishi Eclipse doing sixty on a thirty mile an hour road. I trailed her in my Camry with clenched teeth and hands tight on the steering wheel trying to stay close.

We made it to Cedar Street, cut across to Stephen Hands Path and on to the Montauk Highway. She kept her foot down all the way, only slowing down when she got behind a normal driver. When we finally pulled into the emergency room parking lot at Southampton Hospital I was able to relax. My hands were so wet I had to dry them on my pants.

The waiting room chairs were filled with an assortment of people and kids, some crying, some with obvious cuts and bruises. There was a TV mounted on the wall showing Dr. Phil dispensing smarmy accented advice. We spoke to a woman at the entrance desk. She asked if we were relatives and could provide insurance information. Nolan showed her ID and she sent us to the triage nurse who made a phone call. "You can go inside and talk to the doctor."

The emergency room had a common area taken up with computers, a water-and-ice-dispensing machine, and shelves with supplies and equipment. Off this section were doctors' offices, a series of cubicles with drawn curtains around them, and private rooms for the more distressed patients. Every bed was taken and nurses and doctors and assorted people in scrubs were rushing back and forth, all looking anxious and overworked.

McCleod was in one of the private rooms with a doctor and nurse on either side of the bed. We saw that he was hooked up to monitors and oxygen and IV drips. The doctor looked up. His gloved hands were red. "Wait outside," he said. "I'll be with you in a minute."

We left and stood around with not much to do except try to keep out of the way. A man wheeling a machine asked us to move. Then a nurse had to use the computer we had gotten in front of. Then it was the ice machine. After about twenty minutes the doctor came out. He couldn't have been more than five-five, but he had huge biceps and a bulk to his upper body that marked him as a weight lifter.

"How is he?" I asked.

"He's got a chance to make it," he said. "But there were some bad wounds. We've done all we could, and replaced the blood he lost. Does he have a relative we should notify?"

"Not any that I know of," I said. "I could ask his rabbi."

The doctor's eyes opened wide. "His driver's license said his name is McCleod."

"It's a long story," I said.

"Then get in touch with the rabbi. If there's family, it's appropriate to call them."

"If he survives, what chance is there he might wake up enough to talk to him?" Nolan asked.

"It's a long shot. He'll be out at least four to six hours, I'd guess. We shot him up with a lot of morphine."

"We'll come back then."

"Even if he survives I wouldn't count on his being able to talk."

"We'll be back anyhow."

Before we left one of the forensic guys came in with a kit. He spoke to the doctor and looked at Nolan at the same time. "My boss said I should check his fingernails as soon as possible. He might've scratched the attacker. Is that okay?"

The doctor nodded his approval.

We watched the lab guy put a swab under each nail and put each swab in a plastic bag. On the second hand, he grunted, "Something here for sure."

"Skin?" Nolan asked.

"Don't know what it is until we test it."

"Call me as soon as you know anything, okay?" Nolan said.

"I'll tell my boss what you said."

She gave him her card and we left the hospital and headed back to the parking lot. "Did you hear that little shit? Even the crime lab guys patronize me." She looked at her watch. "Forget I said that. It's almost eleven. I'll be back here at four, just in case he wakes up early. If he makes it, good. If he can talk, even better. If not . . ." She shrugged.

"Okay. I'll wait here for a while. I was just wondering, do you think there ought to be a cop near him, just in case?"

"I'm slipping," she said. She got out her phone and made arrangements. "Go home," she told me. "Call his rabbi and get some rest."

"I think I'll hang out a while."

She peered at me as if she were trying to read what was inside my head. "You feel responsible, don't you? Why? You didn't do anything to cause this."

"I know. I just want to hang for a while. Make sure he's doing okay."

"I have to wait for the uniform, but you don't."

"I know. If you want, I can point the cop in the right direction."

"I don't think that'd be a good idea. Nobody knows you, remember?"

"How could I forget?"

We waited until the uniformed cop showed up. She detailed him about McCleod and explained me by telling him I was a friend of the victim.

I sat around for an hour, then got back to where McCleod was and found the weightlifter still on duty.

"How's the patient?"

He looked at me, puzzled.

"Sorry," I said, abruptly realizing he had lots of patients. "The guy with the stab wounds."

"Vitals are functioning. He's still with us. We're going to send him up to ICU."

I thanked him and decided to take Nolan's advice and go home. I was worn out.

When I got home I found Dr. Morty Adler sitting in his Benz

in my driveway.

"Thank God you finally showed up," he said. "I've been waiting an hour for you. Don't you ever stay home?"

"What are you doing here?"

"Sherri said the other day we haven't seen hide nor hair of you like forever. Every time she calls to invite you to dinner you make some sort of lame excuse. So I came over in person to find out how the hell you are."

"I'm fine."

"You look like shit. Let's go inside. We need to talk."

I wanted to be alone but how could I say no to my best friend?

CHAPTER 24

My throat was dry. I went into the kitchen and got a bottle of water out of the fridge. "You want something to eat or drink?" I asked.

He shook his head. "Tell me what's going on."

I took a long pull of ice water. "What do you mean?"

I knew exactly what he meant. Morty and I had a history going back to childhood. But as couples we had a history, too. I'd been avoiding these friends ever since Rosalind died. At first it had been an unconscious thing. Sherri, Morty's wife, would call to invite me to dinner. My response was to thank her and say that I didn't feel up to it. That was the truth. I didn't want to be with anybody. I didn't want to talk, or smile, or tell stories or listen to stories. She said she understood that I was still upset and we'd make it another time. They kept inviting me and I kept turning them down until I finally couldn't refuse anymore. But afterwards, when I was home, old memories would come back at me with more intensity than before.

"Stop stalling," Morty said. "You know darn well what I mean. Are you hiding from us?"

I shook my head. "Of course not."

"I don't believe you."

"Believe what you want to believe."

"Jake, in my practice I've seen lots of widows and widowers over the years. What you're going through is a classic period of bereavement."

"That's what I like to hear. That I'm a classic."

"You know what I mean, Jake. You're in denial. You're in fucking denial."

"Denial of what?" I snapped at him. "That Rosalind's dead? You don't think I know that?"

"That's not what I mean and you know it." He grabbed my arm. "Come over here and sit down. We have to talk."

"I thought that's what we were doing."

I let him lead me to a chair in the kitchen. "It's bad for you to go on like this. You've got to work through it."

"I am."

"How?"

"I'm working for Toby Welch. I'm looking into her father's murder."

He smiled. "Stop kidding around."

"I'm serious."

"For real? Tell me about it."

I gave him a general idea of what had happened and what I'd done up to this point, leaving out a lot of the details.

He didn't say anything for a while. Then he got up, took a glass from the cabinet and poured water into it. "That's good. But it won't alleviate the situation. It just buys you escape time."

"What's wrong with that?"

"You don't get it," he said. "Escape isn't the answer. You have to deal with the problem. And the best way to do that is to join a bereavement group."

"Is that what this is about? The hospital called me about one after Rosalind died. I told them I wasn't interested."

"Why not?"

"I didn't feel like spilling my guts to a lot of strangers."

"That's not how it works. Yes, you spill your guts. But to people who are feeling the same pain as you. They might be strangers at first. But they become your friends. Because they understand like nobody else understands."

I sighed. "Morty, I appreciate what you're telling me. I'm sure it's good advice."

"But I should fuck off. Is that it?"

"You know what Shakespeare would say?"

"No. But I'm sure you're going to tell me."

"What fates impose, that men must needs abide; It boots not to resist both wind and tide."

"And you know what Morty Adler says to that? Bullshit."

"Nobody says bullshit to Shakespeare. Not in my house."

I went over and put my arms around him. "I know you love me. I love you, too. But I can't do it."

"Think about it. Promise me you'll think about it."

"Okay," I said. "I promise to think about it."

After Morty left I stretched out on the couch in the den and was asleep almost immediately. I dreamed a lot of incoherent dreams with faces of unknown people and shadowy figures and no context. I woke up an hour later, my mouth drier than before and my body still lacking energy. I thought about what Morty had said. He was probably right. Joining a bereavement group might be exactly what I needed. But I didn't think I could do it. Maybe I had to feel worse than I already did, sink lower into despair, like the alcoholic who panics when he finds himself seeing pink elephants.

I wasn't there. Not yet. I still believed I could fight my way through this. I'd progressed to at least doing something useful. It might even turn out to be important. And the possibility of its being dangerous, if that late-night phone call meant anything, only made it more attractive. In essence, I felt I had nothing to lose. But even while I was thinking this I was also aware that submerged somewhere under all this positive reasoning was the nagging thought that I might be kidding myself.

I took a shower and changed my clothes before heading back

to the hospital. I felt better because I'd kept my promise to Morty.

I'd thought about it.

CHAPTER 25

The local news carried the story. Landis heard it on the radio in the afternoon. McCleod was still alive. Landis couldn't believe it. He'd seen the man die before his very eyes. It didn't make sense. Were the police lying to the media, pulling some kind of scam?

He knew he had to find out the truth. He'd go to the hospital and see for himself. He'd already had his morning meeting with Mergenthaler so he was free. To make sure, he called Mergenthaler on the house phone and told him he had a dental appointment he'd forgotten about.

"Careful, Landis," Mergenthaler said. "Forgetting appointments is a sign of old age. Maybe you'd better start taking vitamin supplements."

"I'll take that under consideration, Mr. Mergenthaler," Landis said. "I'll return as soon as possible."

"Just kidding, Landis. Take your time."

On the way to Southampton Hospital he stopped at King Kullen and got the makeup kit out of the trunk. He'd bought the kit a long time before when he'd first thought about finding Cormac Blather and killing him. At the time he'd thought of it all as fantasy. He'd practiced with makeup, changing his appearance in different ways. He made himself look old, or swarthy, added a moustache, beard, sideburns, glasses, even a mole on his cheek. It was quite amazing how he could transform himself into a different person. He'd never actually used a disguise before but now was the perfect time.

He put the case into a shopping cart, tossed some items into the cart, then wheeled it over to where the bathroom was. He'd been there before and knew the bathroom was used one person at a time so privacy was assured. He left the cart with the other items in it outside the bathroom and took his case.

The suitcase had a mirror pasted to the inside of the cover. He made his skin very dark and added a black moustache and goatee. That should be enough, he thought, to make him impossible to identify if it ever got to that point. The Beretta, of course, was safely tucked away in the right-hand pocket of his suit.

He abandoned the cart, got back into the car, called the hospital and asked about the condition of Mr. McCleod.

After a wait, the operator said, "There's no information on him. Is he a patient here?"

"I must have the wrong hospital," Landis said. He assumed they were restricting all information.

He parked in the lot across the street from the hospital and carried the kit with him, thinking it would pass as a doctor's case.

The entrance doors opened automatically and he went in. Some twenty paces ahead was an information counter. He walked over to the young woman stationed there wearing a peach volunteer uniform. He asked about the condition of McCleod.

She checked her computer and then looked up at him. "Are you a relative?"

"Yes. I'm his brother."

"I'm afraid his condition is serious."

"Is it possible to see him? What room is he in?"

"He's in three-ten but no visitors are allowed. Sorry."

"Why not?" he asked.

She shrugged. "I don't know. That's what it says."

Landis nodded. "I understand. Thank you very much."

He turned and left the way he had come in.

While inside he'd seen people enter from another side of the building. He went out, walked around to that side and went back, going directly to the elevators. The elevators were in sight of the information desk so he turned his back to avoid being recognized if the girl he'd spoken to before happened to glance in his direction.

On the third floor he walked purposefully through the corridors as if he were a doctor looking for his patient. It was easy to find Room 310 because a uniformed cop was sitting on a chair at the entrance to the room.

"Is this Mr. McCleod's room?"

The cop didn't get out of his chair. "That's right. Who are you?"

"I'm Dr. Rosenfeld. I was sent by his family to see what I can do. I'm a specialist."

"Sorry, Doc. Nobody's allowed in."

"What do you mean? I was sent by the family. I'm just going to examine him."

The cop shook his head and stood up. "Nobody's allowed in. Those are my orders." He crossed his bulky arms in front of his chest and stared into Landis's face.

Landis turned away and went to the nurses' desk. There were three of them, all occupied with paperwork. He waited a moment for someone to look up. When no one did he said in a loud voice, "Excuse me."

One of them stopped what she was doing. "Yes. Can I help you?"

"I'm Dr. Rosenfeld. I was asked by the McCleod family to examine Mr. McCleod. The policeman in front of the door won't let me in."

"We have instructions that no one's to be admitted."

"Not even a doctor sent by the family?"

The nurse was flustered. "I'm sorry, doctor. But those are the instructions. I can call my supervisor if you want."

"By all means. It's taken me more than two hours to drive out here from New York. I'm in no mood to turn around and drive back."

The nurse picked up the phone. She turned away from him so that he couldn't hear what she was saying.

He thought he might have gone too far. He'd tried bullying his way past the cop and that hadn't worked. Now, if anyone came they'd want to go into the room with him.

The nurse finally got off the phone. "If you care to wait, the supervisor will check with the police to see if it's all right."

"How long will that take?"

The nurse shrugged. "I've no idea."

"Very well," Landis said. "You do that. In the meantime, can you tell me where I can get a cup of coffee?"

She explained where the cafeteria was and how to get there.

He took the elevator back to the main floor and left the hospital. He'd accomplished nothing more than let the police know someone had tried to get into McCleod's room.

Good. Let them worry.

CHAPTER 26

When I got out of my car at Southampton Hospital I noticed Nolan's red Eclipse already there. She was sitting bent over behind the wheel so that it looked as if she were asleep. I tapped the window. Her head jerked up and she stared at me, the expression on her face changing from surprise to consternation. She pushed open the door.

"Sorry if I startled you," I said.

"I was daydreaming. Tough couple of hours, that's all."

The way she said it made me guess it was personal so I made what I hoped was a sympathetic grunt. "Anything I can do to help?"

She shook her head, causing her hair to shimmer, and gave me a weary smile. "I spent the afternoon getting rid of my ex."

"Ex-husband?"

"Boyfriend. Cleared him out of my apartment and my life."

"Oh," I said, feeling unexpectedly pleased. "Must've been tough."

"Very."

She began walking, shutting off the conversation.

Inside the hospital we learned they'd moved McCleod to a room on the third floor. We found the uniformed cop standing in front of his room.

"Everything all right?" she asked.

"Hunky dory."

"How's the patient?"

142

He shrugged. "I ain't the doctor."

She glared at him.

"A guy was here before. Said he was a doctor and wanted to examine him. I didn't let him in."

"When was this?"

"Sometime this morning, about nine, I think."

"Did he tell you his name?"

"Dr. Rosenberg or something like that."

"That's funny. Nobody told me any other doctors were coming."

We went to the nurses' desk and asked if anyone knew about the doctor who wanted to examine McCleod.

One of the nurses spoke up. "I talked to him. He said his name was Dr. Rosenfeld and that the family sent him. When I told him I'd have to call the supervisor he said fine. I called the supervisor and she said she'd contact the police."

Sienna shook her head. "I never heard a thing about it. Do you know who she called?"

The nurse said, "I don't know but I can give you her number and you can ask her."

Sienna took the number and was about to use her cell when the nurse said, "Sorry, no cell phones allowed in the hospital."

"We'll go downstairs. I want to check this out."

"The funny thing is," the nurse said, "the guy went down to the coffee shop but he never came back."

Sienna took out her notebook. "Tell me what this man looked like."

"He was medium height. Good-looking. Very dark skin, like olive. He had a moustache and a goatee. And he was carrying a doctor's bag."

"Anything else?"

The nurse shrugged. "He had on a nice suit. Pin-stripe."

"What color?"

"Dark gray."

We went back outside so that Sienna could call the supervisor of nurses. When she got off the phone she said, "This idiot called the Southampton Town Police who of course don't know a damn thing. That's why I never heard anything. The call got swallowed up in red tape somewhere."

"Sounds like it could've been the killer trying to finish the job."

"Sure does. And now he's long gone. No point in putting out an APB on him. But I'm going to get this nurse to visit with an artist. We can get a sketch and circulate it."

We went back to the third floor and Sienna spoke to the nurse about the sketch artist. She didn't want to go to Hauppauge in the worst way but Sienna wouldn't let her off the hook.

We sat in the waiting room, not much larger than a walk-in closet and with distinctly uncomfortable chairs. For a while one other person kept us company, then she left and we were alone. For whatever reason I was acutely aware of Detective Sienna Nolan. Maybe it was her scent. It made me think of Irish Spring soap. Or the way her reddish hair had glistened in the sunlight.

"If I'm being too nosy, say so," I said. "How long were you together?"

"A little more than a year. But I think I knew it wasn't going to work the day he moved in."

"Did you know him long?"

"A few months. I fell hard and fast."

"He must've been quite a guy."

"He was. Tall. Good dancer. Smooth." She stopped. "Too smooth."

I didn't feel I could ask any more but I hoped she'd go on. She didn't. I decided to change the subject. "I get the Nolan. But where did Sienna come from?"

She turned towards me. I knew her eyes were green but I'd never noticed they had specks of black in them, making them look like gemstones. "Italian mother. She never said, but I think that's where I was conceived."

"What was she doing in Siena?"

"Honeymoon."

"Romantic. I was in Siena once. I hitchhiked through Italy on a summer break."

"You were a backpacker?"

I nodded. "You can only do it when you're young. What about you? Ever traveled anywhere?"

"Does Binghamton qualify as traveling?"

"Let me guess. You went to SUNY-Binghamton."

"Give the man a cigar."

I had my mouth open to say something more but she cut me off. "Enough family history for one day."

My mouth abruptly closed.

"I'm sorry," she said. "I didn't mean that the way it came out. It's just that I don't feel like talking anymore."

"Sure," I said. "Don't worry about it."

I assumed she was thinking about her boyfriend. I was thinking about her. What was she really like under that protective coating she'd constructed for herself? I had the feeling there was another person inside. Not so hard and tough.

An announcement on the intercom interrupted. It sounded urgent, some code mentioned as well as the number 310, McCleod's room. The corridor was suddenly filled with people in scrubs rushing to McCleod's room. All we could do was watch, wait, and hope.

After some time, maybe fifteen minutes or less, a doctor came out. He saw us standing there, along with the uniformed cop. "He didn't make it," he said.

Neither one of us had anything to say. We went down in the

elevator and outside. "Want a cup of coffee?" I asked.

She took her time thinking about it. "Okay."

I drove us to Sip N' Soda on Hampton Road, an old-fashioned ice cream parlor that still had homemade ice cream and sandwiches like they used to have in the fifties. We sat in a booth and ordered two coffees.

"And a bran muffin," she added.

I watched as she poured two packets of sugar and what looked like a quarter cup of milk into her cup.

"You call that coffee?" I said.

"For me, it is."

"You have no idea what real coffee tastes like."

"You know what? I don't care."

She slathered butter and strawberry jam on her muffin and took a healthy bite. I remembered how she'd devoured the pie in the diner. "You do like to eat, I can see that."

"Food is good. Satisfies the body and doesn't screw you over."

"Unless you eat too much."

"I've never had that problem."

It was almost five o'clock and the place was getting ready to close. There were just a few stragglers like us and a couple of women with shopping bags at their feet treating themselves to ice cream sodas.

"What I want to know is, why kill McCleod?" Sienna said, between bites. "He must have known something."

"Somebody thought he knew something, anyway. Remember he told me he thought he saw Cormac's murderer leaving the store the day of the murder."

"You mean maybe the guy caught a glimpse of McCleod? He was holding a painting, right? That would make him easy to recognize."

"How would he know who he was just because he was carrying a painting? There are tons of artists out here."

"Obviously this guy knew Blather enough to want to kill him. Maybe he stalked him beforehand and saw McCleod in the store or going in and out of it. So the night he kills Blather he's walking away and spots a guy with a painting across the street. He puts two and two together. He figures McCleod might remember him for some reason. If he kills him, that takes care of that possibility. If he's wrong, he killed an innocent person, but murderers don't worry about that."

I drank my coffee and watched her swallow the last of the muffin. She licked her lips and patted them with a napkin. Her lipstick had mostly worn off but her lips were still pink. She suddenly looked like a schoolgirl.

"What was it made you throw the guy out?" I said.

"I told you I didn't want to talk about it."

"It might do you good to talk. It's not a good idea to keep things bottled up. They can fester like a boil and explode."

"Are you a shrink now?"

"Just a concerned human being."

She emptied her cup, patted her mouth again and sighed. "He cheated."

"One of the oldest stories in the world."

"Not what you think. It wasn't another woman. Although I wouldn't bet on that either. He used my credit card without telling me. And spent a lot of money."

"He had to know you'd find out, didn't he?"

"That was the worst part. Of course he knew I'd see it on my statement. But he was so sure he'd be able to fix it. He had a story ready. Flowers, a bottle of wine. Candles. The works. He was going to seduce me all over again." Her cell phone rang. She listened to the voice at the other end and looked at me at the same time. Her eyes seemed to tell me that something interesting was being said. "Thanks, Harry. I really appreciate your calling me with that." She snapped the phone closed.

"They found skin under McCleod's fingernails. They're pretty sure it's from the back of the guy's hand. Caucasian with type O blood. When we catch him we can do a DNA and have all the proof we need."

"Great. All we have to do is find a guy in a pin-stripe suit with scratches on his hand. That shouldn't be too hard."

"Funny. How about we drop the soap opera talk and get some work done. You ready to take on an interview?"

"I sure am. *I have no spur to prick the sides of my intent, but only Vaulting ambition . . .*"

She shook her head. "I hope I'm not making a big mistake."

CHAPTER 27

Sienna didn't want to waste any time. She called a woman by the name of Velma Matheson, one of Cormac's many customers, to set up the first interview where I was to observe and learn. Because Matheson lived in my vicinity, Sienna followed me back from the hospital to my house where I left my car. We then drove together in Sienna's red Mitsubishi. Her scent filled the interior. There was a small object suspended from the rearview mirror, a smiley face made of felt.

The Matheson house was on Wickatuck Drive, a street of tall leafy trees and cottages built for summer vacations forty to sixty years before. Now the cottages had been transformed into year-round homes yet still managed to maintain an old-fashioned look, with brick and stone and driveways unfettered by Belgian block and front yards unobstructed to their view.

The woman was about sixty, gray hair pulled back into a knot. She wore a loose housedress and slippers. After Nolan identified herself (I was introduced as an assistant), she invited us in, offered us coffee, tea, or a cold drink.

"No thanks," Nolan said. "I want to ask you a few questions about Cormac Blather. You were one of his customers, weren't you?"

"Terrible," Mrs. Matheson said, "to die in such a violent manner. He was such a nice man."

She had no useful information to give us because she was out of town visiting one of her children at the time of the murder.

After Velma Matheson we made two more stops that produced nothing better than a view of the kind of customer Cormac specialized in: elderly, affluent, and sorry to lose such a nice man and such a good antique shop.

After the third one, Nolan said, "It's late. I'm going home." She handed me a list. "You watched me, right? Heard the questions? You should have no trouble. The only problem you're going to have is getting them to talk to you. You can't show any ID, meaning that fake detective card you have. What you do is tell them the truth—you're a civilian assisting the police. If anyone objects, say thank you very much, and leave. Make a note of the person who doesn't want to talk to you. And that's it. Okay? Capeesh?"

I nodded.

She drove me back to my house. I got out of her car and watched her drive away, thinking about "made out" and "making out."

I walked up the driveway to the front door. It had been dark a couple of hours and I was thinking about what I was going to have to eat, which might explain why I didn't see them until they stepped out of the shrubbery. Two guys wearing black. They each held something in their hands. I hoped they weren't guns, but whatever they were, it was easy to assume they were not going to be beneficial to my health.

The men spaced themselves on either side of me. I have to admit I was scared. At the same time I was kind of cool. I knew I was in deep shit. I could run but knew I wouldn't get far. I could try my best to fight them, but I also knew I didn't have much of a chance. For fun and exercise I'd done a bit of training in karate and judo, but I wasn't Chuck Norris or Steven Seagal. Nothing was going to help me except maybe the element of surprise.

"What do you guys want?" I said.

The taller of the two, the one on my left spoke, "We pay you a visit, that is all. From an old friend." It was a familiar Russian accent, possibly the same man who had made the late-night threatening phone call.

My idea of surprise was to attack first. I threw a kick at his knee but before I made contact something slammed into my right shoulder and sent me stumbling backwards. I put up my arms to defend myself but couldn't stop the next whack to my side. My driveway had solar lamps along the edges that threw enough light for me to see they were using some kind of club on me, like a shortened nightstick. I went down to the ground and tried to roll up into a ball. It was clear I was meant to be beaten but I didn't know if they meant to kill me as well. It was their choice because there was absolutely nothing I could do about it. The blows came one after another. They thudded against my back, arms, legs, head. I yelled as loud as I could. It wasn't hard because they were hurting me bad. I hoped someone would hear me before those clubs broke me into little pieces, and then all of a sudden I didn't feel anything.

I don't know how long I was unconscious. I came back into the world slowly. My head was one massive ball of pain. I could barely open my eyelids. I was able to see just enough to register that it was still night. My body was all bruises and aches, although the word "ache" didn't really tell the story. Every breath I took was painful. Something wet rolled down my forehead. I guessed it was blood. I tried to sit up and felt a stab of fire shoot through my chest so I gave up that idea and remained where I was.

I tentatively moved one leg to see if it worked. I tried the other. They seemed to function. I tested my arms. They also moved, which gave me hope they weren't broken.

I waited a little while and managed to get to a sitting position. Then I tried to stand but my legs wouldn't hold me and the pain in my chest made any movement all but impossible.

I knew I had to do something. Cell phone, of course. I slowly reached into a pocket. I didn't remember which one the phone was in. I was lucky. Found it on the first try. Now I had to hope the battery hadn't gone out on me. I opened it up, saw the face light up, signaling that it was working, and pushed the buttons for 911.

CHAPTER 28

"Nine-one-one, can I help you?" the operator said.

"I need an ambulance." It didn't sound like my voice.

"What's the problem?"

"Someone beat me up."

"Are you calling from home?"

"Right."

"Let me verify your address." She repeated it to make sure it was correct.

"That's it."

"Hang on," she said. "They'll be there in a few minutes."

I guess I passed out again because the next thing I knew I was being lifted onto a gurney and into an ambulance.

I wasn't unconscious in the ambulance but wished I were. The driver must have hit every rut and pothole on Noyac road. I wanted to holler out loud but did my macho best to keep it to a groan. They said they couldn't give me anything for the pain until I was examined by a doctor.

The emergency room doctor was the same one who had first treated Chase McCleod, the guy who looked like a weightlifter.

"Nice to see you again," he said.

I hurt too much to talk or I would have told him to drop dead.

After examination, X rays, and a CAT scan, which took hours, they told me I had two broken ribs along with a concussion. There was no sign of bleeding in the brain which meant the concussion was not serious. I had bruises and lacerations all over me. My fingers were swollen from trying to protect my head with my hands. In any event, there was nothing much to do about it. Everything would have to heal naturally. It would take a few weeks, someone said. All I could do during that process was to be careful and take painkillers when I felt the need. They bandaged the lacerations to my face and head.

"We're going to keep you a while, just to make sure the concussion has no aftereffects."

"Is that necessary? I'd rather go home."

"It's quite necessary. You wouldn't want to be home and pass out, or suddenly start vomiting, would you?"

They wheeled me to a room in the main part of the hospital. The Vicodin they'd given me had worked its magic and I didn't care what they did. Later, in the middle of the night, I woke up in pain and realized the narcotic haze had worn off. I looked around for help and saw for the first time there was another bed in the room, but it was empty.

Desperate, I found the buzzer and squeezed it as hard as I could. I kept squeezing it over and over again hoping it would help bring someone faster. It took what seemed like forever before a nurse finally arrived and gave me more Vicodin. It took a while before it worked and I was able to fall back asleep.

I woke up a few more times. Nightmarish dreams about McCleod, sore body, throbbing head. I wished Rosalind were there to hold my hand and tell me everything was going to be all right.

The next morning I opened my eyes to find not Rosalind but Detective Nolan looking down at me. She looked worried. My head didn't hurt quite as much, my body was another story.

"What happened?" she asked.

"Two guys beat me up. But I gave them hell first."

"Tell me what happened."

"How I gave them hell?"

"Don't be such an idiot." The words were hard but her voice was soft.

"A while back I got a phone call in the middle of the night. Said I should watch out. I didn't pay any attention to it. But I guess I was wrong. Last night two guys showed up and beat the shit out of me."

"You never told me anything about a phone call."

"You would've laughed at me. I should've been more alert, that's all."

"Do you know who they were?"

"No. But the accent was Russian so I'm pretty sure they were sent by Jascha Solofsky."

"Who's that?"

"Russian Mafioso. A guy I helped send to jail. I think he was paying me back."

"The guy with the Fabergé eggs?"

"Right."

"He's in jail, you said."

"Ten years."

"So why is he after you now?"

"I don't know. I cost him a lot of money and also helped put him away. Maybe he thinks I deserve a little pain to make up for it."

She frowned. "I don't know. You'd think he'd have more important things on his mind."

I tried to adjust my position in the bed and felt that fire flash through me.

She noticed. "Anything I can do?"

I shook my head. "You don't know this guy. He's bad news."

"How long is it since he was sent up?"

"About eight months."

"I wonder why he didn't get to you sooner."

"I'm glad he didn't," I said. "You think they might come back?"

"I doubt it. If he'd wanted you dead, you'd be dead. My guess is he just wanted some payback."

"He sure got it," I said. "I don't think I'll be able to move for a week."

"You don't look so bad," she said. "I've got work to do. I'll check back on you later."

After she left they came around with my breakfast. It was pureed. My jaw wasn't broken but they must have felt it would hurt too much to chew. I managed to spoon it down. At least the O.J. was good.

Later that morning, my friend Morty stopped by. "I was in the hospital visiting one of my patients when one of the nurses told me you were here. She knew we were friends. What the hell happened?"

I told him in as few words as possible.

"You're lucky they didn't kill you."

"Right now I don't feel lucky."

"I looked at your chart. Couple a fractured ribs. You're going to be okay. Just a few aches and pains, is all."

"Pain never bothers the one who doesn't have it, right?"

He laughed. "Got to go. Want Sherri to bring you anything?"

"How about some opium?"

After he left I found I couldn't keep my eyes open. The pain had vanished once more due to the painkiller. I allowed myself to drift off and slept until they woke me for lunch: pureed turkey accompanied by pureed spinach, and pureed applesauce. Yuck!

Sometime in the afternoon Toby swept in. *O queen of queens! How far dost thou excel* . . . She was accompanied by a severe-looking woman in a man-tailored suit sporting a butch haircut and black-rimmed eyeglasses. Toby was carrying a bouquet of yellow tulips and a box wrapped in purple paper and tied with a pink bow.

"Would you find a vase for these, Philippa?" she said, handing the flowers to the woman.

Philippa went to find a vase.

"Darling," Toby said. "I heard you were attacked."

"How did you hear?"

"It was on the radio. You're a local celebrity, remember? I brought you some candy, too." She put the box with the pink bow on my bed.

"I can't chew," I said.

"You will, though, right? Eventually?"

She sat on the side of the bed and took my hand. "How are you feeling?" Her hand was soft and warm and the perfume she wore filled the room like a dozen bouquets.

"Better. Really nice of you to visit. I know how busy you are."

"Don't be silly. I rushed down here as soon as I heard. You're more to me than just a friend. I hope you realize that."

"You are so . . . sweet," I said. I didn't know if it was the Vicodin, perfume, or her soothing words, but my eyes were beginning to close again.

"Poor boy," she said. "You need to rest and I'm keeping you from it."

I caught a glimpse of Philippa coming back with the tulips in a vase and heard Toby say something to her. I didn't hear what it was because my eyes closed and I was once more asleep.

CHAPTER 29

A resident came in after dinner and told me I could go home the next morning.

"We can't really do anything for your ribs but there is something to wear that will keep them from moving. It's like a vest."

"I don't think so."

He shrugged. "Your decision."

During the day, they'd gotten me out of bed and had me walk up and down the corridor with a walker. After a few steps I felt I didn't need the walker but they insisted.

"You should use one at home for a few days," the nurse said. "Just to make sure you don't have an accident."

"My legs don't feel too shaky," I said.

"You're in good physical condition. How old are you, about fifty?"

"Bless you," I said.

For most of the afternoon I watched CNN, reruns of *Law and Order* and *Everybody Loves Raymond*. But my thoughts kept coming back to Blather, the attempt to murder McCleod, and the fucking Russians who beat me up. It was a vicious beating but it could have been worse. I couldn't help wondering if there were more to it than just revenge. The other thing that was really hard to take was that I'd finally been able to get into a small piece of the investigation and now that this happened I was forced out of the action. Nolan might decide never to use me again and I'd be back where I was at the beginning.

Morty's wife, Sherri, came by with a couple of brownies from Schiavoni's. There was once a bakery called the Gingerbread Bake Shop but they'd sold out to a burger joint. Alas, Sag Harbor. Progress was going to kill us.

I didn't hesitate to try eating one. To my delight I was able to chew without effort and gobbled it up in a hurry. "Man, that is delicious. You were an angel to bring it. I'll save the other one for later."

She smiled. "I know hospital food is not the most enjoyable stuff in the world."

That night I didn't sleep well again, due to the drug wearing off as it had the previous night (although the pain was not nearly as bad) and also to my anxious desire for the morning to come so I could get out of the hospital—away from the room, the food, the smells, and an atmosphere full of germs, disease, and chemicals.

I'd decided it was simpler not to ask anyone to drive me. I managed to dress myself and was happy to let them take me to the exit in a wheelchair where the taxi I'd arranged for was waiting. When the driver dropped me off and pulled away, even though it was mid-morning, I couldn't keep myself from looking around to make absolutely sure no one was hiding in the shrubbery.

My legs were wobbly but I found that by taking small steps I was able to manage. Once inside, in familiar surroundings, I took a deep breath—it only hurt a little. It was good to be home.

The answering machine light was blinking in the den. Did I want to hear messages or did I want to chill out for a while? Who was I kidding? I pressed the button.

"How did you get out so fast?" Sienna Nolan's voice demanded to know. "Call me right away. Important."

"Jake, I called to see if you wanted more brownies but they

told me you were discharged. Call me if you need anything, okay? This is Sherri, but I'm sure you know that."

"Welcome home, Meestair Wanderman. We hope you enjoyed the hospital. It could have been the morgue. I remind you that we can visit you at any time of our choosing. To prevent this, we recommend that you disconnect yourself from anything to do with Mr. Blather's departure from this world. Do we understand each other?"

Jesus H. Christ! These guys were seriously on my case and it had nothing to do with payback. How did they know I was involved with the Blather murder investigation? Obviously they didn't know much because they were warning me off something I was barely on the edge of. But what could it possibly matter to them? How could they be tied up with it? The whole thing didn't make sense.

I was suddenly weary. I sat in my leather recliner, and tipped it back. The physical movements involved in getting dressed and the ride home had exhausted me. It seemed like a good idea to rest before doing anything else. I didn't even remember closing my eyes.

I woke up hungry. A couple of hours had passed. It was most definitely time for lunch.

In the kitchen I cracked three eggs, added some milk, pepper, salt, and a healthy dose of *herbes de Provence,* and began beating the eggs. Ouch! The motion must have moved my ribs because I got that fiery pain again. I very carefully finished the stirring, tossed a pat of butter in the pan and made an *omelette fines herbes.* It was so delicious I didn't even mind the pain. I took two Vicodin anyway.

I decided to let the call to Detective Nolan wait and check my computer for e-mail. There were 189 messages, most of them spam, but I was excited to see one from Herbert War-shavsky, the NYPD cop in Jerusalem my father had hooked me up with. I opened that first.

"Nice to hear from you, Jake. Your Dad's a great guy. What's on your mind?"

Short, sweet, and to the point. Now I had to ask myself what *was* on my mind? At the moment, nothing that had to do with Jerusalem, for sure. What I would have to do was concentrate and figure out why I thought I could use this NYPD cop in Jerusalem in the first place and how he could fit into the picture. Certainly the stolen burial box or ossuary was a factor.

It had been nine days since Cormac's murder.

CHAPTER 30

I called Sienna while trying to relax in my recliner and stared at the walls of bookshelves that lined the room. I wondered how many books there were crowding those shelves, probably more than a thousand. I was sure I'd read every one but if I were asked what each was about I was equally sure I wouldn't have the answer.

"I went back to see you yesterday but you were asleep," she said.

"I apologize."

"You know you can be infuriating sometimes?"

"I apologize again. You said you had something important."

"That was just to get you to call."

"Well *I* have something." I told her about the message from the Russians. And I told her about Herb Warshavsky.

"What could those goddamned Russians have to do with this? As for the cop over there, it shouldn't be too difficult to think of what he can do to help."

"Fine. Tell me what to ask him and I'll ask. Right now I'm a complete blank."

"I'll get back to you."

A few seconds later the phone rang. "Maybe I should come over there and we can bounce ideas off each other? Two heads better than one kind of thing? Are you up to it?"

"Sure. I ain't goin' nowhere."

I wasn't about to tell her I didn't have the ability to walk

162

around the house without pain, much less leave it.

I opened the front door a crack and went back to the recliner. If the Russians came back a locked door wouldn't make any difference. Fuck them, I couldn't do anything about it anyway.

I tilted the chair and remembered there was something in the house that would dull the aches in my body and head better than most painkillers. A bag of pot wrapped in aluminum foil in the refrigerator. The stuff came from my California nephew who visited us once a year, never failing to bring a gift from that great state. The first time Jon came for a visit he asked if we minded if he lit up a joint.

"Hell no," I said. "Can we share?"

"I didn't know you indulged," he said.

We smoked his joint, had a few drinks, and gave him dinner. Rosie got real sexy afterwards which led to a wonderful night. When he left the next day, he said, "I have a present for you." And he'd done the same ever since.

I heard tires crunching the gravel in the driveway, then Sienna's footsteps coming up to the front door. "Hello? Where are you?"

"Back here," I said. "Walk straight ahead. You'll find me."

The moment she came into the room I felt better. She wore a navy blue pantsuit, the jacket open revealing a pale-gray open-necked shirt and a strand of colorful beads. Glittering earrings dangled. Her lipstick seemed brighter and her face flushed, or was she wearing more makeup?

"I've been here before," she said. "Remember our first meeting?"

"I sure do. You were Miss Bitch that day."

She came over and stared at me. "You look like hell."

"Looks can be deceiving."

"Oh, are we being macho? You got hammered, Jake. Admit it."

"I admit it."

"Good. Before we start, can I get you anything? Like an aspirin or something to drink?"

I thought about the pot. I knew I'd better not smoke in front of her. After all, she was an officer of the law. Whether she approved or disapproved, it wouldn't be fair to put her in that position. But I had something to look forward to. A Stoli on the rocks crossed my mind. "I took painkillers so a drink is out but a glass of cold water would be great. There's some in the refrigerator."

She came back with two bottles and handed me one. "Tell me about the Russians. What's going on?"

I pointed to the answering machine. "You can hear it yourself."

She played the machine and heard all the messages, including her own. "Then they didn't beat you up as a payback. It was to warn you off. It means they're connected in some way with Blather. Maybe they were the ones who killed him."

I shook my head. "But that doesn't work with McCleod. They don't operate that way. They wouldn't have made phone calls, set up a meeting . . . they would have waited for him to leave his house and then shot him. The guy who tried to kill McCleod couldn't be one of them."

"You might be right. I got the sketch made of the man who came to the hospital. It's out. Maybe someone'll recognize him."

"Maybe."

"Whatever. But the bottom line here is you have to get off the case."

"The hell I will. They tried to scare me off before and couldn't do it."

She sighed. "I can freeze you out completely, if I want. You know that. It's for your own good."

"Let me worry about my own good. I can still do a lot on my

own. I've got the cop in Jerusalem, remember? There's a lot of information he could find."

"I can get the same cop to cooperate with me."

"I doubt he'd do for you what he'd do for the son of his friend."

"Maybe. But that's not the point, is it? Why put your life in danger? Why would you do that?"

"I promised Toby I'd help find her father's murderer."

"I guarantee if you told her that these guys who beat you up said they'd kill you if you kept on investigating, she'd be the first one to tell you to stop."

"Maybe."

"So do it. Drop out. Find something else to do."

"I'll think about it."

"While you're thinking I recommend you close your eyes and take a nap. You look as if you need it."

"I can live with that," I said, closed my eyes and promptly fell asleep.

I woke up to find Sienna sitting in the chair opposite me. I was surprised she was still there, and glad of it. The lamp next to her was on. The light from it reflected on her silken skin. She looked very good.

"How long did I sleep?"

"An hour and a half. Feel any better?"

"I think I do." I reached over for the lever to make the chair straighten. "What did you do while I was asleep?"

"I checked out your refrigerator. I'm impressed. Most single guys would have a hunk of moldy cheese and a six-pack of beer but you have all kinds of good stuff. Then I looked in your medicine cabinet."

"Not much in there."

"Correct. How about I get some takeout for dinner?" she said.

"That's very nice of you, but don't you have other things to do?"

"I have a right to help my former partner, don't I?" She smiled at me. "After all, you got beaten up in the line of duty."

"You called me partner," I said. "I'm touched. *O happiness, enjoy'd but of a few!*"

"I can always count on you to come up with Shakespeare when I least need it."

We ordered a Gorgonzola salad and a half plain, half pepperoni pizza from Conca D'Oro, my favorite Sag Harbor restaurant. She did all the work: set the table, served the food, cleaned up, rinsed the dishes and put them in the dishwasher. My only contribution was opening a bottle of Santa Christina.

We ate in the kitchen. There was a table tucked into one corner. It was cozy. Rosie and I used to have all our meals there. Now I sometimes ate standing up.

I watched her polish off every bit of the salad and pizza that I didn't eat. She didn't finish the bottle of wine only because she knew she had to drive.

"You know," she said. "I have a feeling that the stolen ossuary is connected to Blather's murder. There's too much coincidence here. It was probably a fake which was why Bryson Mergenthaler gave me such a hard time. First his ultra-slick secretary tried to keep me from interviewing him altogether. I had to turn on the pressure to get him to allow the interview. And then he stonewalled me when I tried to question him about it."

"Absolutely right," I said. "It had to be a fake. We know Cormac was into forging paintings again. Why not antiques?"

"Okay. But where would he get the expertise to do it?"

"Jerusalem. Didn't your search of his computer turn up e-mails from Israel?"

"They didn't say anything incriminating."

"You wouldn't expect them to lay it all out in an e-mail,

would you?" I said.

"Of course not. But maybe your guy in Jerusalem could help in this? Why don't you give me his e-mail address? I'll write him, introduce myself, and see what he'll do for me."

"I think it would be better if I contact him first. I can bring you in after we establish some kind of rapport."

"You don't trust me. Okay. What're you going to tell him?"

"I'm not sure. My first idea was to lay out the whole story, then I thought it might not be a good idea to do it in an e-mail for security reasons."

"Got a point." She frowned. "How about this? Just tell him about the ossuary. A friend of yours sold one that supposedly came from Jerusalem. There was a possibility it was a fake. Could he look into the faking of antiquities over there? How they do it? How they distribute it? That sort of thing. That doesn't say too much, does it? Nothing about a murder. Just about the faking business."

"Sounds okay. I'll get right on it." I couldn't keep the discontent out of my voice.

"Hey, I know it's tough for you to drop out of this. But it's the smart thing to do."

I didn't answer.

We went to the door. In spite of everything I felt a strong urge to kiss her. At the same time I thought of Rosalind. I hesitated. We stood there and looked at each other. I was sure she was feeling something, too, that I wasn't imagining it. Didn't matter. In the end I wasn't able to make the move toward her and she didn't make one toward me.

CHAPTER 31

I sent the e-mail off to Warshavsky, the cop in Jerusalem. I sat in front of the TV and stared at the blank screen. I didn't turn it on, didn't want pictures or sound. I didn't want anything. A kind of lethargy had taken over my body. I felt as if my arms and legs weren't functioning. My brain felt frozen, numb. Even the pain in my ribs had temporarily dulled.

I sat for a long time without moving. Eventually I got up. The thought of eating brought a wave of nausea. All I could manage to do was get into bed and pull the blanket over my head.

I didn't sleep well. In addition to the broken ribs, my body had locations all over it that reminded me of the beating. When I turned from one side to the other during the night, the pain woke me and then thoughts skittered through my mind at random speed so that I couldn't keep track of any of them.

At six o'clock in the morning I dragged myself into a hot shower. Hydrotherapy. It worked enough to allow me to get dressed and make some coffee. I still had no appetite. I recognized what was happening. Depression. Was I going to do anything about it?

The answer to that question was to once again climb into bed, this time with my clothes on. But I did take my shoes off.

I stayed in bed all day. The phone rang but I didn't answer it. Didn't turn on the radio or watch TV. Had my eyes closed or stared at the ceiling.

I was deep into it. Allowing myself to sink into a swamp in

the bayous. Foul air. Unearthly smells. Hoped I would stumble and drown. Wished for some slithering snake to pierce a leg with poison.

In the middle of all that shit I still couldn't help remembering Richard II:

> *My grief lies all within;*
> *And these external manners of laments*
> *Are merely shadows to the unseen grief*
> *That swells with silence in the tortured soul.*

The doorbell woke me. I looked at the clock. Nine p.m. How could I have spent that much time in bed doing absolutely nothing?

I stumbled to the door to find Morty Adler, a concerned look on his chubby face. My friend had gained a lot of weight over the years.

"What the hell is the matter with you? Why don't you answer the phone or return a message?"

"I wasn't feeling good."

He took hold of my shoulders and peered into my face. "You look like shit."

"I've been told that already."

"What's the matter? Is it the pain? Or is it some other effects of the beating?"

"More or less all of the above."

"I'm going to get my bag from the car. Go and sit down."

"You don't have to do that."

He was already on his way and paid no attention to me.

He came back with his medical bag and ran his stethoscope over my chest and back. Then he got a blood pressure kit out of the bag. He squeezed the rubber ball and I felt the wrap tighten.

"Nothing out of the ordinary," he said.

"Too bad. I was hoping for cancer."

"That's not the least bit funny, Jake. What's going on?"

I didn't feel like talking or explaining anything. But he was my best friend, wasn't he? Didn't he break a window when we were kids so that I had to hide him in my mother's closet? And didn't we go all through school watching each other's backs? I told him about the Russians. I told him that Nolan had dropped me. I tried to tell him about my feelings but couldn't manage to get the proper words out.

He listened to my stumbling speech without interrupting. That was impressive and showed how concerned he was. I used to call him *Mortus interruptus* because he never let me finish a sentence.

"It's obvious you're depressed," he said. "I don't want to say 'I told you so,' but I told you so. You never worked through your grief about Rosalind. Working with the detective was good for you—it gave you an outlet—but now they're kicking you off the case. That's a lot to deal with. Remember what else I told you before? That you ought to try a support group? It might really help."

"I don't think I can handle that."

"What's there to handle? You just go. You don't even have to talk."

"Then what's the point?"

"Look," he said. "This is not my field. But I do know it's helped a lot of people. There must be something to it."

"I'll think about it."

He gave me a skeptical look.

"No. I mean it," I said. "I really will."

"Call me in the morning. If you decide to do it I'll find out what I can. I know they have meetings around here someplace. I think maybe the Whalers Church in town might do it."

"Thanks, Mort. You can go home now."

"You're sure you don't want me to stay a while? Keep you company?"

"Not unless you want to get in bed with me."

"I'll pass," he said.

As he left the siren went off in Sag Harbor. I was three miles away but it sounded like next door. It meant a fire, an accident, or a medical emergency. The siren also went off supposedly at noon every day, but typical of the charm of Sag Harbor it was usually a minute off.

"Watch out for those volunteer firemen with the blue lights," I said. "They'll drive right over you if you don't get out of the way."

CHAPTER 32

I had no intention of doing anything about a support group. I'd only told Morty I'd think about it to get him to stop bugging me.

After another poor night's sleep I was pleased to find in the morning that I had an appetite. I decided to have coffee first and see what I felt like eating. I took an "everything" bagel out of the freezer, defrosted it in the microwave, scooped it out, toasted it, spread a little butter, and only ate half. It turned out I wasn't hungry, after all.

Morty's suggestion was still on my mind. In the local Yellow Book, under "Grief," I was directed to go to "Counseling." Below that heading was a long list of therapists. The only specialty was marriage counseling, nothing about grief. The Whalers Church that Morty had mentioned was not listed. But I noticed that East End Hospice was there and remembered someone telling me that they did "bereavement care."

Maybe Morty was right. Maybe it would help me to get into something like this. There wasn't anything else for me to do anyway. I was out of business. Besides, I had to wait for my body to heal. I could also use the time to get some healing for my soul.

I called and was referred to a social worker who told me that the first step in the process was that I had to come in for an interview. They wanted to assess me. I assumed they wanted to know what kind of shape I was in. I could've told her over the phone I was in lousy shape but I guessed what they wanted had more to do with the techno-psych jargon stuff. The earliest appointment they could give me was three days away.

After specifying the time, I said, "Okay. I'll be there."

Immediately after hanging up I asked myself, what was I doing? Why was I doing it? What did I need it for?

You know why, I answered. Because you're a sorry mess. Simple as that.

I went into the den to see if there was anything on the answering machine from the day before when I hadn't picked up the phone. There were messages from Sienna, Toby, Morty. They were all more or less the same: testy, annoyed with me. Why wasn't I answering the phone, and where could I possibly be since I should be at home recuperating? I pushed the button hard to erase them.

The house was closing in on me. I slipped on a sweat jacket and went outside to walk in the garden. Rosalind had been the gardener supreme, planning, reading books on layout, which shrubs would do well in shade or sun, how to get blooms in every season. She used perennials and combined them with annuals so that the eye was always taken from one place to another with pleasure. We'd spent hours on our hands and knees, weeding, planting, transplanting. Lots of backaches and dirt under the fingernails but all of it worthwhile.

I wandered slowly and saw the petunias fading, the impatiens still bright, the mums popping out in yellows and whites and pinks. It was her vision but it didn't make me feel worse to think of her in this context. In fact, it made me feel better. I breathed in the crisp October air and went back inside in time to hear the phone ringing.

I answered and heard Toby Welch say, "Darling. I'm so glad to hear your voice. You really had me worried. When you didn't answer the phone yesterday I thought you might have had a relapse so I called the hospital, but you weren't there. I didn't know what to think. You're home now, though. Are you all right?"

"Dandy."

"I'm sure you're not but I do hope you're being wise and making sure to take care of your body."

"I don't have much choice. I hurt too much to do anything else."

"Poor boy. I have an idea. How would you like me to bring you a wonderful dinner? How does that sound?"

I tried to be enthusiastic. "Sounds great."

"What would you like to have?"

"Anything will be fine."

"I'd like to bring you something you love. What's your favorite food?"

"I like everything. All nationalities. Whatever you bring'll be great."

"All right then," she said. "I'll think of something. Is seven o'clock okay? Or is that too late?"

I told her seven was fine and looked at my watch after I hung up. It wasn't even ten in the morning. What was I going to do with myself for a whole day?

I went back into the den and tried to think logically . . . about everything, all the stuff I hadn't consciously thought about before. With Rosalind life had been rewarding. Lots of pleasuring after working all those years. And then had come the fantastic adventure of the Fabergé eggs. It had all seemed too good to be true.

But Rosalind died. Abruptly. I went through all the stuff that the sudden death of a loved one does to the person left behind: numbness, disorientation, anger at her for leaving me, and the worst kind of disbelief, thinking she might still be alive. I sometimes thought I saw her across the street, or in another aisle in the supermarket, even heard her voice.

I'd gotten over most of it. But it was still hard to be alone. I'd had no interests until the involvement with Cormac's murder. Was there anything other than that I might care about?

I settled back in the chair and tried to disregard the stab of pain I got every time I moved. I closed my eyes to help me concentrate. After a while I realized there wasn't anything else. All my old interests from tennis to Shakespeare were no longer important. The only thing I wanted was to be in on finding Cormac's murderer. But I was out of it. Dumped. And the cause was those fucking Russians. I wished I could get my hands on them, one at a time, of course.

Once again I thought about what I was going to do for the rest of the day. Obviously I couldn't exercise and I was too worked up to read. It was too early to go to the movies, not that I really wanted to anyway. I flipped on the TV and watched CNN for a while, then a rerun of *Everybody Loves Raymond,* then the Food Channel. There was an old WW II movie on AMC with a lot of guys sweating in the jungle. Couldn't stay with that, either.

I thought about making myself another cup of coffee when the doorbell chimed. I opened the door expecting to see the UPS guy or FedEx but it was Sienna Nolan at my doorstep with a strange expression on her face. I wasn't sure if she was smiling or not.

"Hey," she said.

"What are you doing here?"

"That's not a nice greeting."

Without even trying this woman had a way of getting under my skin. "Come on in."

She was wearing tight jeans and a sweater in place of the pantsuits she usually favored. She brought her scent with her. I followed her into the den unable to keep my eyes off the plumpness of her behind under the jeans. Amazing, I thought, how quickly a man's thoughts could shift from earth-shattering self-pity to enjoying the sight of a woman's ass.

"What brings you here?" I said.

"Is it all right if I sit down?"

"Sure. Have a seat. Then tell me why you're here."

She didn't sit. "You don't sound like you're glad to see me."

"Are you surprised? You kick me off the case and you want me to give you a hug?"

"Would a hug be so bad? Actually, this is what I had in mind." She came close and kissed me lightly on the lips.

"What's that all about?" I said.

"What a strange response. Didn't you like it?"

"Of course I did."

"Then why don't you kiss me back?"

I hesitated, not sure why, but guessed it was probably fear. Was this a game she was playing? Was it a test of some kind? And if so, why? If it was not a game, then I had reason to be nervous. This was entirely new to me. Would I be able to handle it? My next thought was, don't be a schmuck.

I kissed her back.

I hadn't tasted a woman's lipstick or felt the softness of a woman's lips for a long time. It was sweet. It was delicious. The kiss went on and on and on.

Finally, we stopped to breathe. I could feel my heart banging around in my chest like a loose bowling ball.

"You're a good kisser. I thought you would be," she said.

"Now what?"

She smiled. "In my experience, at this point, the man grabs the woman by the hair and drags her into his cave."

"I'm not the caveman type."

"Too bad."

"Come on," I said. "I'm flattered. I really am. But I can't

help being skeptical."

"Why? Can't I just be attracted to you?"

"You never gave me a clue that you were *attracted,* to use your word. Where did it come from? When did it start? And why now?"

She took a deep breath. "Okay. Let's sit down and talk."

She sat. I stood with my hands clasped protectively in front of me.

"I think I felt something for you from the beginning," she said. "I just didn't realize it until the other night. You know. We had dinner together and I was leaving. I thought you wanted to kiss me then, but you didn't."

"True. I did want to kiss you."

"Then I was right."

"So what? That doesn't explain the sudden change. Why the interest in me now? It couldn't be you're feeling sorry for me, could it?"

"My feeling for you has nothing to do with anything except wanting to go to bed with you."

"Did you just say what I think you just said?"

"You don't need a hearing aid, do you?"

"My hearing is first rate."

I took her hand and led her upstairs to a bedroom.

CHAPTER 33

I woke up with her head on my chest and her hair in my nose. I sneezed, which woke her, too. She yawned, slid her warm, smooth body over on top of me and kissed me.

"Ouch!" I said.

"I'm sorry," she said, rolling off. "I forgot."

Her getting off me added another dose of sting. "It's okay. I wish you could stay there, believe me. But it hurts too much."

"So you told me. Several times." She grinned. "I thought you managed quite well, in spite of your problems."

"Amazing, isn't it? How you can bypass the injuries when you're in heat? I know you're being nice. And I appreciate it. But I can do better. Much better."

"There goes Mr. Macho again."

"I don't mean to sound that way. I'm just a humble male, lady, trying to do my best. *My duty pricks me on,* as Proteus said to the Duke of Milan."

She laughed. "Now that's a quote I can appreciate."

"What time is it, anyway?"

She leaned over me to look at the clock on my night table. "You won't believe this. It's almost twelve o'clock."

"No wonder I'm starving," I said.

We went out to eat. I had her drive us to the Corner Bar at the foot of Main Street in Sag Harbor. Good food, and a great place for a casual lunch. At night, the bar was jammed with the noisiest bunch of bar flies on the East End. And a Friday night

178

after work? Don't even try to have a conversation. But I liked it. No bright young things with iPods and cell phones ringing. The only thing the Corner Bar had in common with the upscale restaurants favored by thirty-something so-called movers and shakers was the noise. Otherwise, the food was better and the prices lower.

I wasn't the only one who liked it. Even though it was well after the season, almost every table was occupied by working men and women from local banks and real estate offices, young mothers with kids, and other assorted types. The noise level was not low but we were able to talk.

In between bites of our burgers, Sienna said they had the DNA from the skin under McCleod's nails. I drank some of my Diet Coke. "Why can't I still do something? It doesn't have to be obvious. Maybe I can make phone calls, check lists." I hoped it didn't sound like begging. "Just so I feel I'm still helping in some way."

"That's an idea. Let me look into it."

"Good. I need to tell Toby Welch what's going on. She's the one who got me into this in the first place."

I didn't see any reason to tell her that Toby was coming to my house that night.

"You could tell her the truth. Your life was threatened."

"I don't want to do that." I reached over and put my hand over hers. "Get me something to do. It's important."

Instead of answering me, she removed her hand and brought the burger back to her mouth. The Corner's hamburgers required two hands. Her mouth full, she chewed with a happy smile on her face. "This is so good. I'm glad you introduced me to this place. I'll definitely be back."

"I'm glad you like it. But that's not an answer."

"Sure," she said. "I'll look into it. I sure will."

179

"Are you stiffing me?" I said. As soon as I said it I started to laugh.

She almost choked on her food as she laughed, too. "It's supposed to be the other way around, is that it?"

"And so it was," I said.

She took another bite and stuffed some fries into her mouth. After she swallowed every bit, she said quietly, "The bedroom we were in wasn't your bedroom, was it?"

I blinked at the non sequitur and was surprised by how smart she was. "How'd you know?"

"Obvious. It was decorated like a guestroom, not a master bedroom. The colorful pillows, the bedspread, the curtains. Besides, I knew you wouldn't want to go to your own bed."

This was getting more uncomfortable by the minute. "How did you know that?"

She put down the burger and wiped her hands and mouth with her napkin. There was that small smile around her mouth again, the same one she'd had when I'd answered the door. "Did you think I was going to let you work with me without my checking you out? I know everything about you. Well, maybe not everything, but a lot. I know where you grew up and where you went to school. I know the names of friends from the past as well as the present. I know what you taught and where. And all that stuff about you being freaked out on Shakespeare. And I know about your wife."

A teacher gets used to being a talkative person. You stand in front of a class for years and have to stimulate minds that are closed down or shut off. I had to learn how to wake them up so I'd tell stories or deliberately say outrageous things to get them going. Rarely was I ever without words to roll trippingly off my tongue. Until that moment.

Finally, I was able to say, "I should have known you'd do that. I don't know why it comes as a surprise."

She shrugged, then looked at her watch. "Omigod. I gotta go. I'm supposed to be at a meeting at two o'clock. It's with my boss so I can't be late."

"I'm not finished," I said. "And neither are you."

She stood up, glanced down at what was left of her burger, then picked it up and took one more bite. "Umm. I hate to leave the rest, it's so good. But I guess I could say my hunger has been satisfied."

"I wasn't talking about food."

"Neither was I. Sorry. Have to go."

She drove me home, gave me a peck and all but pushed me out of the car. Hey, wait a minute, I thought. This was a role reversal I didn't like. The *guy* is the one who wants to move on after sex, not the woman.

I went around to the driver's side, leaned in the window and kissed her fully on the mouth. "When can we get together again?"

"I'll call."

"What does that mean?"

"Let's see how it goes," she said and drove away.

I watched her car disappear down Noyac Road, my self-esteem somewhat eroded.

Toby was due to arrive in a few hours. No doubt there'd be all kinds of questions about her father's murder and about how the investigation was going. What could I tell her? The truth was too demeaning. I was also concerned that Toby possibly had something else in mind besides dinner. That was not something I wanted to deal with. Especially now. On the other hand, the early part of the day had turned out to be a lot better than I could have expected, so I decided not to be discouraged. The end of the day might turn out to be better than expected, too.

CHAPTER 34

Landis Kalem was in the bathroom of his room in the five-star Excelsior Hotel in Rome. The bathroom was the size of a New York City studio, with ornate mirrors, marble sink, floors, walls, and tub, towels thick enough to use as blankets, toiletries of every description. The lights were bright but adjustable to low. In addition to the usual hair dryer, outlets for American appliances and Jacuzzi-sprouting serpentine coils of tubing, there was a plasma TV on the wall to watch from the tub.

But Landis was not paying attention to any of those things. He concentrated instead on squeezing a thin layer of ointment out of a tube of Polysporin. He gently applied it to the back of his right hand.

Having to fly to Italy just now with all that had happened was disconcerting. He was glad to have the rest of the evening to himself. He had gone with Mergenthaler to a deluxe affair high up in the Appian Hills. Only some of the world's most powerful billionaires had been invited. Warren Buffett from the United States, Silvio Berlusconi of Italy, Rupert Murdoch, the Australian, Li Ka-shing from Hong Kong, Prince Alwaleed from Saudia Arabia, Carlos Slim Helu from Mexico, Mikhail Khodorkovsky, the oil baron from Russia. Somehow Donald Trump and his gorgeous wife, wearing her usual extreme décolletage, had managed to get invited as well, even though it was well known his net worth was mostly fiction. Ostensibly it was just a celebration of wealth but the hidden agenda was old-fashioned networking, pulling strings and ferreting out weaknesses that could be exploited in the future. They were all masters but Mergenthaler was the best.

Before they left New York Landis had had to cover the back of his hand with Band-Aids. He was annoyed with himself because he'd thought the scratches would heal naturally and so had not paid proper attention to them. When he'd noticed the redness and the subsequent infection, it was too late.

"What happened to your hand?" Mergenthaler had asked.

He'd conjured up a story about dropping his cell phone near one of the rose bushes in the garden in North Haven, and that when he'd tried to retrieve it, had gotten scratched by the thorns. It was a plausible story and accepted.

Not by Mario, the butler. He'd been scornful of the explanation. They were in Landis's bedroom in the North Haven residence, sometime after midnight.

"Since when you ever go near the rose bushes? I never seen you in the garden even."

"How would you know?" Landis said. "I go into the garden quite often. I love the smell of roses."

"It's too cold. There ain't no roses this time of year."

Landis sat on the side of his bed. He wore only his pajama top. "Stop arguing, will you?" he said. "Kneel down like a good boy and give me a kiss where it'll do the most good."

Mario followed his instructions. Landis leaned back on his elbows and closed his eyes. He thought how foolish he'd been to go to the hospital and put himself in danger. All for no good reason since it had worked out anyway. McCleod had not survived, after all.

"Ahhh," he said out loud, as Mario's astonishing mouth and tongue continued to delight. He leaned forward and ran his hand over the top of Mario's head. He didn't think he'd have to worry about Mario. Who would he tell and why would he talk about it?

He took Mario's ear between two of his fingers and pinched it as hard as he could.

"Ow!" Mario stopped what he was doing. "That hurt."

"That was my intention."

"You do that again I might bite your cock off."

Landis leaned forward and put his hands gently around Mario's throat, then pressed his thumbs against the larynx. Mario made a sound, and tried to pull the hands away. He fell over with Landis on top of him still pressing hard, his fingers shutting off the air to Mario's lungs. Mario struggled but couldn't break the hold on his throat. He was turning blue when Landis finally let go.

"Don't ever threaten me again," he said.

"Jesus, I was only kidding." Mario was still gasping for air.

"I wasn't." Landis returned to his place on the bed. "Get up and finish what you were doing."

Now here Landis was, in Rome and still applying Polysporin. He was safe, or was he? He had to hope that McCleod had not been able to speak before he died. If he had, there wasn't anything he could do about it here. But no one had come after him before the trip to Rome which meant all his precautions had been effective. His disguise had certainly worked. He'd seen the sketch in the post office of the man wanted by the police in connection with the case. There was no way anyone could look at that sketch and see Landis. Being away, he suddenly realized, was a good thing. It would give his hand time to heal so that when he returned the telltale marks would be gone. But there was one more worrisome factor. What to do with the miniature he'd taken from the antique shop the night of the murder. He'd placed it inside one of his many sweaters stacked in a closet but he knew he couldn't leave it there. The sighting of that small painting had been the catalyst for what had happened. He'd been at Blather's shop several times after Mergenthaler had commenced doing business with him. On occasions when Blather was interrupted by a customer he'd wander around and look at the various items on display. And then one day he saw it. It took all his powers of self-control to keep any sign of his recognition hidden. The moment his eye took it in he knew immediately what it was. He hadn't thought about it in years but seeing it again jolted his memory.

It must have been sometime around 1967. He was either five or six years old. It was his parents' anniversary. Landis remembered the smile of pleasure from his mother when she saw it. The original had always been her favorite painting. "It's so beautiful, Ben," she said. "And I'm glad you put your initials on it, too, BJK."

Only later did Landis understand the significance of that remark. It meant his mother knew what her husband was doing. She knew why he painted masterpieces.

One day the miniature was gone. "I had to give it to him," his father explained. "He wanted it badly, even with my initials on it. Besides, he gave me a thousands pounds for it."

So it was gone, and soon his father was gone, too, in jail for forgery and fraud. His mother tried to explain it to him but he was too young to fully understand. What he did come to understand was that his life had changed. His mother had no income. They were always short of food, and everything else. She began drinking. Strange men were in the house. His father was let out of jail. He came home a broken man, unable to work. They both drank. Before Landis was ten his father had hanged himself. His mother had been put into an institution. Landis was placed in a foster home.

He'd never been told the name of the man responsible for his father's going to jail. He determined to learn it as soon as he got old enough. In time he was able to go to old newspaper files and there found the story. But the guilty man, the one truly guilty, had never been found guilty of anything because there was no proof, other than his father's word, that Blather had authorized the forged paintings. He claimed he himself had been duped.

Landis, however, knew the truth. He knew one day he would find this man and make him pay for what he had done to his mother and father.

Strangely enough, once he'd located Blather, Landis was in no hurry. He could choose to eliminate him from the earth any time he wished. In fact, there'd been a certain amount of pleasure knowing that he held the man's life in his hands.

But everything changed the day he saw the miniature. For reasons he could not explain to himself, he knew he would not wait any longer.

CHAPTER 35

After Sienna left I took a couple of aspirin. My body had held up fairly well considering what I'd asked of it, but the effects of the beating were still with me. On my way to the den for a rest I stopped to check my e-mail. There was a message from Herb Warshavsky, the cop in Jerusalem.

Picked up something that may interest you. Seems the Russian Mafia here has gotten into other stuff besides prostitution, extortion, credit card fraud, and general thievery. They've made a big dent in the fake antique market. Apparently big bucks there. Sources tell me they've set up a worldwide distribution network.

The light bulb clicked on. What this new information had to mean was that the hammering by the Russians must have been connected to the ossuary sold to Mergenthaler and then stolen. They apparently knew of my closeness with Cormac and how I'd helped him in the past. Could they have been the ones who murdered Cormac? But then why McCleod? And the way it was done to McCleod was definitely not the Mafia way.

It struck me as hard to believe that Cormac would have gotten involved with the Russians after all the trouble they'd given him with the Fabergé eggs, but what other explanation could there be? He was the one who'd sold the ossuary to Mergenthaler and if it wasn't phony why would someone have gone to so much trouble to steal it? Sienna thought the item was a fake, too. She'd brought that up when she interviewed Mergenthaler but he'd given nothing away about how he felt about it. After the robbery Sienna told me nothing else had been taken, only the box, so that put a seal on it. If the item was not available to be examined no one could prove anything.

I settled into my recliner to think about the implications and the next thing I knew the doorbell was waking me up. I got out of the chair feeling a little groggy and wondered how long it would take before I was normal again.

All six feet of Toby were at my door. Up close her height was imposing, but her smile was warm and sincere and her obvious concern for me, genuine. She wore a peach-colored cashmere sweater that looked so soft you'd like to roll around in it. A single strand of pearls was her only adornment.

"Meals on Wheels, sir?" she said. "Steaming hot. Bound to make you feel as good as new." She leaned forward and touched my lips with hers.

"This is so nice of you," I said.

"Nonsense. You'd do the same for me, wouldn't you?"

Maybe, I thought, maybe not. She had so much more help at her disposal.

She was carrying a large plastic bag. I was disappointed. I'd expected her to bring something elegant, more on the order of chafing dishes and bottles of champagne, the way they did in those depression era movies when everyone wore dinner jackets and gowns and had a martini in one hand and a cigarette in the other.

She breezed past me. "Which way's the kitchen? I want to get this into the oven."

I showed her the way to the kitchen. "What did you bring?" She was the TV guru of cooking as well as everything else to do with home management.

She was opening kitchen cabinets until she found the baking pans she was looking for. "I was going to prepare something really special for you and then I had a brainstorm. I remembered you lived right near Cromer's market. And they have the best southern-fried chicken on the East End. What better treat, I thought, than to bring you wonderful chicken along with their great mashed potatoes and gravy. Coleslaw, too, of course." She put her hands on her hips and smiled at me. "Are you pleased?"

"Fantastic!" I lied. Not that I didn't like Cromer's chicken. It was just that I had it so often it wasn't all that much of a treat. I'd been hoping for one of her fabulous creations like homemade gnocchi or papardelle with pancetta.

She put the food in the oven. "You're to rest," she said. "Just point me in the right direction and I'll take care of everything."

She found the dishes, silverware, glasses and set the table. She got a bottle of Pinot Grigio from the wine rack and put it in the freezer to chill. She put ice cubes in the water glasses before filling them with water, then asked where the wine glasses were. She went out of the kitchen and came back with a vase full of artificial flowers that I didn't even know I had and made them the centerpiece.

I don't know what else she did but by the time we sat down to eat the kitchen was filled with delicious aromas and the table was beautiful.

"You're a wonder," I said.

"I know," she said, smiling.

Cromer's chicken tasted even better than usual which made me suspect she had done something to enhance it but I decided not to ask, just eat and enjoy. I was also wondering how much to tell her about the investigation of her father's murder when she got around to asking. I knew it was only a matter of *when* she got around to it, not *if*.

I was barely into my second wing when the question came. "I know you've been sidetracked by what happened to you," Toby said. "And I do feel that your health comes first, before anything really, but I wonder how much you can tell me about . . . you know. Are the police getting anywhere?"

Time to bite the bullet. "I wish I had a definitive answer for you, but it's just not that simple. Are they getting anywhere? I'd have to say they're working hard but other than that . . ." I shrugged. "The police won't tell me much. But I know they're looking into all aspects of your father's business."

"Why?"

"It's possible the murder is connected in some way. I have my own theory. I've been in touch with a guy in Jerusalem. He's a New York cop, friend of my father. He just sent me an e-mail telling me the Russian Mafia is involved with forged art and antiques."

"What does that have to do with my father?"

"Come on, Toby. You know your dad's history. The guys who beat me up spoke with Russian accents."

"So?"

"I wasn't going to tell you this but you might as well know. The Russians beat me up to scare me off the case."

"What does that mean? Why you?"

"My guess is they know about my connection with your father and that I had something to do with another Mafioso going to jail. I'm also guessing it's because of an ossuary your father sold to a guy named Mergenthaler. Do you know what an ossuary is?"

She shook her head. "No, but I know Bryson Mergenthaler. Only I didn't know he'd done business with my father."

"You know Mergenthaler? Your father sold him a ton of stuff. One of the things he sold him was an ossuary, or burial box from the time of Christ. And much as I hate to say it, the burial box he sold him may have been a fake. How well do you know this guy?"

"Socially. Charity affairs, that kind of thing. I still don't understand how any of this could lead to my father's murder."

I swallowed some Pinot Grigio. "I'm not sure myself, but I'm positive there's a connection."

Her blue eyes opened wider. "Do you think Mergenthaler may be involved in this? That he could have had something to do with my father's murder?"

"Anything is possible. But I don't think it's likely. What motive would he have? Even if he thought he'd been sold a fake, would he have someone killed for it?"

"Rich and powerful people don't follow normal rules. They think they own the world and can do anything they want without penalty. I'm anything but poor, but Bryson Mergenthaler lives on another planet entirely."

I'd suddenly lost interest in food. Ideas were crowding into my brain. What Toby had said about Mergenthaler was part of it, and what Warshavsky had e-mailed me about the Russian Mafia was another part. "Listen," I said. "Could you talk to this guy?"

"Mergenthaler? Of course. There's no reason he wouldn't take my phone call. What do you want me to say to him?"

"I don't know yet. I have to think about it. But there's something else. How would you feel about paying my way to Jerusalem?"

"Jerusalem?"

"There are answers there." Suddenly I was excited again. "That's where the ossuary came from. That's where the faking of the antiquities is being done. That's where my friend, the New York cop is, who knows a lot about this. I think the key to the whole story might be there."

"We talked about this before. Don't you remember? I offered to pay for you then. In fact, I wish I could go with you, but with my schedule it's impossible."

I felt so grateful to her that even though I was worn out I got up, went around to her side of the table, and kissed her. She reached up, put her hands around my neck and pulled my mouth hard against hers. After a long moment, we separated.

"Jake," she said. She was breathing hard. "I'm not sure what this means."

I knew she was referring to the kiss and all of its possible combinations and permutations. But I wasn't thinking about that. I wasn't even thinking about Sienna. I was now hot on the trail of something much more important. A way to get my life on track again by heading off to Israel and the ancient city of Jerusalem. I was back in the hunt and I wasn't about to let anything interfere with that.

CHAPTER 36

The first thing I did next morning was call East End Hospice and cancel my appointment with the grief counselor. I went about deciding what to pack, and thought of a few things for Toby to ask Mergenthaler:

1. What did he buy from Cormac besides the ossuary?
2. Did he ever have a suspicion that anything he bought could have been a forgery?
3. If yes, did he ever discuss this with Cormac?
4. If so, did Cormac ever acknowledge there might be a problem?

A few days later Toby called me back to tell what she'd learned. "I wasn't able to speak to him directly. His secretary told me they'd only recently got back from Europe and that Mr. Mergenthaler was too busy to talk to me at that moment. But if I would tell him what I wanted to speak to him about, he would relay my message."

"Son of a bitch," I said.

"I was too polite to say it. I told his secretary that it was personal. I wasn't about to tell him anything else. He was very courteous, actually, more like unctuous. But who knows, that's probably what Mergenthaler wants, a buffer between himself and the world."

"So he hasn't gotten back to you?"

"Not yet."

"What's the secretary's name?"

"Kalem. Landis Kalem. Why?"

"Suppose I call him, and tell him I'm *your* secretary. No, that won't work. Once I start asking him questions he'll want to know why I'm asking and not the police. I know, I'll tell him the truth. I'm a private investigator working for you. Maybe I can get something out of him that way."

"You can try."

She gave me the number. I didn't really expect to get anywhere, but I wanted to see what we were dealing with. I'd gotten an inkling of Mergenthaler from Sienna's notes of her interview with him but I felt it would be a good idea to get an impression of the secretary as well. You never knew when information, any kind of information, could turn out to be useful.

"Landis Kalem," was the way he answered the phone. Very businesslike. I told him who and what I was and that I was calling on behalf of Ms. Welch.

"What may I do for you?"

"I understand that your employer is a busy man and might not have the time to respond to Ms. Welch at the moment. So Ms. Welch thought that perhaps you could help out in this situation."

"Of course. I am eager to do everything I can to help. What situation are you referring to?"

"The murder of her father."

There was a distinct pause. I imagined an intake of breath.

"How can Mr. Mergenthaler be of any help in that regard?"

"It would be useful if he could provide me with a list of everything he bought from Mr. Blather."

"You realize that I am not free to give out any information without Mr. Mergenthaler's permission."

"Of course. But while you're asking about that, there are a few other things I'd like to know." Then I presented him with the same list of questions I'd given to Toby.

"I shall pass your request on to my employer."

"Do you think I'll get an answer?"

"I'm afraid I can't respond to that, Mr.—what did you say your name was?"

"Wanderman. Jake Wanderman."

"Mr. Wanderman, I've worked for Mr. Mergenthaler many years. The one thing I've learned is not to try to predict anything he might or might not do."

Then the prick hung up on me.

CHAPTER 37

I wanted to get going. I wasn't about to wait around for a call back. Besides, I could always call Kalem from Jerusalem if I had to.

Toby had her assistant, Philippa, make all the arrangements. First class on El Al for a start. It was great. My body needed all the pampering it could get. The pain was lessening but it was still there to remind me I had a way to go.

I was met at the airport in Tel Aviv by a limo. An hour and a half on expressways much like the LIE and I was deposited at the American Colony, a luxury hotel favored by diplomats and celebrities. They'd booked me into a suite: sitting room, four-poster bedroom with painted ceilings, plasma TV and wireless access. I checked out the rest and found a grotto-like bar, a couple of restaurants, fitness room with ultramodern equipment, and a heated pool with shimmering blue-green water. I had a late breakfast outdoors in a flower-filled patio with the sun shining warm rays down on me like a blessing. Rosalind would have loved this place.

I went back to my room to wait for the call from Herb Warshavsky. I'd e-mailed him my arrival time and told him where I was staying. He'd e-mailed back to say he'd get in touch with me.

I switched on the TV and ran through the channels to see what was on. There were talking heads in Hebrew, game shows in Hebrew, soap operas in Hebrew, French, Chinese, and a language I didn't know, a BBC sports show discussing cricket and rugby. My eyes were closing as I found CNN international weather.

I woke up in about an hour, had a shower, got dressed, and went out to the patio. There were only a few others out there, business types wearing suits. I ordered coffee. When the waiter brought the coffee he said there was a phone call for me inside.

It was Herb Warshavsky. "Sorry not to have called sooner, but I've been busy all day."

The New York accent was happily familiar, but I could hear stress in his voice. "No problem, Herb. I'm glad to finally hear from you. When can we get together?"

He offered to meet for dinner, gave me the time, the name of a restaurant, and advised me to take a taxi.

"I'll be there," I said. "In the meantime, I have a question. I hope it doesn't sound silly but I'd rather be silly than stupid. I thought I'd take a walk around the old city this afternoon. Is it safe?"

He didn't laugh. "Yes. There are soldiers everywhere. But even without them, there's no need to worry."

"If I go into the Moslem quarter, that's okay, too?"

"Absolutely."

"Okay, then. That's what I'll do. I'll see you tonight."

I'd decided that since I was there I ought to check out the famous old city of Jerusalem. And while I was at it, try to find some stores that sold ancient objects. I'd done some Internet research and knew there were places in old Jerusalem where these things had been sold. Whether in stores or by individuals, wasn't clear. Would it be possible to locate an ossuary? I didn't think so. But why not look around anyway? I finished my coffee, went back to the main desk and told the girl there what I had in mind. She gave me a map, drew a line on it for me. "Twenty minutes' walk," she said, smiling.

"Are there any antique stores in the area?"

"What are you looking for?"

"I'm interested in ancient objects."

"Just a minute." She reached under the counter and brought up a small book. "There's a place in the King David Hotel that advertises ancient art, and another called Sassoon. But they are far from here."

"Nothing in the old city?"

She thought for a moment. "If there is, I don't know about it. I'm not much interested in those things myself."

Of course not. Young, beautiful, what interested her was the present, not the past.

Map in hand, it took me only a little more than fifteen minutes to get to the Damascus Gate, one of eight gates to the old city. The walk took me past stone buildings, some residential, some commercial, and roads full of traffic. When I went through the Damascus Gate I found myself on a narrow street paved with rough stones and immediately felt as if I were in another world. I was surrounded by people who seemed to be moving in all directions. Most of the men were bareheaded but they were uniformly small with swarthy skin. Many of the women wore long dresses or robes which covered every part of them down to their feet, leaving only the eyes showing or sometimes also the nose and mouth. The younger women wore jeans and blouses, their arms and faces exposed, but had their heads covered with a kerchief. There were tourists, too, looking like tourists everywhere, with digital cameras, sunglasses, and sunburned noses.

Shops lined the street on both sides. A pair of Israeli soldiers in olive drab stood together with machine guns cradled in their arms, observing the crowd. Nobody seemed to pay any attention to them. Two teenaged boys were in front of me. They wore jeans and sleeveless T-shirts. The soldiers stopped them. The boys pulled papers from their pockets and showed them. They were waved on.

I went over and asked the soldiers if they knew of any antique shops in the area.

One said in excellent English, "You might try Hatzariah Haadom."

"What's that?"

"The name of a street. It's not far, over there." He pointed.

I thanked him and headed in that direction. It was identical to the street I'd come in on. Narrow, crowded with people and shops. The stores all looked the same on the outside, narrow fronts open wide, counters and tables set out on the street overflowing with all kinds of tchochkes: silver, gold, and olive wood crosses, a set of painted candles portraying Jerusalem, Bethlehem, and Nazareth, an olivewood box containing a cross and bottles of holy oil, water from the Jordan and earth from the hills of Bethlehem, a stone with a hand-painted inscription from the New Testament. There were stores selling shoes, sneakers, cheap-looking luggage, Jerusalem key rings, pens, sunglasses, postcards.

Many of the merchants, all men, were outside observing the traffic. Some of them called out to me in English as I passed by. "Hello, sir. Would you like to look at my shop? Come inside. I have coffee for you. Tea. Come in. It will only take a minute."

I paused in front of a store that had some good-looking jewelry on display. I thought about buying presents for Toby and Sienna. I wasn't there ten seconds before I felt a hand on my arm. A clean-shaven man with a big smile on his face. "Come inside, sir. I have much more to see inside." He tugged at my arm. I didn't like him doing that, then I thought, what the hell, when in Jerusalem, so I went with him.

In the store was a large display of necklaces. I fingered one of them. "How much is this?"

"How much do you want to spend?"

"Never mind how much I want to spend. Just tell me how much you're asking for it."

"Four hundred shekels. Not even a hundred dollars."

"I don't want to spend that much."

"How much do you want to spend?"

He thought he was smarter than me. "I don't know. Show me something cheaper."

"Please to sit down," he said. "I will bring you some coffee."

"No thanks. I don't want any coffee." I picked out another necklace. "How much is this one?"

"Ah, that one is five hundred shekels. It is handmade by Bedouins. But I like you. I will give you both for eight hundred."

"I'll give you four hundred."

"Please sir. Please. I have to make a living. I cannot give them away. Let me bring you some coffee."

"Three hundred."

He laughed, displaying large white teeth. "Please sir, do me the honor to sit down. I will show you others. I cannot sell these at such a price." He took another one off the display. "This is worth four hundred shekels. I will throw it in for nothing. You give me eight hundred shekels for all three."

I was having fun. This guy was good. "I don't want three. I'll take the first two for four hundred."

He shook his head. "Ah, sir. You are very persistent. But I need the business. I will let you have them for five hundred."

"Four hundred fifty," I said.

He shook his head sadly as if I'd just caused him pain. He put the two necklaces in a bag and I counted out the shekels.

When I left his store and was back on the street I had the annoying feeling that in spite of my so-called smarts I'd been taken, and that the merchant was probably smirking at how he'd outsmarted another dumb American.

The ground under me was a combination of bumpy cobble-stones with smooth stretches every once in a while. Occasionally, a couple of steps would appear and have to be negotiated before the flat surface resumed. Hatzariah Haadom was no more than ten feet across and made narrower by the merchandise displayed in front, as well as by the hordes of men, women, and children walking behind me, towards me and around me, all of them seemingly in a huge hurry. Dust rose up from the dry street.

Every shop looked the same, the only difference being the merchandise displayed. So far I hadn't seen anything that looked like an antique shop. Two young men passed wearing the Hassidic uniform of black suit, black shoes, white shirt and no tie, black fedoras, curls hanging below their ears. I thought I was back in Brooklyn. I guessed they were headed for the Wailing Wall. I wanted to go there, too, but that would have to wait. A few minutes later, I saw what definitely looked like an antique shop. Unlike the other places that overflowed with merchandise, this one had a restrained look. There were no tables set out in front, no merchandise to be ogled and touched. The only display was just a few objects in the window. A hammered copper necklace with turquoise stones, some clay pots with decorative designs. Bowls of metal and ceramic. A piece of stone with a drawing of a rabbit on it. All of them looked ancient indeed. But no ossuary. The one similarity to the other stores was that the door was open.

Incense was burning, filling the air and clogging my nostrils. I didn't see anyone at first, then a deep voice said, "Welcome, welcome."

A slender man came toward me wearing a western-style suit, his shirt open at the neck. He held an enormously long cigarette holder, smoke escaping from a brown cigarette at the end of it.

"Come in." His velvet-toned voice flowed over me. The accent was English and very polished. He had a small black moustache, the rest of his skin was as smooth as his voice. "Make yourself at home. May I offer you some Turkish coffee?"

"No thanks," I said. "I just had breakfast."

"Ah, you Americans. What does coffee have to do with eating? Coffee is not food. It is elixir, to be savored."

"Maybe later," I said.

"That will be fine," he said. "Are you looking for anything in particular?"

"Ah," I said. I hadn't thought it through, as usual, but if anything illicit was going on here, it seemed prudent not to mention the ossuary, at least not right away. "I'm not exactly sure."

He put the holder in his mouth, took a long drag and exhaled the smoke through his nose. "You have nothing definite in mind, but you are looking for something of an antique nature, is that it?"

Was he being sarcastic? I'm in an antique store. What else am I looking for? "Something like that."

"Have you been in Jerusalem a long time?"

"Not very long."

"I am delighted you have come to my shop. Were you perhaps told about me? I would be so pleased to know if one of my customers recommended my shop to you."

"No. I was just strolling through the old city and noticed your interesting window."

"Just strolling. I see," he said, looking at me as if he were studying me. "Well, dear sir, why don't you stroll around and see if anything appeals to you? Then we can proceed further."

"Sure." I walked slowly through the shop pretending to study the various items on display. There was pottery, jewelry, even some furniture. It appeared that not all of what he sold was ancient, and possibly not even antique. I looked in vain for something that might be considered an ossuary but didn't see anything that came close.

The owner hadn't followed me. Instead, he'd seated himself on a chair and had just finished inserting another cigarette into his holder when I returned.

"Did you see anything that might interest you?"

"Not really." I considered whether to ask, then thought, what the hell, why not? "Do you have anything like a bone box?" I used that term hoping he'd think I was an ignorant tourist.

He behaved as if he hadn't heard me. He put the holder into his mouth and lit another cigarette with a gold lighter. After dragging in a lungful he exhaled once again, the smoke wafting from his nostrils. He smiled at me. "You are referring perhaps to an ossuary?"

"That's right."

"Do you know anything about ossuaries?"

"Not much. I saw a program on TV and it caught my interest."

He got to his feet. "Let me get you a coffee and then I will tell you something about ossuaries."

He gestured for me to sit, went away, and returned in a few minutes holding two china cups and saucers, the cigarette holder clamped between his teeth. He handed me a cup, pulled over another chair and sat next to me. After taking a sip, then another drag on his cigarette, he said, "An ossuary is a very ancient object. One would not expect to find one for sale in a shop. Are you aware of that?"

My research had taught me a lot about burial boxes and other ancient stuff. I'd also learned there were a few ongoing investigations into the authenticity of several things that were already in museums, the biggest, a question about a box supposedly containing the bones of James, a brother of Jesus. "I had no idea," I said.

"They are usually sold privately to collectors and to museums and they are quite expensive."

"What do you mean by expensive?" I sipped the coffee. It was nothing like the coffee at the hotel. This was very sweet and thick as pea soup.

"Perhaps in the hundreds of thousands, perhaps a million or more. American dollars."

"That much, huh? As I said, I had no idea." I drank more coffee. It was good. I drained the cup.

"Would you care for another?"

"No thanks, but it was excellent. I enjoyed it."

"I am glad," he said.

"So what else can you tell me about ossuaries? I'm really interested." He might tell me something I didn't already know.

"In Palestine, during the period of time from about one hundred years before and one hundred years after Jesus, or Yeshua, as the Hebrews referred to him, there was a shortage of burial space. There were no formal cemeteries as such. Therefore, when a person died he was buried for a period of about a year, or until the body disintegrated and only bones remained. The bones were taken and placed in a box, usually of limestone. These were the ossuaries, also known as bone or burial boxes. Some were plain, some quite elaborate, even with claw feet and beautiful engravings. Quite a few have been discovered over the years, by archeologists and by farmers, and by nomads who stumbled over them in old caves in the desert. All kinds of specimens have been found in this manner. Each and every one is an exceptional find."

"Very interesting," I said, suddenly aware that I was feeling sleepy. I guessed that jet lag was catching up to me again.

"Some of the discovered objects were quite remarkable. Some time ago an ivory pomegranate was discovered. It was thought to have come from Solomon's Temple. An inscription on it read in part, 'Belonging to the Temple of Yahweh, holy to the priests.' The Israel Museum paid five hundred and fifty thousand dollars for it.

"That same year, the existence of an ossuary purported to contain the bones of James, the brother of Jesus, turned up. It provided the earliest tangible evidence of the existence of Jesus. Have you heard of any of these things?"

"Not really."

"There was quite a lot of publicity. The Royal Museum of Toronto put the ossuary on exhibition. While there, however, its authenticity was challenged by the IAA, the Israel Antiquities Authority, as was the pomegranate. Are you quite sure you never heard of it?"

"Never heard," I said. I could feel my eyelids getting heavy. That time difference was getting to me. "You know what? I'm feeling really tired. I think maybe I'd better go back to the hotel." I got to my feet but my knees were wobbly and I became dizzy. I sat down again.

"Are you all right?" the shop owner said, putting his hand on my arm.

"I guess I might have done too much. I only got in a few hours ago."

"No doubt," he said. "It's quite common."

His voice sounded different. It seemed as if he were speaking to me from the end of a tunnel. I could hardly hear him.

"Why don't you just rest until you feel strong enough to return to your hotel? Where are you staying, Mr. . . . what did you say your name was?"

"Wanderman," I said. I was now feeling light-headed and I could feel my tongue getting thick in my mouth. "I'm at the American Colony. I'm really feeling funny, not good, in fact . . ." My mouth suddenly froze in place, my lips wouldn't move. Even though I was sitting down I felt as if I were standing. Then it hit me. The fucking coffee!

I tried as hard as I could to keep my head from spinning. At the same time I was struggling to keep my eyes open.

That was the last thing I remembered.

CHAPTER 38

My throat was too dry to swallow. My mouth felt as if it were filled with Brillo. I needed water. I tried to move and discovered I couldn't. I was in a chair. There were ropes around my chest, arms, legs.

"Hey!" I tried to yell but it came out more like a squawk. I managed to get some saliva into my mouth and tried again. This time the sound was better but nobody answered.

It looked like I was in a storeroom. There were brooms and shovels and pails along with cleaning supplies. There were wooden crates, some of them opened and empty. Lined up against one wall were several rolled-up rugs.

I couldn't believe this had happened. What did I get myself into? Why would the guy with the cigarette holder do this? I didn't have a clue. I was angry, not scared. My father had brought me up not to be afraid of anything, not people, animals, or anything else. I was bullied once in fourth grade and told my Dad about it. *Kick him in the balls,* he said. It worked. Females made me nervous, but other than that I'd gone through life without fear.

I heard something. Voices, low at first, then getting louder as they came closer. The door opened and the shop owner came in, cigarette holder in hand. He was accompanied by two men who looked like toads: small, beady eyes, even lumpy green skin.

"You are finally awake." He flashed my wallet. "It says here that your name is Jake Wanderman. I am so pleased to meet you. Allow me to introduce myself. I am Ahmid Ben Bey, purveyor of antiquities."

"What did . . . you do to me?" My mouth and tongue weren't quite coordinated "Why . . . am I tied up?"

"Allow me to explain. It is all your doing. I am most disappointed in you. You are not the innocent abroad. You are, in fact, a liar."

I blinked a few times trying to clear my head. "What makes you say that?"

"You have a card identifying you as a private detective."

Great, I thought. I'd never been able to get myself to throw that card away. He'll never believe me if I tell him it's not real. "That doesn't mean anything. I'm still a tourist." I was beginning to feel better. "I advise you to untie me and let me out of here."

"Perhaps later. First a few questions."

"Could I have something to drink? I'm dying of thirst."

He spoke in what I imagined was Arabic to one of the toads who left the room and came back with a cup of water which he tossed in my face. While I licked the water off my lips, Ahmid Ben Bey barked at him. "I apologize for that. We are not so uncivilized as to deny a man a drink when he is thirsty." He made the guy get more water and hold the cup to my lips. "I know you are not a simple tourist. I knew it when you came into my shop. Now tell me, who sent you here to spy on us?"

"Nobody." *How did he know?*

"Who is Toby Welch?"

"What? What do you know about her?"

"She paid for your stay at your hotel, didn't she? I had someone look at your computer. You seem to know quite a bit about ossuaries, after all." He took a drag on his cigarette and as usual blew the smoke out through his nose. "I am not playing games, Mr. Wanderman. I have the ability to cause you much hurt if you persist in lying to me."

"I'm not lying. I was under a lot of stress back home. My wife died not long ago. Toby Welch is a friend of mine. She's rich. She offered to pay for a vacation. I always wanted to see Jerusalem, so I came here."

"And what about your interest in ossuaries?"

"It's a hobby of mine. I'm an antique buff. Nothing else. I swear that's the truth. Now why don't you let me go?"

Ahmid Ben Bey abruptly left the room. The toads remained. In a few minutes he returned with a grim expression on his face. "I spoke with my associates," he said to me. "I'm afraid the response was not good for you."

He said something to the two men. They went to a corner of the room, came back with one of the rugs I'd seen before and proceeded to unroll it on the floor. "We are going to move you."

"Where are you taking me?" Ben Bey's manner had changed. I suddenly had a bad feeling. A really bad feeling. These guys weren't fooling around. I had to do something. All I could do was plead. "Listen to me, will you? Please! I'll tell you the truth. Okay, I'm not a tourist. I'm in Jerusalem trying to find out about an ossuary. A particular ossuary that someone back home bought and then had stolen. That's all I was doing. I'm not spying on anybody. I swear I'm telling you the truth."

Ahmid Ben Bey fitted another cigarette into the holder. "Perhaps," he said. "I'm tempted to believe you, but at this point it no longer matters."

CHAPTER 39

They slapped a large piece of tape across my mouth, untied me and forced me down on the rug. I was rolled over and over until I was wrapped inside. I tried keeping my elbows out as they turned me so I wouldn't be squeezed. It helped. I was able to move a little and could breathe. The fibers of the rug were scratchy and the wool was full of odd odors. I could smell cigarette smoke, spices, a hint of urine. Some light came in from each end so I wasn't entirely in the dark.

I felt them lift and carry me for a few minutes before I was dropped, not too gently. I could tell I was on an uneven surface because my legs fell below the rest of my body. The next thing I knew I was jiggling, bouncing up and down. They were moving me on some kind of a dolly and every time it went over a bump I could feel the vibration.

I thought about what he'd told me. They could know what hotel I was at because I had the map the hotel had given me with "American Colony" stamped on it. But the only way they could know who'd paid for my stay at the hotel was for someone who worked there to tell them. It wasn't on my computer. The ossuary information was, but nobody knew I was going to this antique shop. The only one I'd spoken to was the pretty girl at the desk. I'd told her I was interested in ancient art. I hadn't said anything about ossuaries. And she said she didn't know of any antique stores.

Unless she was lying. Duh! If these guys were involved with

forgeries they had to be on high alert. Maybe she was a spotter for them. The American Colony was a high-profile hotel, a good place to have one. She did ask me what I was looking for. She could have called them just to let them know about me. And of course, after I left she could have easily searched my room and my computer, too.

When they first put me in the rug and were transporting me I didn't hear a sound. Later, I heard murmurings that I guessed were Ahmid Ben Bey and his henchmen talking to each other. Now I could hear actual voices. I could make out words, occasionally an English one. I realized they were rolling me along on a public street, maybe the same street I'd entered the old city on.

I could still feel the effects of the drug. That, the tape across my mouth and being crushed inside the rug made it difficult to breathe. I didn't want to speculate on what they were arranging. I tried to keep my self-control. I thought of what I could do. I had a little movement inside the rug. If I were able to move my body enough I might be able to make the rug fall off the dolly. I didn't know if it would help but I had to try.

The bouncing went on. I didn't have much time. I had to do something while I still heard voices, which would mean people around. I took a deep breath, tensed myself and threw my weight to one side. Nothing happened. I couldn't make the rug move at all. I tried again. Same result.

The bouncing continued for a while longer, then it stopped. There were no longer any people sounds. It was quiet. I thought they must have gotten me out of the old city through one of the gates and were now going to put me in a car or a van. Then what?

Suddenly I heard shouts. I couldn't make out what they were about but the shouting was loud and there was a lot of it. I was suddenly jolted out of whatever I was being transported on and felt myself drop and hit something hard.

The shouting stopped but the voices continued. They were much clearer. They were speaking Hebrew. Then I was being rolled over and over until the rug opened and I was exposed to the air. Fresh air that I could breathe. I was on my back, surprised to be looking up at a night sky full of stars. I realized I must have been in that shop a long time.

People were standing over me in a circle. Two men and a woman. Even in that poor light I could see she was good-looking. She leaned over and jerked the tape from my mouth.

Aieee! I kept the yell inside.

"Are you all right?" she asked.

"Thanks, I'm okay." I wasn't going to admit how much it hurt.

I tried to get to my feet. My legs were tingling and unsteady. The woman reached down and helped me. When I was standing I saw that they were all in civilian clothes with no ID showing. They stared at me and said nothing. The two henchmen were handcuffed together with another man guarding them. "Thanks for getting me out of this. Where's the guy who did this to me?"

"You mean Ahmid Ben Bey? He remained in the shop," she said. "He's too smart to get involved in something like this."

I heard an American voice. "Excuse me." Someone pushed past the circle. He was tall, beefy, and fair-skinned in contrast to the Israelis. "Jake Wanderman. I'm Herb Warshavsky."

Relieved, I held out my hand. "We meet at last. What a break you guys were around. I was getting worried."

He shook my hand but not happily. "You didn't do either of us any good by going to that antique store."

"What do you mean?"

"You blew an operation that's been on for almost a year."

"I did?" I felt like he'd punched me in the stomach. "Hey,

I'm sorry. I thought I'd scout around. I didn't see any harm in that."

"You didn't. But there was."

"I'll say it again. I'm sorry. In the meantime, are they going to arrest the guy who owns the shop, this Ahmid Ben Bey?"

"On what grounds?" the woman who'd ripped the tape off me said. She seemed to be the one in charge.

"He drugged me. He kidnapped me."

"It would be a waste of time. How are you going to prove it? Besides, he's only a bit player. He is not important."

"But he serves up a mean cup of coffee."

"We will go back to headquarters now to debrief you. Those two will not tell us anything." She indicated the handcuffed men.

"Do you mind if I come along?" Warshavsky asked.

"If you wish, as long as you know you are not privileged to do anything but observe. You understand?"

Warshavsky shrugged. "I'm used to that."

CHAPTER 40

The Israelis took the prisoners and I went with Warshavsky in his little Toyota. Not surprising that his car was tiny. Gas was expensive even though we were surrounded by most of the world's oil reserves. I remembered what Prime Minister Golda Meir once said: It was too bad that Moses dragged the Jews through the desert to the one place in the Middle East where there was no oil.

Herb was a big guy, but with a bit of maneuvering, managed to squeeze himself in. We were both silent while he drove. I rolled the window down to breathe in the fresh air. After a few minutes he said, "Look. I'm not trying to beat up on you. There was no way you could have known about their operation. But do me a favor and try not to wander by yourself anymore. At least, not without telling me where you're going. Okay?"

"Sure. I'm not anxious to get on the wrong side of anybody. But I'm curious to know how you found me."

"When you didn't show up for dinner I called the hotel. They thought you'd gone to the old city. So I got in touch with the local cops. That's when they told me the shop was under observation and that a Westerner had been spotted going in but had never come out. They didn't have a clue who you were. You could've been one of the bad guys. But they called in a description. Even though we'd never met I told them it was probably you."

"Lucky for me they were there. I don't know what they

planned to do with me but I don't think it would've been good."

"How'd you get there in the first place? I thought you were just going to look at the old city."

"I was. But I'd learned that archeological stuff was available so I thought I'd look for a shop that might have some."

"Did you say anything that might've made them suspicious of you?"

"Nothing. All I said was that I was interested in ossuaries."

"That's all? You're sure?"

"Absolutely. I tried to act like a dumb tourist. It didn't work because this guy already knew about me. Why else would he give me spiked coffee? He took my wallet after he drugged me. He also knew a lot more about me than he could've learned from just my ID. He knew what hotel I was at and he knew that Toby Welch paid for my room."

"Who's that?"

"She's the woman I'm trying to help. Her father was murdered. He was also the one who sold an ossuary that could've been a fake to a very powerful industrialist."

"Hey! Slow down. You're going too fast for me. You never said anything about a murder before."

"I didn't want to say too much in an e-mail. I was planning to tell you everything when we met."

"I think you better tell me as much as you can before we get to the police station. And be quick about it. It's only a couple of blocks away from here."

I filled him in as well as I could in the few minutes we had. I managed to let him know about Cormac Blather, Chase McCleod and his forgeries, Toby and my investigation, Bryson Mergenthaler and the ossuary, and the threat made to me by the Russians.

"So you see why I think it's all connected?" I said. "When

you told me the Russian Mafia is big in Israel, it all came together."

"You might be right. I'll tell you more about the Russian Mafia later. Right now, we're here. Let's go inside."

There was no place to park. Herb put the car half on the street, half on the sidewalk and put a police ID in the window. I looked around and saw a huge church directly across from us.

"That's the Russian Orthodox church," he said. "This whole area was known as the Russian compound. All the buildings in the square were owned by the Russian embassy. They used to house their staff here. The police station is where one of their buildings used to be."

As we headed toward the station he said, "Let me give you some advice. Answer all their questions as directly as you can. But you don't have to tell them everything you know. Just tell them what they ask for."

"How come? I'm the victim here. Am I under suspicion?"

"Trust me," he said. "Just do what I say."

We entered into a sort of anteroom: a counter with a cop in civilian clothes behind it. He asked for ID. I didn't have any because my wallet was back in the antique shop. I hoped the cops could get it back for me. He made me empty my pockets into a basket and walked me through a metal detector. He did the same with Warshavsky. No special treatment for him. I had a feeling he wasn't particularly well-liked by the local fuzz.

"They're waiting for you upstairs in the back," the cop said.

We went from the anteroom into a courtyard that seemed to be a parking lot for police vehicles to a building about fifty yards away. Inside was a stairway directly ahead and an office to the left. Nobody paid any attention to us. On the second floor we found a large circular area. One wall was taken up by a gallery of photographs of police brass posing with famous dignitaries. Some generals in fancy uniforms, President Clinton, even

John Paul II. Offices filled the rest of the circle.

"Do you know where they are?" I asked.

"Don't have a clue," he said. "But it's not unusual. They operate differently over here."

We poked our heads into every office until we finally spotted the beautiful policewoman and one of the men who'd been on the street with her. They were sitting behind a dinged-up metal desk. The top had a tape recorder on it and a couple of ashtrays choked with butts. The air was appropriately full of smoke. Two chairs for us.

"At last," she said. "We've been waiting for you."

Nice friendly greeting. "Well, here we are," I said cheerily.

Glumness was the response.

When we were seated the woman said, "I am Sergeant Liat Olshef. I am in charge of this investigation. This is officer Asher Goren. I will ask you some questions. Please answer as fully as you can. Leave nothing out."

"Before we start," I said. "This guy who owns the shop has my wallet and some jewelry I bought."

"We will retrieve them for you." She spoke in Hebrew to the other cop who got up and left the room. She pushed the button on the tape recorder. "Let us commence."

She took me back to the beginning. Who was I? Meaning she wanted my background. When did I come to Israel? Why? I gave her minimal responses following Herb's directions. Then she had questions about the antique store: how did I come to go there, did anyone tell me about it, what happened in the store, what did Ahmid Ben Bey do, what did I do, what did he say, what did I say? Question after question until I was getting dizzy.

After an hour had gone by she leaned back in her chair and lit a cigarette. "Would you like a cold drink?"

"No thanks. What I'd like is to get out of here and go back to my hotel. I'm beat."

Warshavsky added, "He's been through a lot. And this is his first day in Jerusalem."

"We have almost concluded," Superwoman said, showing no sign of being tired or under strain.

I was about to say, *what else could you possibly ask?* but remembered Warshavsky's advice. Instead, I said, "Lucky for me you were keeping watch over there. What's your operation about, anyway?"

She smiled for the first time, as if showing me she could read my clumsy attempt to pick her brain. "You are indeed lucky. I suspect they were going to kill you."

"Kill me? Why?"

"That's what I'm trying to find out. Why did your presence cause this extreme reaction. Not that the Mafia is hesitant to kill. They do it all the time. But why you?"

I shrugged. "Beats me." I felt better because I'd gotten something important out of her. Confirmation that the Russian Mafia was in this big time.

Asher Goren, the cop who'd left, now came back into the room holding my wallet and the bag with necklaces. He put them down on the desk and spoke to Liat in Hebrew.

She translated: "Ahmid Ben Bey had them ready. He said he was prepared to return them to your hotel. And he sends his apologies."

"That's really sweet," I said. "The next time I see him I'll have to express my gratitude."

"I suggest that will not happen. I advise you not to go there again."

Her skin was the color of toffee, her eyes dark, slanted, almost black, above high cheekbones. Her hair was also black, cut short, with bangs to her eyebrows. Without makeup she was drop-dead gorgeous and had to know it, but so far had not shown any sign that she knew or cared.

"Okay," I said. "I hear you."

CHAPTER 41

We left the station through a gate with a full length turnstile just like the ones in the old New York subway system. Nobody was going to get of there in a hurry. On the way back to my hotel I asked Herb if he knew why the police had been staking out that shop.

"I don't know. I wouldn't even ask this woman who's in charge because she'd brush me off. The local cops want me to stay off their turf. But I'll find out. I know a few people. Get yourself some sleep and I'll see you in the morning."

After he left I stretched out on the bed with my clothes on. I had a debate with myself about whether I should climb into the Jacuzzi or stay where I was. I was just about convinced that I had barely enough energy to remove my shoes when I thought I heard a knock at the door. The entrance to the suite was in the other room so I wasn't sure. But then I heard it again. I dragged myself off the bed and went to the door. I was still spooked so I didn't open it. "Who's there?"

"Sergeant Olshef."

I heard the voice clearly enough to know I wasn't dreaming. *What now?* I opened the door.

The beautiful Israeli cop with the serious attitude had disappeared. She now had a friendly smile. "Hello," she all but purred.

I couldn't help being curious. "What can I do for you?"

"May I come in?"

I stepped back and she went past me. "May I sit down?" she asked.

"Of course." We were in the sitting room. "Can I get you something from the bar?"

"No thanks. I know you're tired so I won't keep you long. I just wanted to ask you a few follow-up questions." She took a pad and pen out of her purse.

I sat across from her and noticed she'd changed from a tailored shirt and pants to a soft blouse and skirt. She'd also done something with her eyes to make them look more dramatic, added lipstick, and was now more beautiful than I'd thought possible. I couldn't help wondering if this was for me, or just her usual routine after leaving the office?

"Where do you live in the United States?"

"I don't know what that has to do with the man in the moon, but I'll tell you anyway. I live in a small town called Sag Harbor. It's in New York on the eastern end of Long Island."

"Man in the moon? I don't think I've ever heard that before. An idiomatic expression?"

"Right."

"And what do you do in Sag Harbor?"

"Didn't you already ask me this?"

"Please be good enough just to answer."

"I don't do much. I'm retired. I used to be a teacher."

"What did you teach?"

"English. You already know this. To high school students."

"Are you married?"

"I was. My wife died."

"How long ago was that?"

"Seven months." And four days, but I didn't tell her that.

"I'm sorry."

"Look. I don't want to sound disrespectful, but would you tell me what you really want?"

She searched in her purse and took out a pack of Marlboros. "Do you mind if I smoke?"

"Yes." I was irritated and didn't care if she knew it.

"I'm sorry if I've caused you distress. You are entirely correct. I've done a bad job of it."

I waited.

She put the Marlboros back. "You want to know why I came here? I'll tell you. I know you are not just a tourist. You did not stumble into that antique shop. And furthermore, you have connections to Warshavsky, a policeman from New York. So I ask myself, why has this man come to Israel, to Jerusalem? What is he looking for? What does he want? What is his relationship with Warshavsky?"

"You're very sure of yourself. But on what evidence? That I know Warshavsky? He's an old friend of my father's. My father asked me to look him up. As for the shop, what's unusual about a tourist going into an antique shop?"

"When that tourist is drugged, then it becomes unusual."

"Touché."

"Please don't embarrass yourself by continuing to insist on your *innocents abroad* pose. When Detective Goren picked up your wallet he examined its contents. You have a Private Investigator license."

She had me, of course, even without the phony license. "All right then, I came here for a reason. But it has nothing to do with you."

She looked down at her purse. It was obvious she was dying for a smoke. "You may derive some benefit by talking to me. Perhaps I can be of help to you. Perhaps we can help each other."

"That's a lot of perhapses."

She smiled. My God, those perfect white teeth and her dusky skin. I suddenly thought of Sienna Nolan. Sienna was a different breed in looks, if not so much in personality. Liat was an exotic beauty. Sienna was good-looking, not striking but wholesome. Where they were alike was in their attitudes and professionalism. "One more perhaps," she said. "Perhaps I could have something to drink?"

"Sure." I was glad not to have to decide right away what I should say to her. "What'll it be?"

"Coke?"

I opened the mini-bar. "Sure you don't want anything stronger?"

"Quite sure."

"Well, I need something. I think I'll try a bit of this Remy Martin."

I handed her the can of Coke and a glass. The polite thing to do would have been to open it for her but I was too worn out to be gracious. I opened the bottle of brandy and poured it into a snifter. "Cheers."

"L'chaim."

I let the brandy run down my throat, leaned back and closed my eyes so that I could enjoy its effects.

"You must be very tired," she said.

"Dog tired. Bone tired. Every kind of tired you can think of. I'm so tired I don't even feel the pain anymore. *To die; to sleep, to end the thousand natural shocks that flesh is heir to.* That's not an accurate quote but it's good enough."

"Hamlet," she said. "I love Shakespeare. But why are you experiencing pain? Did they hurt you back there?" She leaned forward intently. "If they did I'll make them pay."

"No, no. Thanks for the offer, but they didn't hurt me. It's pain from another source. Don't worry about it." I wasn't ready to spill. But I was impressed that she knew Shakespeare.

She wrote something, tore out the page and handed it to me. "A phone number where you can reach me. Think about what I said. One hand washes the other, no?"

She was gone. Her scent remained, a mixture of perfume and cigarettes. I swallowed the last of the brandy, turned off the lights, and went to sleep.

CHAPTER 42

Landis had been painstaking in his efforts to leave no clues behind and was sure he'd been successful. He assumed he was not under suspicion by anyone, so the call from this man Wanderman had upset him. There'd been no sign of the police ever since the first interview with Mr. Mergenthaler. A private investigator was something else again. And why was he asking about the stolen ossuary? Was he really concerned about it or was he just reaching for any connection he could find to Blather?

After the phone call Landis decided it would not be a bad idea to keep track of this man Wanderman and see what he was up to. Of course he would be careful. He would call Toby Welch by making use of the questions he'd been given for Mr. Mergenthaler. He would tell her that he had every intention of helping her but had misplaced the questions that Mr. Wanderman had given him and would she be able to supply them again. In that way Landis would not have to inform Mergenthaler about the inquiry. He did not want to mention the word forgery to Mergenthaler even though he was quite sure Mergenthaler might have had his own ideas about the subject. Perhaps during the course of the conversation he might learn something.

In fact he remembered the questions well. Did Mr. Mergenthaler buy anything from Cormac Blather besides the ossuary? Did he ever have a suspicion that anything he bought could have been a forgery? If yes, did he ever discuss this with Mr. Blather?

If Landis ever had to answer, he would, of course, deny any possibility of forgery. The denial ought to quiet that part of the inquiry. Unless this Wanderman person didn't believe the answer. Unfortunately, that was entirely possible. Why else was he asking in the first place? No doubt the break-in and burglary played a role in that thinking. He'd thought of that, too, but had decided it was in his own interest to just let the incident go. Insurance would pay for the loss and the less said about the whole affair the better.

When he reached Toby Welch on the phone she was almost apologetic. "I do so much appreciate your calling me back," she said. "But I'm so sorry. I don't recall the questions. I don't know what to say."

"Perhaps you could ask Mr. Wanderman to repeat them to you. That shouldn't be too difficult."

"That's a good idea. He's away. In Jerusalem, as a matter of fact, but I should be able to reach him."

"Excellent. He told me he was working for you in the matter of your father's demise. I suppose that's what he's doing there?"

There was a moment of hesitation before she answered. "Actually, he's there on a vacation. He said he needed to get away."

"I see," Landis said. "I myself would have preferred a less stressful locale for a vacation, but to each his own. I hope that he is at least in a lovely hotel. Tel Aviv has some good ones. In Jerusalem, the only one for me is the American Colony."

"Oh yes, he's in a nice place," she said. "I'll get back to you with those questions."

"And I will supply the answers as quickly as possible."

It couldn't have been easier, although it was obvious that she'd held back after telling Landis where Wanderman had gone.

The moment he was off the phone he explored his Rolodex for contacts in Israel. He had traveled the world with Bryson

Mergenthaler, and because of his association with this powerful man had been able to meet key people everywhere. Prominent individuals in all parts of the world had befriended him. He had also gotten close to many like himself: secretaries, assistants to powerful people. But also like him, they had access to information in all spheres of business and social life that made them quite influential in their own way.

He found a few names. There was a diplomat's secretary based in Tel Aviv. There was a professor at Hebrew University who'd become sort of a superstar. He was young and handsome and had made some major academic breakthrough. They'd met at an affair to raise money for Hadassah Hospital. There was also an assistant to the CEO of a technology company.

He thought the diplomat's secretary would be the best bet to locate Jake Wanderman. He would be discreet. It was his business, after all. When Wanderman was located, Landis would have to hire someone to find out what he was doing there. That part would not be easy but perhaps the secretary could help out there as well. In any event he had no doubt it could be done.

What he learned about Mr. Jake Wanderman would help determine his next move. Landis had the profound feeling that Wanderman would not find it to be a pleasant one.

Later that night he entered Mario's room. He had Mario lie on his stomach and tied his hands and feet to the bedposts. He opened the blade of his Beretta knife and made fine cuts along Mario's back and buttocks, then licked the blood that oozed from the incisions.

Mario groaned with pleasure.

CHAPTER 43

A good night's sleep had taken away the aftereffects of the drug and all the rest of what had happened the day before. The pain from the beating back home was still with me, mostly in the rib and lower back area. The color purple had infiltrated the black and blues, but the colors were fading and the pain was lessening. I went directly to the front desk. I wanted to talk to the girl I had suspicions about. She wasn't there.

"You mean Hasiba?" another clerk said. "She won't be in today. She called in sick."

Coincidence? I'd have to wait and see.

I had breakfast on the outdoor patio. It wasn't the same as when I'd arrived. Hard to believe it was only the day before when I'd been able to relax and enjoy the surroundings. At the moment I was nowhere. I could do further research into ossuaries but that would only get me what I already knew. I could try the IAA but doubted they'd give information to someone without credentials. I had to decide what to do about Liat Olshef, the beautiful cop. Did she really want to help me, or was she just digging for anything she could get that would help *her*? If Herb Warshavsky didn't come across with something I'd be forced to turn to Liat. Otherwise, I might as well go home.

While waiting for Warshavsky I wandered around the grounds. They had a gym with all the machinery you could ask for. I hungered for exercise but my body still wasn't ready for it. I had nothing better to do so I walked through the rest of the hotel. It was larger than I expected with a bar and lounges below the first level. I picked up a brochure about the hotel's history. It was founded in the late 19th century by a spiritual couple named Spofford. They were good people who reached out to all Jerusalem's citizens. The booklet had photographs of their family and friends and a copy of a hymn Horatio Spofford himself composed.

The waiting was making me anxious and frustrated. I felt like taking a running jump into the pool with my clothes on when I saw Herb Warshavsky come in through the front entrance. You couldn't miss the guy. He was linebacker sized, six-four, two hundred seventy-five, at least.

I was so glad to see him I almost gave him a hug. I restrained myself and took him back to the patio where I ordered two coffees and forced myself to wait for him to speak first. I had to clamp my teeth together to do it.

Herb sipped his coffee and leaned back. "Do you know what I do here in Jerusalem?"

"Not really. My dad said it had something to do with terrorism."

"It's all to do with terrorism. Suicide bombers killing civilians is nothing new in Israel. This is the front line. Whenever there's a bombing I get a call. My job is to observe and report back to New York on everything that happened. Who was the bomber? How did he or she do it? Why weren't they caught beforehand? I've seen more blood and body parts in six months here than I saw in twenty years on the job in New York." He drank more coffee. "Sorry about that. I need to let it out sometimes. My wife usually gets the brunt of it. Today you got it." He smiled. "So tell me about your dad. How is the old lover supreme?"

"My dad's great, Herb. And he thinks very highly of you. He couldn't stop telling me what a great guy you are and what a great family you have. But could we cut to the chase? I need to know if you found out anything."

"It's lucky I have friends in high places," he said. "It took a lot of phone calls and some arm twisting, but I was able to get some information."

"That's great."

"The Russian Mafia is here in a big way. They're into a lot of things. Art forgery is just one of them. There's also drugs, extortion, prostitution, credit card fraud, identity theft, you name it. The cops staking out the antique shop where you were are limited to the art forgery. They're not involved with any of the other issues."

"So what I did yesterday really fucked them up."

"You better believe it. They're mighty pissed off."

"Not completely pissed. I had a visitor last night, after you left." I told him about Liat and her offer. "What do you think?"

"I wouldn't go there. I don't believe she has enough authority to help you. Sex discrimination is alive and well in Israel. Women are at the bottom of the ladder. It's pretty amazing that she made sergeant. And I'll bet she's a university graduate. But even with a degree it's rare for a woman to get a grade. As for the male cops, most of them never went to college, and that includes the brass."

"So where do we go from here?"

"I told you I'd help if I could. I got a name. He's afraid to talk to the cops because he thinks they're corrupt. And who knows? I'm sure some of them are."

"But he's willing to talk to you?"

"My source said he wants to talk because he thinks he can trust me. Apparently he's scared shitless."

"Is he one of the forgers?"

"I don't know." He took out his cell. "I'll call him now and let him know we're on the way. You'll be my associate."

"I'm used to that."

After making the call, he said, "He thinks he's under surveillance. He wants to meet us at the Israel Museum. He goes there all the time so he figures whoever is watching him won't be suspicious." On the way, Herb told me a little more. "It seems there's the equivalent of a forgery industry here. Breaking it is complicated. The men at the bottom, like Ahmid Ben Bey, are no problem. But there are others, archeologists, dealers, wealthy collectors, people of influence. It's hard to get at them. Some of these people are very well known in Israel. Real muck-a-mucks."

"Like this guy?"

"Exactly. This man is supposed to have a major collection of ancient art."

"What's he afraid of?"

"That's what we're going to find out."

CHAPTER 44

There was a line at the booths where tickets to the museum were sold. Herb showed his credentials to the guard at the entrance enabling us to enter without them. When we were inside I asked Herb what the guy's name was and where we were going to meet.

"His name is Aren Brotman. We're going to meet him in the building that houses the Dead Sea Scrolls. Have you ever been there?"

"Never."

"It's fantastic. It's designed to make you feel like you're going into the cave where the scrolls were originally discovered. Too bad you won't have the time to appreciate it, but you should make an effort to come back when all this stuff is over and done with."

I followed him along a path of gravel and stones. Directly ahead was an enormous white dome shimmering in the sun. The top of the dome rose only about twenty feet, the rest of the structure hidden by a body of water. A winding walkway brought us to a small wooden door that appeared to be cut into a wall of concrete. There were no signs to tell anyone what was on the other side of the door.

"Through there," Herb said.

The day was bright and sunny which made the darkness inside intense. It took a few minutes of squinting before my eyes could make the adjustment.

"This way."

I followed him along a narrow corridor, both sides of which were lined with displays. The lighting in the glass cases was normal but the corridor lighting was a deep blue which helped to emphasize the feeling of being underground. We went through another doorway into a large circular room. I realized we were now under the dome.

"This is called The Shrine of the Book," Herb said.

It was like being at the bottom of a well, looking up from darkness toward light. The walls surrounding us were a continuous glass circle behind which were manuscripts, pottery, fragments of stone with Aramaic characters etched into them. Steps before us led to a brightly lit display at the top. The scrolls were up there locked behind more glass or Lucite, securing them from contamination. The sight was so stunning I almost forgot why we were there.

"There he is," Herb whispered. "He told me he'd be wearing a blue *kippa*."

We began walking toward a slight man farther along the wall. He examined us as we approached. There were other visitors to the Dome of the Rock but the room was not crowded. Nobody was near us at the moment. "Mr. Brotman? I'm Sergeant Warshavsky and this is my associate, Jake Wanderman."

"Don't say my name again," Brotman said.

He held out his hand and we both shook it. It was like shaking an empty glove. He was a small man, dressed casually in brown corduroy pants and a tan sweater. He wore glasses and appeared to be in his sixties.

"I hope you can help me," he said. "I don't know if you can. I don't know if it is at all possible. But I am desperate."

"I'll do my best," Herb said. "Suppose you tell me what your problem is."

There were now people in our vicinity. Brotman waited for

them to go by. "A man named Grigori Palkovich," he said. "He is the number-one problem. Then there is another man, Eli Semontoya. He is problem number two."

More visitors went past us. "It's hard to talk here," I said. "Isn't there someplace else we can go where we won't have to look over our shoulders all the time?"

"There is," Brotman said. "I wanted to meet you here first because it would be easy to see if anyone followed me. I am a big donor here. They will let me use one of their offices. But to be safe, you two go back to the main building where you came in. Wait for me. You will see me go into a small office. After I go in, knock once and enter."

We did as he said. Herb said, "I wouldn't bet that he wasn't followed. If they were professionals, he wouldn't have a clue. They might be waiting right here for him to come back. Look around. Try to spot anyone who doesn't look as if he belongs. You never know. Even pros forget to dress the part or don't have a chance to. We used to laugh at the FBI trying to infiltrate long-haired student groups using agents with crew cuts and black shoes."

I looked at everyone hanging around. Mostly there were women in groups, some couples, some people with *tourist* all but stamped on their foreheads, but no slouching types in black hats and trench coats.

"I don't see anybody suspicious," I said.

"Neither do I."

We saw Brotman arrive, go to a counter and speak to someone. He nodded, walked to the opposite side of the room, knocked on a door and entered. In a little while, a woman came out and walked away.

"I guess that's our signal," I said.

CHAPTER 45

The office was about the size of a walk-in closet. There was a desk with a computer on it, one chair behind the desk and one other in the room. Brotman was standing when we entered.

"Sorry, only two chairs in here," he said.

"Don't worry about it," I said. "I have no problem standing."

"Okay, Mr. Brotman," Herb said. "Tell me what's on your mind. Why did you specifically want to talk to me?"

Brotman moved the chair from behind the desk to the side of it. He sat on the edge with his hands clasped, fingers interlocked. "Yuval, the man you spoke to, told me who you were and that you were inquiring about forgeries. I know a great deal about them. I have been a collector for more than thirty years. Let me assure you right away that I myself have never been involved in any forged art. But I know many people who are and many who were but have since dropped out."

"Go on."

"I am willing to provide my information but I need something in return."

"And that is . . . ?"

"Protection. I don't trust the local officials. Corruption is rampant. My life is threatened. My daughter's life is threatened. It's a nightmare." He covered his face with his hands. After a while he took out a handkerchief, wiped his eyes and blew his nose. "I'm sorry. The last two weeks have been dreadful."

I didn't know why but I wasn't convinced the handkerchief

thing was real.

"Mr. Brotman, I'd like to help you," Herb said. "But I don't know what I can do. I don't have any resources here. I'm on my own."

"You can help get me and Naomi out of the country, can't you? That would do for a start."

"You're free to leave anytime you want, aren't you?"

"It's not that simple. I'm being watched. They won't let me go."

Herb looked at me and raised his eyebrows indicating a question: *Should I say I can help this guy get out of the country?*

I nodded as enthusiastically as I could, trying to indicate back, *Hell yes, tell him anything, just so we get to hear what he has to say.* Maybe that wasn't the nicest way for me to behave but in my defense I didn't doubt for a minute that Herb could somehow use his connections to help him.

"I can't promise to succeed," Herb said. "But I'll try my best, if that's what you want."

"Right now that's exactly what I want," Aren Brotman said.

"You've got his promise," I said. "Please go on."

He took a deep breath. "It all began with my daughter. She's a difficult child. Along with many other illnesses she has rheumatoid arthritis. She's always in pain. Because of that she's always looking for relief. She became addicted to pain killers, one in particular, called Oxycontin. She tried to get off it but couldn't manage to do so until she heard about this man I mentioned before, Eli Semontoya. He claims to be a guru who can heal people. He has a place he calls the Institute for Healing. She went to see what it was all about and came back a convert. She told me she no longer needed Oxycontin, all she needed was his healing touch, the herbs he sold her, the spa treatments and all the rest of it. To help pay for his outrageous charges she signed my name to one of my checks for five

thousand dollars. She also fell madly in love with him."

"Is he the one who threatened her life?" I asked.

Brotman shook his head. "It's a complicated story. Allow me to tell it in my own way."

Chastised, I decided to keep my mouth zipped.

"I was approached by this man, Grigori Palkovich. He claimed to be close to a member of academia, a professor at Hebrew University. I'd rather not mention his name at the moment. If you agree to help me I will tell you everything. To continue, he claimed that this man had authenticated a tablet found in the desert, purported to be more than a thousand years old and wanted me to add my seconding opinion. I said I would be glad to look at it. He came back the next day with a tablet that I immediately perceived to be counterfeit. I couldn't believe that this professor, whom I know quite well, had authenticated it. When I told him what I thought he said that was why he needed me. To help make it look genuine, and of course, to add my name to the certifiers. I refused.

"That was when he told me Semontoya worked for him. He would tell Semontoya to get Naomi back on Oxycontin for a start. After that, Semontoya could do anything he wanted with her. And if I didn't believe it he could prove it to me quite easily by having me meet Eli Semontoya and talk to him myself. But of course I did not have to meet this man. I knew my daughter was completely under his spell."

I'd been leaning against the wall while listening. I was full of questions. I couldn't be like Herb, the consummate professional, who would have allowed Brotman to tell the story in his own way, no matter how long it took. "Who is this guy who owns Semontoya?" I asked.

"Grigori Palkovich is one of the main people in the Russian Mafia in Israel."

Bingo!

"I should mention," Brotman went on, "that this was not the first time Palkovich tried to get me to work with him. He knows I have much expertise. I always refused. But now he has a club over my head. I thought about offering to do what he wanted if he would leave me alone after that, but I knew it would be foolish. He could promise and then break the promise. I would still be in his hands. This is the only thing I could think of."

"Do you have any kind of proof about these forgers?" Herb asked. "Papers, memos, photographs, anything like that? If you have, I could get them to the right people and possibly break the ring. If we lock up this Palkovich character, you're off the hook."

"I can give you names," Brotman said. "I can tell you about some of the items I suspect they forged and sold to collectors and museums. But I have no specific proof. After all, I wasn't doing any of it."

"Do you know a man named Blather? Cormac Blather?" I asked.

He looked at me then quickly looked away. "Cormac Blather? No. I don't think so."

"It's not a name you would easily forget," I said. "He was doing business with a dealer or a collector over here. In fact, he bought an ossuary from that person. It was supposed to be from the time of Christ. He sold it for a lot of money."

"He probably got it from one of the people I've been telling you about."

"All right," Herb said. "Let's discuss where we go from here. Did this Palkovich guy give you any time frame as to when you have to do this work?"

"He gave me a week. That was two days ago."

"Good," Herb said. "That buys us a little time. The first thing we have to do is get you to make up a list for us. Write down what you know about the forgery people. Names, places, items, rumors. Anything you've got. We don't know what the key is so we have to look at everything. Will you do that?"

"Of course. I have records in my safe at home. I will do it right away."

"In the meantime, I'll put out some feelers to see what I can do about getting you and your daughter out of the country."

"I don't want to be a naysayer, but what if his daughter doesn't want to go?" I said.

"She must go," Brotman said. "She will have no choice."

You haven't been able to do much with her so far, I thought. *What makes you think you'll be able to talk her into leaving her lover?*

"Hold on," Herb said. "Let's cross that bridge when we come to it."

"Sorry," I said. "I'm not trying to create problems. *I humbly do beseech you of your pardon.*"

Aren Brotman gave me a funny look.

We all shook hands and left separately.

CHAPTER 46

"I have an idea," I said to Herb Warshavsky. "How about my going to the Institute for Healing and checking out this Semontoya character?"

We'd left the Israel Museum and driven back through heavy traffic and bright Jerusalem sun to my room at the American Colony.

He didn't immediately object which I saw as a good sign. It meant that he might be accepting me as a full-fledged colleague in this endeavor and not some stumbling schlemiel. "Let's think about it for a minute," he said. "How would that help us?"

"We get to know what kind of person Semontoya is. We find out if Brotman's take on the man is correct, or if he's being deluded by his daughter in some way. And we also ascertain if this is a legitimate outfit or a scam."

Herb had a big beefy face and a wide boyish smile. "I admire you, Jake. You've got balls. After what happened to you in the antique shop, you're still offering to go into the lion's den?"

I shrugged. "Maybe it's stupidity. But I'm really not afraid. I'm just going to look around. I can't imagine they would do anything to me for that. And I've got a legitimate reason for going. I have pain they can help me with."

"How come? Did Ahmid Ben Bey do anything to you?"

"The beautiful cop asked me the same thing. The answer is no. I didn't tell her who did but I can tell you." I told him about the Russians.

"Sounds like you've got an extra stake in this."

"I'd say it would give me more motivation if I needed any. But I don't need any. I'm hungry to go after these guys. I'm positive it ties in somehow with the murder I'm investigating. What do you think about a fake identity and cover story?"

"It would be great if we could do it. Before the Internet it was much easier. But now there are problems. We'd have to create one and there's no time for that, not to mention the amount of effort it would take. We could get you some phony ID's but they wouldn't work. Anything you tell them can be checked out almost immediately. If you make up a name, a business that isn't real, they'll find out pretty quickly and then you'd be worse off."

"Then I go as myself. No problem."

"You realize that if this man is connected with Ahmid Ben Bey, he'll probably know about you. At least your name."

"What would he know? That the cops rescued me. He might also think the cops are watching. That might make him think twice about doing anything. Besides, I didn't tell this Bey character much. Just that I was looking for an ossuary. On the other hand, we don't know if Semontoya's connected to this bunch, do we? That's what we want to find out."

"I don't think it's a good idea, Jake. You just got yourself knocked out by doing more or less the same thing."

"I was a teacher. I taught high school kids. I can handle it."

He shook his head. "Negative. Definitely too dangerous. Forget it."

I stopped arguing. "By the way, I've been meaning to ask you something; did you pick up a vibe from Brotman when I asked him if he knew Cormac Blather?"

"What do you mean?"

"I don't know. Just a feeling that the name was not unfamiliar to him."

"Where did that feeling come from? A hunch?"

"Right. But I trust my hunches."

"What if he did know the name? Why is it significant?"

"If he knew Cormac Blather's name it might mean he knew who sold the ossuary to him. And knowing who sold it might be a clue as to whether it was real or a fake. And besides all that, if he did know the name, why would he say he didn't?"

"A lot of conjecture," Herb said. "First let's see what I can do about getting Brotman and his daughter into the States. No reason they can't go as tourists, but as for staying, that's another ball game."

CHAPTER 47

It was a little after three o'clock in the afternoon when the taxi let me off. Ethiopia Street was a shaded thoroughfare with parked cars, leafy trees, and no pedestrians in sight. I'd left the Jerusalem traffic and the multitude of walkers, eaters, shoppers, and doers behind. Residences were hidden behind walls but not completely. I could make out enough to see that the homes were built of stone, were quite substantial in size and well kept. There were flowers blooming everywhere in landscaping and in pots.

I was disregarding Herb's order. What did the kids say? *You're not the boss over me!* The sun was bright, the temperature a pleasant seventy degrees. I'd called the hotel desk and asked where the Institute was. They said it was not far from the Deir es-Sultan monastery which housed the Ethiopian Orthodox Church. I'd read that the Ethiopian Church was unusual in that it was built in the round, and said to house ancient artifacts and paintings. I made a mental note to add that to my list of places to see before I was done with Jerusalem.

I had made myself look like a man with money, not some ordinary zhlub. I wanted to look prosperous enough so that if Semontoya was indeed a swindler my looking like a patsy would be more enticing if I had gelt than if I didn't. I wore my Ralph Lauren blazer, blue buttoned-down shirt, khaki twills, and mocs. I figured that waspy outfit ought to identify me as someone with class.

243

A bronze plaque attached to a metal gate spelled out the Institute's name. The gate was unlocked. I pushed it open and went along a cement walkway that led through a lush garden to the entrance door. A small sign written in English, Hebrew, French, Italian, and German said, "Welcome. Please push button." I obediently did that and waited.

It was not a long wait. A young blonde woman in a full-length white dress and wearing open-toed sandals opened the door. She smiled at me, put her hands together as if in prayer and gave a slight bow.

I remembered from a trip to Thailand that her greeting was called a *Wai* and that I was required to *Wai* her back. I did.

"Welcome," she said. "You are American, no?"

"Sure am," I said, trying to sound casual.

"Welcome," she said again. "Would you come with me, please?"

I followed her into a small office, just large enough for her desk and a visitor's chair. She sat at a computer. "My name is Elira. May I ask your name?"

"Before we bother with all that, can you tell me anything about this place?"

"I shall be delighted to tell you everything you wish to know, but these are my instructions. I must follow procedure."

"No problem." I answered all her questions, including where I was staying, date of birth (I lied), that I was retired and that I was in Jerusalem as a tourist.

"What did you do before you retired?"

"I was a teacher."

She keyboarded the information into her computer. "Thank you, Mr. Wanderman. Would you care to tell me why you have come to the Institute for Healing?"

"It's simple, really. I'm in a lot of pain."

"What is your problem?"

I described my real symptoms from the beating and added some for my lower back.

"How did you learn about the Institute?"

"I heard a clerk at the hotel talking to another guest."

"Would you know that person's name?"

"Afraid not."

"Don't worry. It is not significant." She finished typing and smiled at me. She was young, pretty, and glowed with well-being. "Now what would you like me to tell you about the Institute?"

"Everything."

She began reciting a speech she'd obviously given countless times before. "The Institute for Healing was founded by our Master, Eli Semontoya. He studied in India for five years at the ashram of the guru, Maharishi Dwivedi Yogi. There he studied the Indian art of healing, known as Ayurveda. Later, the Master added his own healing power of touch. What he has achieved is remarkable."

Her eyes were bright, her expression rapt. This was not an act. This kid was a believer.

"You mean he's going to heal me by just touching me?"

"Not at all. The Master's treatment is different for everyone. But you are in luck. The Master is in residence today. He himself will evaluate you. What a blessing!"

"I guess I am lucky then," I said. "How much is this going to cost?"

"It all depends on the treatment prescribed. But the minimum fee is five thousand dollars. You will find out more after you are evaluated."

"That sounds like a lot of money."

"Many people say that but when they have had the treatments they are most grateful. Bear in mind that our Master is a guru. You have no doubt heard the word guru, but do you know what it means?" She didn't wait for my response. "A guru is one who can lead you from darkness into light."

She stood up. "Before meeting the Master, I will have someone take you on a tour of the Institute so that you can see what a lovely setting you will be in."

She pressed a button on her phone and almost immediately there was a tap on the door. A young woman came in. She was identical in dress and in looks to Elira. She *Waied*, smiled, and indicated I should follow her.

Good taste and lush appointments were everywhere. Plants and flowers inside and out. An indoor pool, hot tubs, yoga rooms, meditation rooms, massage rooms. There was some kind of music in the background that sounded like chanting. Although it was a little hard to see because the place was kept quite dark, the furniture and décor were all top of the line. There were quite a few people in hallways and lounges. Everyone was dressed in gauzy tunics and pants or dresses like the girls. The rooms that were being used by clients were off limits. When we were heading back to the main building I got a glimpse of a familiar face in a small room off to one side. It was Liat Olshef. The Israeli policewoman was speaking animatedly to a young woman across from her. The woman looked at me as I passed. I couldn't avoid eye contact with her but I was grateful that Liat did not look up as I passed.

My guide brought me to an anteroom. "Please wait here. In a short while the Master will receive you. May I bring you some Chai while you are waiting?"

"Is that tea?"

"Yes. It is quite flavorsome." She brought the tea in a cup and saucer of beautiful china and left me alone. I sipped the tea and found it had some kind of spice in it that I didn't recognize but it was delicious. I had time to think. And the first thing I thought about was Liat. I very much doubted she was a client.

This was a high-end operation, not the kind of place a lowly cop could afford. So what was she doing at the Institute? And just who was she talking to? I couldn't hear anything she said but her manner of speaking indicated that she was excited or upset about something.

The door in front of me opened and the man they called Master stood there. He looked to be around forty. His eyes were a disconcerting royal blue and seemed to pierce my skull like twin lasers. He was tall, his head shaved and gleaming. He wore a gauzy white tunic without a collar that closed at the neck. Matching pants, almost like jodhpurs completed the outfit. Diamonds glittered in each ear. He put his hands together in a *Wai*. I got to my feet and did the same.

"I am Eli Semontoya, Mr. Wanderman." He had a slight accent, his voice richly textured and musical. "It is a pleasure to meet you. Come in."

I'd expected his office to be luxurious and I wasn't disappointed. It was a spacious room, large enough for a desk and chairs at one end and a suite of furniture at the other. There was an oriental rug covering part of a hardwood floor. A leather couch in a mahogany color with a couple of matching leather chairs. Three flat screen TVs, stereo system with floor speakers. His desk was also mahogany, intricately carved, with a huge leather chair behind it. He sat in that chair and I sat in one of two chairs on the other side. My chair was much lower so that I was looking up at him. I was pretty sure that was deliberate.

"Why are you here, Mr. Wanderman?" he said.

"I'm hoping you can help get rid of my pain."

"Of course. What I am asking is, why here? Why my Institute?"

"Simple, really. I've tried all sorts of remedies, been all over. Chiropractors, orthopedists, spas, clinics, you name it. When I heard about this place, I thought, why not give it a shot?"

"A familiar tale," he said, looking past me, not directly at me.

"I was privileged to sit at the feet of Maharishi Dwivedi. He believed that compassion for the individual could bring forth their wisdom and creative spirit, so they could transcend their present difficulties and find peace. From him I have learned what I have learned and have added to that learning. I have also been given his great gift. I began by studying Ayurveda, a system of healing that originated in India thousands of years ago. Ayurveda is made up of two Sanskrit words. Ayu means life and Veda means the knowledge of."

The richness of his voice and his manner of speaking produced an almost hypnotic effect. In spite of myself I found that I was listening to him with complete attention.

"In ancient texts over sixty preparations were mentioned that could be used to help cure various ailments. Essentially, however, Ayurveda is more than a medical system, it is to do with life itself. Understanding what is meant by life is the core of the Ayurvetic philosophy. I have spent many years in this endeavor and believe I have found the true inner core of this understanding."

"Sounds very impressive," I said.

"Maintaining a balance of the four essential parts of what the scholar Charaka defined as life is a part of this core. Mind, body, senses, and soul. That's what it's all about, Mr. Wanderman. Mind. Body. Senses. Soul."

"But how does it work? What will you actually do for me that will get rid of my hurt? I was told you could cure people by touch. Is that true?"

"You are getting ahead of me," he said. "I have been expounding to you the philosophy of my Institute, not the detailed methods I employ. That will become known to you when you begin your series of treatments."

"You're not going to tell me how you do it, you mean? I just have to trust you?"

He smiled. "You are skeptical. That is good. What did you do for a living, Mr. Wanderman?"

"I was a teacher, mostly. I also dabbled in the market. That's where I made my money."

"Two most stressful occupations, I would think."

"You have no idea."

"And at some point in your various careers, and in your private life, didn't you have to put your trust in someone? Didn't you have to give up something of yourself and then hope it would come out right?"

"Yes. What you say is true enough. But the trust wasn't always returned. I got burned a few times."

"If you want to be cured, Mr. Wanderman, trust will be necessary. If you have no faith that I can do what I promise to do, I cannot help you."

"I see. It's a pretty expensive trust. How much is it, exactly?"

"After I evaluate I tell my assistant what the treatments will consist of and that determines the final cost. If after four treatments, you are still not cured, the next four will be offered to you at half the initial cost. The treatments require several hours each and are given every other day."

He came around the desk and approached me. "Do not get up." He held his right hand palm outward and moved it toward me, stopping it about an inch away. Then he moved it above my head, around both ears, across my face and down over my body, crouching so that he could get as far as my knees. He straightened up and returned to the chair behind his desk.

"You have had a severe injury," he said. "You are in much pain."

"That's right."

"We will be able to help you, if you so desire."

"I would like to give it some thought. Is that okay with you?"

He smiled and stood up. "By all means. Take your time.

Ponder your decision. It is best not to rush to judgment. The Institute will be here waiting for you." He pushed a button. "It has been a pleasure meeting you. I hope we shall meet again."

Elira appeared.

"Would you show Mr. Wanderman out?"

He put his hands together.

CHAPTER 48

Okay. I'd met Eli Semontoya. He was unusual. The Institute was impressive. No way yet to get a handle on him or the setup. It looked like I would have to fork over the money and start the process if I wanted to get more information.

But what about Liat? I wanted to know what she was doing there. How could I find out about that? I had her card. I could get in touch and offer to talk. Herb had warned me against doing that but he was too cautious. It seemed like a good option to me.

In any event I had to get in touch with Herb and let him know the little I'd learned. I didn't have a local cell phone and had no idea how to use the public phones. I had to go back to the hotel to call him.

When I got to my room the light on my phone was flashing indicating a message. I called the desk and heard that Toby had called and that I should call her back. She picked up on the first ring.

"I thought you ought to know that I heard from Mergenthaler's secretary. You know, the stuffy one."

"What did he want?"

"He claimed he wanted to submit your questions to his boss but that he didn't remember them. I told him I didn't either so he said I should ask you. I told him you were away in Jerusalem. Then he started asking me about where you were staying. Something about the way he asked gave me the feeling he was looking for information. I might be wrong but I thought you ought to know about it."

"You didn't tell him where I was, did you?"

"No."

"Thanks, Toby. I don't like that guy."

"Me neither. How are you getting on there? Have you learned anything?"

"Lots. But so far I feel like I'm still on the surface."

"I wish you'd hurry and get below the surface. I miss you."

"I miss you, too," I said. And I did. I didn't think I had any romantic feeling for her but I liked her a lot and I really did miss her. I also missed being home so maybe that had something to do with it.

Not long after we'd disconnected there was another call. This one from Herb Warshavsky.

"I had Semontoya checked out," he told me. "He's clean. No rap sheet. Not even charges. His family came here from Morocco. His father was a doctor, a pediatrician. He didn't go to college. Worked at a series of jobs of no account. He started the Institute a few years ago. Nobody knows where he got the money."

"Did he ever actually go to India? I was told he stayed there five years."

"How'd you learn about that?"

I told him what I'd done.

"You took a big chance, Jake. You were lucky nothing happened."

"I didn't feel threatened at any time."

"I repeat, you were lucky. Don't think of going back."

"But there's a lot more to be learned. Besides, what's life without a little excitement?"

"I don't need any more than I already have. More important, Brotman wants us to meet his daughter. She'll be at his house tonight. I assume you want to go, correct?"

"Of course."

"I'll pick you up at eight o'clock."

Chapter 49

Roger Bouvie, the secretary to the English ambassador, had been extremely helpful. The consulate was in Tel Aviv because of the West's refusal to have any in Jerusalem but as he had assured Landis, that was not a problem at all. Roger had contacts all over Israel.

He'd sent a message to Landis's BlackBerry that he had located Wanderman at the American Colony Hotel. Landis messaged back with instructions to hire someone to keep an eye on Wanderman and make occasional reports. He immediately wired a thousand dollars, knowing it was excessive but felt it would help to ensure Roger's further cooperation.

It had worked. Landis knew everything that had happened to Wanderman while in Jerusalem. He had learned the names of all the people with whom Wanderman associated. Landis knew about the New York policeman as well as the Israeli policewoman. He learned about the affair in the antique shop a few days after it happened. The investigator had a contact in the police department who supplied him with information. Thus far it had been a waste of time and money, but Landis felt it was important to continue. He felt he needed to know what Wanderman was doing in the event it might somehow have an impact on him.

Back in New York he had tried to learn what he could about the Blather investigation. He was limited because he did not want to use the sources he had within the police department for fear of compromising his own situation. Eventually, he decided to try one source, an inspector in New York City. Without specifying the actual case, he'd asked if he could learn anything about a murder that occurred somewhere in the Hamptons not long before. The inspector called back to say that without a name he couldn't learn anything and furthermore, the pricks in Suffolk County never did give a shit about giving any information to the cops in the city.

Same old, same old. He'd have to rely on himself, as usual.

CHAPTER 50

The map of Jerusalem showed various parts of the city with individual names. It was a lot like Brooklyn with its Flatbush, Williamsburg, Crown Heights, Coney Island, and so on. Here they were called Katamon, Kiryat Wolfson, German Colony, Mea Sharim, among others. Brotman lived in a part of Jerusalem called Rehavia that according to Herb was quite exclusive. Traffic was heavy. It took us more than a half hour to go what seemed only a few miles.

"A lot of distinguished people live around here," Herb said. "Literary folk, philanthropists, professors, even some politicians. And lots of old money."

The houses all seemed to be built of Jerusalem stone, the same stone that most of the official buildings in Jerusalem were made of, as well as those in the old city. It looked like marble but it was more like limestone. The stone was famous enough to be quarried in different parts of Israel and shipped all over the world. I could see why it was in demand. It almost seemed to glow at certain times of the day according to how the light fell on it.

"I want to do a drive-by a few times before we stop," Herb said. "Check the parked cars for watchers."

We drove past Brotman's house, went around the corner and came back the other way. There was a car a few doors down with two men in it, both slumped down with caps pulled low.

"The gray Honda," I said. "Two guys."

"I see them," Herb said.

"Then they're going to make us."

"My guess is they made us already."

We parked and went to the front entrance of one of the larger houses. There were flowers blooming everywhere, much like at the Institute. Aren Brotman answered the door himself. He looked older than he'd looked in the museum. Maybe the light of day exposed what the darkness of the museum had hidden. He walked somewhat bent over. His hair was sparse and his eyelids drooped and showed red edges.

He took us through several gloomy rooms filled with heavy furniture. I looked for ancient artifacts on display but none were to be seen. We went into a sort of sitting room filled with some ratty-looking chairs and a sofa. The air was musty. The atmosphere all around us was that of a place unlived in. At least in this room the blinds were open enough to let some light in.

"My daughter will be here shortly," he said.

We sat and waited. Brotman sat drooping in his chair and said nothing.

After a few minutes there was the sound of footsteps approaching and Naomi Brotman came into the room. I recognized her. It was the same girl I'd seen Liat with at the Institute. She sat in a chair across from the three of us with her knees together and her hands clasped. She spoke with her mouth all but closed, her voice tremulous. "I just want to say at the outset, that I am here under protest." She didn't smile.

"Naomi, not that again," her father said.

"If you are here to injure Eli in any way, I will do everything in my power to stop you."

Her father started to speak but Herb held up his hand, interrupting him. "Wait a minute, Miss Brotman. Let's get something straight right off the bat. Nobody's here to harm anybody. We're trying to get some facts."

She pointed at me. "I saw this man at the Institute. What was he doing there?"

"I was there to get some facts, just as Herb said."

"You were spying."

"I was there because I'm in a lot of pain."

She snorted, her hesitant manner gone. "Give me a break, will you? Do I look that dumb?"

Anything but. She was a plain-looking girl with coarse black hair pulled tight and held in the back with a barrette. Her eyes were hazel and clearly intelligent. She wore a skirt and blouse, and just a touch of lipstick, but independence showed in the stud planted in her nose and silver rings ornamenting every one of her ten fingers.

"Okay, I was trying to get an idea of what the place was all about. You want to call that spying, go ahead."

"What do you want to know about the Institute? I'll tell you. It's a place for healing, healthy living, meaning diet, exercise, meditation. There's nothing evil going on there. I can swear to it."

"Semontoya has threatened me. I told you that," Brotman said.

"I don't believe it. I asked him and he said it was not so. He said he's never spoken to you."

"No, he hasn't spoken to me directly, but he will do what this man Palkovich tells him to do."

"I don't know who this Palkovich is. Eli says he doesn't know anyone by that name. And even if there was such a possibility, do you really believe Eli would do such terrible things to me? I love him and he loves me."

"I didn't tell you everything. If I don't do what they ask me to do and you don't cooperate, they will kill you. Is that laughable?" Brotman bent over and put his face in his hands.

She went over and knelt in front of her father. "Daddy, I'm

not trying to hurt you. But I can't go along with anything that might harm Eli. He's gotten me off drugs. I'm not suffering anymore. His treatments have changed my life. How can I turn against him?"

"Hold on a minute," Herb said. "Let's try and analyze the situation in a rational manner."

"Great idea," I said. "Just how do we go about doing that?"

"What facts do we have to work with? Mr. Brotman says his life and his daughter's life are in danger. Reason? He's being pressured by the Russian Mafia to authenticate a fake. He doesn't want to do it."

I continued, "And his daughter says that's nonsense, that her boyfriend would not be involved in anything like that. So we've got two opposing views. Which one is correct?"

"I'm telling the truth," Brotman said. "Why would I make something like this up?"

"You asked Herb to get you into the United States," I said. "Maybe there's another reason why you can't go there on your own."

Brotman glared at me. "What are you accusing me of?"

"I'm not accusing, just speculating," I said. "Maybe you're in some other kind of trouble."

"I don't need more than I've already got. Did you see those men out there? Someone is there all the time. They want me to know they are watching me."

"Mr. Brotman, listen to me," Herb said. "I can certainly expedite a tourist visa for you. But it's not going to do you much good. Think about it. The Russian Mafia is not only here. They're in New York, too. They're all over. If they want to find you, they will. The only thing I can think of to help you is to get this guy Palkovich and lock him up. Maybe we can set up some kind of trap."

Brotman shook his head. "They'll find out and kill me and Naomi, too."

"Then we have to make sure they don't," Herb said.

"Can you guarantee that?" Naomi asked.

"There are no guarantees. But I can't think of anything else. Can you?"

"Yes," Naomi said. "Let my father do what they want."

I jumped in. "You know what that would mean, don't you? They'd own him from that point on."

"Don't they already?" said Naomi Brotman.

CHAPTER 51

"What do you think she meant by that?" I asked Herb. We were on our way back to my hotel. Nothing further had been accomplished because Brotman told us he couldn't talk anymore. It was obvious the man was struggling but I wasn't convinced he was being completely truthful with us. "Do you think maybe he's already done something for them and now is sorry and wants to get out of it?"

"Anything's possible," Herb said. "I don't know. I also don't know where we're going with this. To be honest, I'm up a tree here. I'd have to liaison with the local cops and tell them what's going on. No way we could set up a trap without them."

"By local cops I guess you mean Liat Olshef. She's the one in charge of the case. Right?"

"That's right."

I didn't continue the conversation and neither did Herb. I was exhausted. I'd only been in Jerusalem two days and had not stopped moving for one minute. Not to mention what else had happened to me. I needed sleep and lots of it.

In spite of what Herb had said I'd already made up my mind that I was going to disregard his advice about contacting Liat. I had her business card with her phone number. But it would have to wait.

I was too tired to eat. I hit the sack and didn't wake up until morning. I had a continental breakfast in my room and called her while I was drinking my coffee. "Would you like to get together with me and have a talk?"

"About what?" she said.

"Lots of things. The Institute for Healing. Eli Semontoya. Grigori Palkovich."

She didn't answer immediately. I'd taken her by surprise with those names which was what I'd intended.

"Did you hear what I said?"

"I heard you," she said. "Do you want to come to my office?"

"At the police station? Not on your life. How about we meet at the Western Wall? I was there once briefly, but it was a long time ago. Might as well kill two birds with one stone."

"Another of your proverbs?"

"More like a cliché. But it'll do for now. How about this morning, ten o'clock?"

"I can't. I can meet you at three, this afternoon."

"Okay."

"The area at the wall is very large. There are many people all the time. On one side, to your left as you face the wall, you will see some water fountains. I will meet you there."

I stayed in my room most of the day, going out only for a swim and to have lunch on the patio. Of course I wanted to talk to Liat but I was also excited that I was finally going to visit the Western Wall or Wailing Wall, as it was also known. It may not have been on the list of "Wonders of the World" but if not, it should have been. It had been there for thousands of years. It had endured attacks, occupation, desecration, attempts to demolish it entirely, but somehow it was still there, not only a symbol, but the most solid kind of evidence that the Jews had survived and would not be destroyed. The Wall attracted people from all over the world, Christians as well as Jews, the most devout and the atheist.

I walked to the old city again, back through the Damascus Gate, and kept going until I reached a checkpoint where soldiers

looked at my ID. After the checkpoint a short walk along a corridor, then through glass doors and I was at the top of a flight
of stone steps leading down to a square or a courtyard.

The sight was nothing like I'd remembered from the visit
years ago. The area was at least as large as a football field and
filled with hundreds of tourists walking back and forth. The
wall was well behind them and from where I was standing
looked disappointingly small. There were a dozen or so mini-
vans parked at one end of the square which accounted for the
parade. Many were dressed in casual clothes, T-shirts, cameras
around necks, but some were more formal, sensitive to the
significance of where they were. There were people in wheel-
chairs and kids in strollers, orthodox Jews dressed in black
wearing fedoras, others looking as if they'd stepped out of a
medieval time warp, heads covered with wide-brimmed hats
made of fur and dressed in long coats of a shiny material that
went to their knees, their legs covered in white knee stockings.
There were also teams of uniformed soldiers scattered around
with machine guns in their hands.

It was late afternoon and the air was chilly but the sun was
still strong and threw a glaring light over the scene. In spite of
all the activity there was hardly any sound. Or maybe I didn't
hear any because I was so enthralled. As I got closer to the wall
I saw that I'd been mistaken about its size. It was in fact quite
elevated. It was made of huge blocks of stone, many of them
cracked. Vegetation had managed to grow out of some of the
cracks, the green foliage an anomaly but maybe also another
symbol of survival.

On my left I saw the water fountains Liat had mentioned, a
row of faucets, the kind where you pushed a button to get a
flow. She wasn't there. A low concrete barrier separated the area
near the wall from the public square. On the wall side a good
number of people were *davening,* praying, some rocking back

and forth with prayer shawls over their heads. Lots of others stood around in groups, chatting as if they were at a cocktail party. Strewn about the area were dozens of the cheap white plastic chairs that have become universal. A few of them were occupied but most were empty. To me they looked like litter, almost obscene in fact, for them to be in such a holy place.

I felt the urge to get nearer to the wall. In order to do that it was necessary to pass through portable metal gates set up to create a narrow entrance area. At the entry itself was a container filled with white cardboard *yarmulkes*. I saw others without head coverings take the *yarmulkes* and put them on their heads so I did the same.

Before I went further I glanced back at the water fountains for Liat. She still wasn't there. I went closer to the wall. I could hear the praying of the people with *tallit* over their heads or on their shoulders. Some *davened* in loud voices, others were murmuring their prayers. I saw a few individuals stuffing scraps of paper into cracks. I'd heard that these notes were usually prayers or wishes.

I remembered that women were not allowed on this side. They were close by, at another section of the wall but separated from the men by yet another barrier. We could look at them and they could look at us but officially we were separated. Separated, but definitely not equal. The size of their area was one-tenth the size of the male side. Rosalind had been really pissed about that.

I didn't know why but I suddenly felt a need to touch the wall. I'd never been in the least religious. In fact, I was with Marx. Organized religion was *opium for the masses*. Unlike me, Rosalind had been brought up as an observant Jew and celebrated most of the holidays, not just the high holy days. My approach was to fast on *Yom Kippur* and accompany Rosalind to the synagogue when she wanted to go.

In spite of all the people there it was not difficult to find a spot where I could get close enough to the wall to actually touch it. I reached out and put the flat of my hand against the stone. It was smooth and cool to the touch. I closed my eyes and let my hand rest against the stone. I felt my body tremble. Without warning my eyes filled. I didn't try to hold back the tears. I let them come and run down my cheeks. Somehow it was satisfying to be there with my hand against the stone and feel the tears streaming on my face. It only lasted a few seconds. I got a tissue out of my pocket and used it.

Then I went looking for Liat.

CHAPTER 52

When I left the cordoned-off area Liat had arrived at the water fountains. She was talking to a tall soldier with an Uzi suspended across his chest. They seemed to be having an intense conversation. When I walked over his expression changed from complete attention to unadulterated disappointment. It was evident he wished I'd never been born. Liat shook his hand and he turned away.

"Your soldier was not happy to see me," I said.

"What do you mean?"

"Couldn't you tell he was already falling in love with you?"

"Don't be ridiculous."

It wasn't her clothing, (a pale blue blouse and navy pants), or jewelry, (a necklace of clunky beads), or makeup, (just lipstick), but there was an aura about her. She also had a wide mouth and perfect white teeth that showed to advantage against her olive skin. And her eyes got to me, too, somewhere between chocolate and mocha. "Come on, Liat. You must know you're a beautiful woman."

"We're not here to talk about me."

"Okay. What were you talking to the soldier about?"

"I wanted to know if anything unusual had occurred in the last few days."

"And?"

"Nothing. He said it was so quiet he was bored. He wished he could be assigned somewhere else."

"I don't imagine that you're bored."

"Definitely not. I enjoy my work."

"Even though there's a lot of sexism in Israel?"

"Of course. Just as there is in the United States and everywhere else."

"Granted. Let's find a spot where we can schmooze," I said.

Her remarkable smile appeared. "Unlike your other expressions, I know what schmooze means."

We walked to a part of the square that was a good distance from the entrance to the wall. From where we stood we could see the crowds of people moving forward and back in a neverending flow. But we were quite alone.

"All right," she said. "Tell me what's on your mind."

"What's on my mind is that I'd like to know what you were doing at the Institute for Healing, and who you were talking to so intently."

She was cool, didn't even blink. "How did you know I was there?"

"I saw you."

"When? And why? Why were *you* there?"

"Now I know you're definitely Jewish. You answer a question with a question. You answer mine, I'll answer yours."

She opened her handbag and took out a pack of Marlboros. This time she didn't ask my permission. She lit one and breathed in the smoke. "I was there to see a friend."

"And this friend was . . . ?"

"Before I answer that I want to know why *you* were at the Institute."

I knew we weren't going to get anywhere without her help. I was taking a chance but I didn't see any other choice. I told her about Brotman and his daughter.

"Naomi Brotman," she said. "That's who I was talking to. We've been friends since we were five years old. I was doing my best to help her."

"How?"

"By getting her away from Semontoya. I was trying to convince her to go back to her analyst. I was hoping the analyst would give her the strength to at least separate herself from him. At this point she is completely dominated. She will do anything he says."

"Is she doing drugs?"

"She says not, but I'm not convinced."

"I saw her when I was at the Institute and she looked like she was on something. I met her again at her father's house." Liat looked at me with surprise. "That's part of what I have to tell you. I went there with Herb Warshavsky, the detective from New York. Anyhow, she was completely different. Self-assured and confident. She told us that Semontoya has helped her. That's she's clean and without pain for the first time in her life."

"That's what she told me," Liat said. "But when I suggested to her that if that were the case she would be better off going back to work, she insisted that he needs her at the Institute."

"What did she do before?"

"She's a chemical engineer. She graduated with honors. Had an important job at the Technion doing research on complex fluids and macromolecules."

"What happened?"

"She's been sick her whole life. Abdominal problems, headaches, rheumatoid arthritis, you name it. It's understandable she'd have psychological problems as a result. Add to all that her addiction to painkillers. She's had breakdowns. She was given sick leave over and over again. Eventually they were forced to dismiss her."

We'd been standing for a long time and the air was getting colder by the minute. "There's a lot more to talk about," I said.

"Including some ideas I have about Semontoya. Why don't we have dinner somewhere?" I was enjoying my time with her and didn't want it to end.

"Fine," she said. "Do you have someplace in mind?"

"This is your town, not mine."

She laughed. "Let's get out of the old city and I'll take you to a restaurant that has decent food and nice people running it."

"Lead on. As the Duke said to the Master of the Revels, *How shall we beguile the time, if not with some delight?*"

"Shakespeare again? Do you know everything he wrote?"

"I've read everything he wrote but I can't say I memorized all of it."

"Where was that last quotation from?"

"*A Midsummer Night's Dream.*"

"Ah. It is one of my favorite plays."

"Mine, too."

We left the Western Wall and began walking back with Liat leading the way. She took me on a different route from the one I'd taken. It seemed to be residential. There were no shops. The streets were quiet. Only a few people around, none of them tourists.

I suddenly felt the desire to take hold of her hand as if we were on a date. I didn't because I thought she'd think I was trying to come on to her. Then I thought maybe that's what I really did want.

She stopped suddenly and touched my arm so that I stopped too. She looked behind us. I turned but saw nothing other than a few people walking along the street. None of them looked suspicious.

"What's up?" I asked.

"For a minute I thought we were being followed."

"Why, did you see something?"

"No. I think I just felt it, somehow."

"Which gate are we heading for?"

"Jaffa Gate," she said. "It's not far now. We have to turn at the next corner."

I hadn't seen anything remotely out of the way but her remark put me on edge. I was tense and alert when we began walking again. Liat was in the same mode. We were both looking to either side and moving at a faster pace. Even so, we were taken by surprise when two heavies suddenly appeared from behind a parked car. They looked like they belonged in a French gangster film: black leather jackets, huge shoulders, one tall and beefy, the other small but no less bulky, and both of them looking mean, ugly and dangerous. They were holding small objects in their hands. They came towards us moving fast. No one else was in sight.

"You were right," I said. "What do we do now?"

"Run like hell," she said, and took off.

I ran after her. She was faster than me and in no time at all I was breathing hard trying to keep up. I heard yelling behind us and knew they were close. We reached the corner. As soon as we went around it she dropped to one knee and pulled a gun out of her bag. The bruisers came around the corner in a big hurry. Liat fired a shot in the air. Either they didn't hear it or their momentum kept them from stopping. She stood up and pointed the weapon at them. They were no more than three feet away when they saw the gun and stopped in their tracks. They were breathing hard and looking at her with hatred in their eyes.

She said something in Hebrew. They dropped what they were holding and raised their hands above their heads clasping them together. What fell out of their hands were small versions of bats and the ringing sound they made when they hit the pavement indicated they were metal. I had a brief moment thinking of the damage they could have done to us with those super blackjacks.

There was still nobody in sight. Apparently the sound of the gun hadn't been heard or recognized. Or else no one wanted to get involved. I picked up the clubs and held one in each hand. They were light, not much more than a pound. I thought of the wooden clubs the Russians had used on me back home. These were deadlier.

Again she uttered a command and they turned around so their backs were to us. She pulled handcuffs out of her purse. They looked like they were made of plastic. She approached the smaller of the two.

"Wait a minute," I said. "You've got a gun in your hand. I can do this."

She hesitated. "Have you ever put handcuffs on anyone before?"

"No. But I'm sure I can figure it out."

"These have no key. You put it around the wrists and lock it by pulling the strap tight." She handed me a pair. I put the clubs on the ground so I could take hold of it. The handcuffs were lightweight but seemed well-constructed and solid. She said something else in Hebrew and the men lowered their hands behind their backs.

I went towards the shorter of the two. As I pulled his arms backward to get the cuffs over his wrists, he muttered something to his buddy and then suddenly dropped to the ground.

The big one turned and shoved me hard. I went backwards directly into Liat. She staggered and fell. I was still upright but off balance. Liat's gun hit the ground and bounced away from her. I was right next to the clubs. I picked one up and swung it as hard as I could at the guy nearest to me. I got his left arm but it didn't seemed to make an impression on him. He raised his right hand to swing at me but stopped when the guy on the ground yelled. The short one got up and he and his buddy began to run. While this was happening Liat scrambled over on her hands and knees and got hold of her gun.

By this time the villains were around the corner. We started after them. When we reached the end of the building we saw the two of them for a brief moment at the far end of the street heading towards an alley. Then they were gone.

"*Ben zona!*" she muttered. I didn't know what she said but I knew what a curse sounded like. "Stupid," she said, more to herself than to me. "I should have called for backup immediately. But no, I wanted to be a hero and bring them in by myself."

"Look at the positive," I said. "You saved us from a savage beating."

"I didn't get a chance to learn anything. No names, no information. I had them in my hands and I lost them."

"Don't be too hard on yourself. The adrenaline was flowing."

"I'll have to report this."

"Hold on a minute," I said. "Think about it. Nobody knows about this except the two gangsters and us. No need to give your bosses any reason to criticize you."

She put the gun back in her handbag and withdrew the Marlboros. She fired one up and looked at me. "I never supposed that you were a devious kind of person."

"Why should you? You don't know me at all."

"I've always followed the rules."

"This is not so far outside the rules. You didn't do anything bad. It's not like you're corrupt or anything like that."

"If I don't make a report I would be putting myself in your hands. Like you said, I don't know you. Why should I trust you not to say anything?"

"Let's talk about it over dinner," I said.

She didn't object.

On the way I tossed one of the clubs into a trash can. I held on to the other one.

CHAPTER 53

She'd parked her Volvo with its police tag just inside the Jaffa Gate where a few taxis waited. We drove out along Jaffa Road, a busy commercial street with hole-in-the-wall shops selling everything from cheap souvenirs to upscale leather goods. Among the stores were a bunch of restaurants serving a wide ranging assortment of foods from Asian to Italian to Zambesian. We stopped outside one with a large outdoor patio. Most of the tables were occupied even though it was already cold enough for a down jacket. She pointed at a table. "What do you think?"

"Too frosty for me. I'm a wimp."

"As you wish," she said.

"You'd rather eat outside so you can smoke, is that it?"

She laughed. "Very perceptive."

It turned out to be a vegetarian restaurant and served the food cafeteria style. I followed her lead and got a tray and utensils and went along the counter to see what they had. The choices were impressive: three kinds of soup, a variety of pizza and quiches, a full salad bar, hot vegetables, pasta, rice, pastry, yogurt, ice cream, sorbets, and hot and cold drinks. It all looked fresh, inviting, and no different from what could be found in New York. I settled for a slice of pizza and salad. She had a bowl of lentil soup, dark bread, and a bottle of pomegranate juice. The cash register was at the end of the line. I was pleased that she allowed me to pay for her. "Thank you," the cashier said in English.

Then I recognized what was different from New York. Everyone working behind the counter was smiling and pleasant.

We found a small table in a corner where we had some privacy.

We ate in silence for a while.

Finally, I said, "Well?"

"What?"

"Are you going to file a report?"

"I will think about it."

"Fair enough. I don't have to know. Do you know who those guys were?"

"I've never seen them before."

"Not individually but who they're working for. They were there to send a message. I'm familiar with that because I got the same message not long ago."

"You were attacked?"

"Correct. By the same kind of goons. That's their M.O., I guess. They like to beat people up. Do you think these guys were Mafia?"

"I don't know. They could be. They could also have been sent by Semontoya. He knows I've been trying to get Naomi away from him."

"How'd they know where we were? You think there might be leaks in your department? A cop on the take?"

"The take," she said. "I know what that means, too. Yes, it's entirely possible. But I don't think so. I don't distrust any of the people I've been working with. If there is someone, I have no idea who it might be. As for how they knew where we were, they could have been following me. Or they might have been following you."

"I don't think it's me. I suspect you're the one they're worried about. Maybe you're getting closer to busting them."

"I'm not any closer but they might think I am. They obviously are nervous about something. Maybe a big deal is in the making and they don't want me to get wind of it."

"Let me tell you what Naomi's father had to say. I'd like to hear your take on it."

"You just used the word *take* in a different way. Now I am confused."

"I'm sorry," I said. "English can be a perplexing language. What I mean is I want to hear your reaction to what I am now going to tell you."

A busboy came to the next table and began clearing away dishes, making a lot of noise in the process. I waited for him to finish and then told her Aren Brotman's story about being forced to certify a fake and what he'd said about Grigori Palkovich being the big boss. "I know of this man Palkovich. He is not the head of anything. He does not control Eli Semontoya. If anything, Semontoya controls him."

"What are you saying? That Brotman's story is a lie or that Semontoya is using this guy Palkovich as a shield to hide behind?"

"I'm not sure what's going on," Liat said. "But now I'm beginning to wonder more about Mr. Eli Semontoya and his possible role in the forgery ring."

"You mean he might be running the whole shebang?"

"Shebang?"

"The whole operation."

"It's a distinct possibility."

"Does this information help you in any way?"

"Again, I'm not sure. It might. At least it opens up another avenue to explore."

"There's something else I want to ask you," I said. "Is Aren Brotman all that he says he is, only a collector? In plain English, is he kosher?"

275

"Why do you ask?"

"I don't have any evidence, just a hunch. But I wouldn't be surprised if he hasn't done some forging of his own."

I told her about Cormac Blather and the burial box, that Blather had a contact in Israel, that there was something about Brotman's denial of knowing the name that made me think he was lying. And then, as long as I was at it, I filled her in on the rest of the story including Cormac's murder and why I was in Jerusalem.

Liat listened attentively but said nothing. She bent down to her soup bowl.

I had the distinct feeling I'd touched a nerve and that I shouldn't press her.

It wasn't easy but I managed to finish eating without saying another word.

Chapter 54

Outside Liat immediately lit another cigarette. "I'll drive you to your hotel," she said.

"Don't you have something you want to tell me?"

"Not now. I have to think before I talk with you again."

"What's there to think about?"

"If I tell you then I won't have thought about it so I can't tell you."

A Talmudic-like response. More silence while she drove through the now quiet streets of Jerusalem. It was not late, not even nine o'clock, but there were few people walking or driving. The people of Jerusalem were apparently more interested in security than frivolity.

When we got to the hotel she stopped the car and turned towards me. There was enough light coming from the building to delineate the outline of her face. Her eyes were mostly in shadow but I thought I could see enough to observe an intensity in them that had not been there before. I leaned over and kissed her. She didn't turn away. I could feel her lips responding to mine. I moved to put my arms around her when she pulled back. "No," she said. "Not now."

"Why not?"

"It's too complicated as it is. We will speak again. I will call you tomorrow."

I knew her well enough by then to realize there was nothing to do but get out of the car and watch her drive away. I stood at the entrance to the hotel, the taste of her lips still on mine. Confused didn't begin to describe my feelings. I was excited, I knew that much. At the same time feelings of guilt suddenly swirled through me. And then came thoughts of Rosalind, and Detective Sienna Nolan got in there, and then along came Toby Welch. They spun around and around until they eventually blended with Liat, and left me bothered and almost as bewildered as the acne-ridden teenager I used to be.

What was I doing? What was I thinking? Was it the "power of the pecker" syndrome again, my body leading the way when my brain ought to know better? Said Fabian in *Twelfth Night:*

> *If this were played upon a stage now,*
> *I could condemn it as an improbable fiction.*

But this wasn't on a stage. It was here and now, in a real place, in a real time, and as genuine as my hard-on.

CHAPTER 55

I had a rotten night. In fact I spent most of it pacing back and forth. I tormented myself trying to understand what had happened . . . what might happen . . . and at the same time tried to get my emotions under control.

I wasn't successful.

Coffee helped. The next morning I was enjoying a cup in the pleasant outdoor patio of the hotel when Liat appeared. She was wearing the equivalent of a police uniform: dark blue jacket and pants, a tailored shirt under the jacket. As I watched her walk towards me, I noticed that even the fluid way she walked was beautiful.

"Good morning," she said.

"Would you like some coffee?"

She nodded.

I decided it would be better if I didn't look into her eyes because they might turn me into a puddle of mush. I waited until the server had brought her coffee before I spoke. I knew I ought to ask her about Brotman. Instead I said, "I hope you weren't upset that I kissed you."

"I wasn't."

"Why weren't you? Did you expect it?"

"As a matter fact, yes," she said.

"Tell the truth. You wanted me to kiss you."

"Yes."

"I'd be willing to do it again," I said.

"I'd like that, but at the moment there are more important issues to address."

She was right, of course. I had to stop acting like a romantic idiot. "Okay. I'm listening."

Liat had another sip of coffee. "Aren Brotman. You asked me about him, his history. Your instincts were correct. He was indeed a forger. He was also in the business of looted antiquities, disposing of them privately without government knowledge. As you may be aware, this is a worldwide industry.

"I know all this because a long time ago Naomi came to me and begged me to keep her father out of jail. He'd heard that the Israel Antiquities Association was investigating him. I was able to turn the investigation in another direction. I knew I was risking my career but I did it anyway for Naomi's sake. Afterwards, I told Brotman that if he ever went back to it there would be no more help on my part. That, in fact, I would be leading the investigation and would be glad to bring him down."

"I knew it," I said. "I felt it in my gut. Now I'm sure he was connected with my friend Blather in that ossuary deal."

"More than likely," Liat said.

"Do you think he ever quit?"

Liat put her cup down. "I think he did. I never heard even the slightest rumor that he may have gone back into it. But anything is possible. If he didn't, he's a fool, or greedy, or both. If he did give up, and he's telling the truth about being pressured, that's another story."

"How can we find out?"

The waiter returned and poured more coffee for both of us.

"Naomi," Liat said. "She ought to know. If not, I'm quite sure she can find out. Her father will do anything for her. Even tell her the truth."

"Are you going to follow up on that?"

"Yes. I'll let you know as soon as I can. In the meantime, I suggest you become a real tourist and avoid any possibility of another incident."

"I'll try. But I hope you don't mind if I think about you."

She pushed her chair back and stood. "Think as much as you like. Just don't do anything. As a matter of fact, I suggest you stay in the hotel until you hear from me. I doubt anything can happen to you here."

"You make me sound like a bumbling idiot."

"I'm sorry. I didn't mean that at all. It's just that unpleasant things seem to happen when you are in the vicinity."

"There's a semblance of truth to that, I admit. If I hang out here and don't venture outside I should be safe, don't you think?"

She smiled.

"How long will it be before I hear from you?"

Liat's eyes met mine but I couldn't read anything in them. "There's really no way to tell, is there?"

CHAPTER 56

After she left I decided I ought to let Herb Warshavsky know what had happened. Not the amorous stuff, of course, but everything else, including the attack. I reached him on his cell and filled him in. He made no comment but I could feel his irritation. I guessed he resented the idea of my doing anything without his say-so. I couldn't imagine what his reaction would be if I told him *everything*. Well, I had enough to think about without worrying about my approval rating.

Once again I wandered the grounds of the hotel. My mind was full of questions: what was Liat going to learn? What would we do next? When could I go home? I'd only been in Jerusalem four days but I was already homesick. I was tired of dusty dry Jerusalem, full of stone and little green. Even though I'd fallen for the beautiful Liat I realized I wanted to be back in my beloved Sag Harbor again. I yearned for the ocean, the bay, the smell of salt in the air.

I went to my room and turned on the TV. I didn't have the patience to watch it, couldn't sit inside. So back I went to the patio and ordered another coffee. I sat there taking small sips, wondering how long I would have to wait before I heard from Liat.

Two men appeared in the doorway. They wore dark suits and ties. I glanced at them incuriously for a moment, then away. Suddenly I realized I'd seen them before. One was tall and wide and one was short and wide. They were the same two mugs who'd wanted to bash Liat's head and mine in the old city. I started to get up but I wasn't quick enough. They were already at my table. I wished I had the club I'd kept in my hand but it was back in my room doing me no good at all.

"Sit," the short one said. The tall one put his hand on my shoulder and pressed down hard, forcing me back into my chair. Shorty opened his jacket so that I could see a holster with the handle of a gun showing. The big one remained standing while Shorty sat. He looked at me calmly. He had soft-looking brown eyes like a cow.

"Coffee?" I said.

He didn't speak.

I waited for what seemed like minutes, then finally asked, "What do you want?"

"You come with us." His English was slow and heavily accented.

"What if I don't want to?"

It took a few beats before what I'd said translated in his head. In an instant the expression on his face changed from confident and serene to a guy who looked like he'd swallowed something slimy and rotten. "Then I will kill you."

"Here? In front of all these people?"

He turned away from me and we both looked around. I felt stupid because we were the only ones out there. All the tables on the patio were empty. He shrugged. "Even if people, make no difference."

I believed him.

The tall one put his hand on my arm and pulled me to my feet. We went in a sandwich with the short guy in front, the big guy in back and me, the filling. I hoped there might be someone I could turn to for help but the only person I saw was the man at the reception desk. He wasn't even looking up as we passed by. We went out the front entrance and down the street to a gray Honda, probably the same one I'd seen near Brotman's house. I was put in the back with the short guy while the big one drove. No one talked.

I was left to ponder what was going to happen next. I had no idea but obviously someone wanted me. For what, was the big question? I wasn't as frightened as I might have been because except for the assassin next to me I was fairly confident nobody else really wanted to kill me. I didn't think I was important enough for such drastic action. Not that I wasn't nervous about what they did want with me. Strangely enough I had the odd satisfaction of thinking that at least I couldn't be blamed for getting into this particular bit of trouble. Definitely not my fault this time.

They didn't blindfold me but they didn't have to. The car went at a high rate of speed, up one street and down another. Sometimes we were on a wide boulevard lined with palm trees. At others we were snaking through narrow medieval-looking streets where the ultra-orthodox *haredim* lived, those who wore the wide-brimmed hats of fur and long black coats. In some neighborhoods there were lots of people hurrying along on sidewalks, then suddenly there were no people. Scooters ripped back and forth, their tiny motors buzzing, cars beeped their horns a lot. Of course, nobody paid any attention to us. I didn't have a clue as to where we were or in what direction we'd traveled.

Finally, we parked on a street that could be found in almost any city in the Western world. A blue-collar look: attached houses, no yards, no shrubbery, plain entrance doors. The driver knocked on the door of one of these nondescript places and waited. After a while, the door was opened and we went into a small entrance foyer that had a table and a mirror on the wall.

An old woman in a *babushka* stood by the door. She wore an apron and looked down at the floor as we entered. In front of us was a flight of wooden uncarpeted stairs, the varnish on the wood long gone. We went up to the second floor and into a room that was clearly used as an office with a desk, file cabinets, a computer, fax, and printer. The walls were bare except for the one on the right side of the desk. This wall had both a door and a framed rectangular drawing done in black ink or charcoal. It was a caricature of a man with deep-set eyes, a nose like a doorknob, and a chin as pointed as the end of a knife. The expression on his face was that of a man about to pleasurably consume a large ox.

The short guy pointed to a chair in front of the desk. "Sit."

I heard a strange noise and looked to see the cause. On a table behind the desk was a cage with a treadmill. Something large and ugly was running on the treadmill. As the wheel turned it made a squeaking sound, accounting for the noise I'd heard. The animal in the cage was about ten inches long and shaped like a sausage but unlike a sausage it had brown fur and a long tail. It looked very much like what I'd once seen running out of a cellar on the lower East Side with a fat man in an undershirt chasing it with a broom.

The two minders stood, one behind me, the other leaning against a wall. Nobody spoke. We listened to the squeak of the treadmill as the animal ran on his neverending boulevard.

After a while there was a noise in the corridor. The two bruisers all but jumped to attention. In came a man moving as if he was late for an appointment. He brushed past me, went to the opposite side of the desk and paused to look at the treadmill. He picked up a bottle of water that had a long nozzle at the end and poured some water into a bowl in the cage. Then he sat down and turned towards me.

It was the man in the caricature. The artist had gotten him just right. His chin was shaped like a spade, coming almost to a point. What the artist had not gotten was the dark stubble on his face and the gold loop in his ear. Perhaps he'd shaved the day of the sitting and hadn't worn the earring. At any rate, his expression was the same. He looked as if he were anticipating a feast.

He rubbed his hands together. "Ah, good," he said. "Good, good, good."

He had a slight accent of some sort. I thought it was Russian, but I wasn't sure. He was a small man, in his forties, slender build, manicured fingernails. His suit looked Italian. It was black, of course. His shirt was pink and the tie black with tiny pink dots. On one of his manicured fingers was a diamond ring, the stone the size of a zucchini.

"Did you look at my drawing? You like it? It was done in Barcelona. On the street. *Las Ramblas.* You know it? Street musicians. Mimes. Artists. This one was good. I watched him do a few. He did mine for ten dollars. A bargain, don't you think?"

"Yes indeed," I said.

"Ever been to Barcelona? A wonderful city."

"No. I always wanted to go. But never made it."

"Perhaps you will still get there. There is plenty of time. You are not yet very old." He pressed the palms of his hands together. "But much depends on you."

I didn't respond. I knew he would tell me what he wanted from me.

"By the way," he said. "I neglected to introduce myself. I am Grigori Palkovich."

He made a motion with one hand. The next thing I knew an arm was around my neck and my head was being forced back. Both cheeks were pressed hard by powerful fingers so that I had to open my mouth. Then something was pushed into it, all the way to the throat. I began to heave.

"Not that much," Palkovich said.

The object was moved away from the back of my throat but

was still filling the cavity and pressing on my tongue. I was finding it hard to breathe and not gag again. I tasted metal and oil and knew what they'd stuck in my mouth was the barrel of a gun.

"Do you know what that is, Mr. Wanderman? Of course you do. It is a nine-millimeter pistol. Manufactured by a company called Glock. This one holds seventeen rounds. An excellent weapon. Quite reliable."

I closed my eyes and concentrated on breathing.

"You have become an incredible nuisance to us, Mr. Wanderman. More than a nuisance, actually. You don't know what you are doing but nevertheless, you manage to disrupt a great many things. You are in my way and I want you out of my way. Do you understand me?"

The gun was withdrawn and I could breathe again.

"Look at me," he said.

I fixed my eyes on him.

He looked calm, but his eyes glittered and a muscle on the right side of his jaw jumped. "I want to make it clear that I am very serious. The pistol is one method. With it I can have you shot and disposed of. But there is also another method."

Before I had a chance to say anything, he again made a motion and once more I was grabbed from behind, an arm around my neck pressing on my throat. My right hand was pulled out in front of me and placed flat on a board. I couldn't move.

"This method is less crude and almost as effective, I have found." He came around the desk and stood in front of me. One of the goons handed him a knife. It had a long blade that shone in the light. He put the tip between two of my fingers. "What I can do to demonstrate the seriousness of my intent is to cut off one of your fingers a portion at a time. I would start with the first joint which includes the fingernail. The point of this exercise is to convince you that it would be in your best interest to leave Jerusalem immediately. If you hesitate, I can remove the entire finger and then start on another." Now he was smiling.

I found myself drenched in cold sweat. A childhood memory abruptly came back. I'd been terrified at the age of five when a friend of my parents tossed me into the ocean to teach me how to swim. That was the scariest moment of my life because I thought I was going to drown. Until now.

I didn't know if this guy Palkovich was serious about what he was threatening me with or if he was putting on an act. But if it was an act it was the most convincing one I'd ever seen. "You won't have to do that," I managed to get the words out.

"You say that, of course, but can I believe you? I know you are with that police detective from New York. And I know you are also connected with the female from our local police. I don't like any of that. My operation is too important to be compromised by an amateur like you."

"I promise I'll leave Jerusalem the minute you let me go."

He looked at me closely as if to judge whether I was sincere or not. "I think if I remove the first joint with your fingernail it will motivate you more." He raised the knife and held it over my hand.

I shut my eyes tight and waited for the cut and the immense pain that would follow. I could hear the squeak, squeak of the treadmill behind him. I was desperate. "I'm motivated," I said. "Believe me. I'm ready to go anytime you say."

I heard the door and opened my eyes. I saw Palkovich look up, annoyed at the interruption. He abruptly jammed the knife into the board. It landed a fraction away from my fingers, quivering.

Eli Semontoya came into the room. He strode over to Palkovich who was directly in front of me. He was a good six inches taller than Palkovich. He pushed his face close to the smaller man. No *wai* this time. "What do you think you're doing?"

Palkovich didn't back up. "What should have been done before. You wouldn't be bothered about this man, so I had to do something."

Semontoya pointed at me. "And that's your way of dealing with him? Cutting off his hand?"

"Only a finger. And not even the whole finger."

"Do you know what you might have done by bringing him here? This man has friends, you know that. The goddamned police. Maybe they were watching him. He might have been followed here."

Palkovich snapped something at his henchmen in Russian. There was an answer, and he said, "You see? They were not followed. They drove evasively to make sure."

"I can only hope you are right."

An arm was still around my neck. I managed to speak. "Could you ask this man to let me loose?"

Palkovich made a gesture and the pressure was removed.

I stroked my throat, grateful to breathe freely again. "Thanks," I said.

Semontoya looked at me, sorrowfully. "Why did you have to come to Jerusalem? You've caused us nothing but trouble."

"Mr. Semontoya," I said, "I didn't come here to give you any grief. Or to get mixed up in any business of yours, either. I came to Jerusalem to look into the murder of a friend of mine. His name was Cormac Blather. Brotman was connected with him and that's how I got into the picture. I don't care about forgeries or anything else you're doing. I was just trying to get some information about the murder."

"Blather. Of course," Semontoya said. "I know the name. Brotman had a connection with him. He was just an outlet for us. Why would we want him killed?"

"That's what I came to find out. To learn if anything here

was connected to his murder. Now I'm sure it wasn't."

"I couldn't care less about any of that."

"I only want to prove to you that I'm not a threat. By the way, was one of those things he disposed of for you an ossuary?"

"You have chutzpah, I'll say that for you," Semontoya said. "I am going to do you a big favor. You are going to leave Jerusalem right now. We will send you back to the hotel, let you pack, and drive you to the airport. Understood?"

"Absolutely."

"Good." He turned to Palkovich. "See? A much simpler solution."

Palkovich smiled. "Eli, the healer. You think you know everything. He is ready to go only because I scared the shit out of him."

I was thinking, *you're so right,* when there was a booming sound like an explosion that seemed to come from the street.

"What the hell is that?" Semontoya said.

Palkovich yelled and the two henchmen ran out of the room. The short one came back in a few seconds and hollered to Palkovich.

"It's the police," Palkovich said. "They're breaking down the door."

"Let's get out of here," Semontoya said.

Palkovich uttered a command to the burly guy who left the room in a hurry, leaving me alone with the two of them. "They will attempt to slow the police down. The back way is our only chance. We have to hope they don't have anyone there."

They started for the door in the wall next to the painting, with Palkovich leading the way. I suddenly realized that neither one of them was paying any attention to me. I didn't hesitate. I knew without having to think about it that I was bigger than Palkovich and fitter than either of them. I hadn't been working out the last twenty years for nothing. I jumped out of my chair and went after them. I pushed Semontoya aside and shoved Palkovich to keep him away from the door. Semontoya tried to push me back but he was yoga and I grew up in New York. I kneed him in the balls and he went down with a groan. I turned and faced Palkovich. We stared at each other for a bit and then he made for the door again, ready to leave his partner behind. We tussled with each other, neither of us accomplishing much.

He broke away and lunged at me, ramming his head into my chest. I went backwards but was able to grab hold of his jacket and hold on. We wrestled trying to throw the other down but not able to do more than push back and forth. I managed to pull one hand away and punch him in the ribs but I couldn't get enough muscle into it to do any good. He tried hitting me back but he couldn't get in a solid blow either. Out of the corner of my eyes I saw Semontoya getting to his feet. In a minute I was going to be outnumbered.

I grabbed onto Palkovich again, spun him around and propelled him into his partner. The contact sent the three of us sprawling to the floor.

We were scrambling, trying to get free of each other and back on our feet when I heard pounding on the stairs. The door flew open. Liat came into the room two hands in front of her holding a gun. Following her were a bunch of men in riot gear, all of them with weapons.

As soon as we saw them we all stopped moving. I disentangled myself and stood up, pretending to brush myself off. "About time you showed up," I said. I quickly added, "Just kidding. Just kidding. I'm very happy to see you."

"Are you all right?" she asked.

"I'm fine."

She snapped an order and the two men on the floor were lifted up and handcuffed.

Palkovich tried to bluff it out. "What are you doing? What is the meaning of this?"

"You are being arrested, Mr. Palkovich. As is Mr. Semon-toya."

"On what grounds?"

The tension went out of Liat. She smiled for the first time. "We'll begin with kidnapping. I believe this gentleman did not come here of his own free will."

"Who told you that?" Semontoya said. "Why don't you ask him?" He looked at me. "Tell her the truth. You came here on business. You know, the Cormac Blather business we spoke of before."

He was obviously desperate. Still, I couldn't blame him for trying. I said, "Mr. Semontoya, the only thing I can think of to say to you is what Brutus said to Cassius: *Farewell! Forever and forever, farewell . . .*"

CHAPTER 57

Palkovich was uttering a long list of curses as he and Semon-toya were led out of the room. Semontoya said nothing. I followed Liat and the others down the steps. When we got outside, I saw dozens of guys in riot gear and vehicles all over the place blocking the street. Neighbors were on the sidewalk on both sides and looking out of windows. The two heavies were standing near a van, their hands handcuffed behind their backs. They seemed unperturbed and stared into space as if they were waiting for a bus. A man with a machine gun was guarding them.

Herb Warshavsky was there looking anxious. "Are you okay?" he asked.

"I am now, but I have to admit, I was getting pretty nervous. They came close to chopping off a finger."

"I'm not surprised. I told you these were dangerous men."

"Since you're here I'm guessing you had something to do with all this," I said. "What happened? How'd you find me?"

"Pure luck. But it wouldn't've happened if I wasn't mad at you."

"Why were you mad at me?"

"You have to ask? After you called and told me that you'd seen Liat and talked with her and all the rest of it, I got seriously angry. I mean, I was irate. Here I am, trying to help you out, and all you do is not listen to anything I tell you. So I went over to your hotel to read you the riot act. Just as I got there I spotted those two gorillas pushing you into a car. When they took off I followed. It wasn't easy. They dragged me all over the city. Luckily, I was able to stay with them. When you all went inside I called Liat."

"I owe you," I said. "Big time. You really saved my ass."

"I thought you said something about a finger," Herb said. Liat and her crew had led Palkovich and Semontoya over to the police van where the other two were waiting. They were getting ready to put them all inside.

I walked over with Herb and spoke to Liat. "Thanks again. Could I speak to these two guys a second?"

"What about?"

"Something to do with my friend back home."

She uttered something in Hebrew to one of her men who put a hand out and stopped Semontoya and Palkovich from entering the van.

"Mr. Semontoya," I said. "I never got to ask you, what ever happened to the ossuary that was stolen from the house in New York?"

Semontoya looked at me as if I were a piece of dog shit he'd just stepped on. "I have only one thing to say to you, Mr. Wanderman. Go fuck yourself." I had the feeling that if his hands were not behind his back he might also have put them together in a *wai* the way he had when we first met. He then snapped at Palkovich. "Idiot! What did I tell you?"

Palkovich muttered something but it was plain he was no longer the happy warrior at a feast. They disappeared inside the van.

"Lucky for you your friend here saw them," Liat said.

"Believe me, I'm well aware of that. And I can't thank you enough for the rescue."

"I'm sure it was not pleasant for you but it was the best thing that could have happened. We've got them by—how do you say it?—short hairs? We can now file charges against them for kidnapping, extortion, and anything else we can think of. In the meantime, we will search this house and see what we can discover. I am sure we will find a treasure trove."

"Fantastic," I said.

"I shall transport them to the station where I have a lot of questions for them. But first we have to secure the house and begin the search. You and your friend must go. I have much work to do."

"I'd like to stay and see what you turn up," I said.

Liat shook her head. "I am sorry. It cannot be permitted. If my boss hears of it I will be admonished."

"That's too bad," I said. "Any chance of seeing you later?"

"I'm not sure. I am going to be quite busy." She turned away and began issuing orders.

"My car's down the street," Herb said. "Follow me."

When we got in, he said, "What was that all about?"

"What was what about?"

"Don't bullshit me, Jake. *Any chance of seeing you later?* Did I miss something?"

"You didn't miss anything. But I don't feel like talking about it."

"Sure. I'm just the guy who saved your life. Why do I have to know anything?"

"All right, all right. Drive and I'll tell you."

Herb started the car and pulled out into the street away from the action behind us. We'd gone a couple of blocks when he said, "Well?"

"Okay," I said. "You remember I told you we were attacked, Liat and me? It was those same two bastards, by the way, the ones you followed. Anyhow, something happened to me afterwards. We were having dinner together and I began to feel very attracted to her. I felt something and I think she did, too. But now I don't know."

"Listen, Jake. I'm not your brother, and I'm not your father, and you didn't ask. But I'm going to tell you anyhow. If you're thinking about getting involved with an Israeli cop you are out of your fucking mind."

"I never heard you curse before. It wasn't anything I planned. But these things happen."

"What things? Did something significant happen?"

"Not yet. Just a hint that maybe our relationship might develop."

"Go home," Herb said. "There's nothing more for you to do over here. Go home and enjoy your life."

"The investigation isn't over. I still don't have a clue as to who killed my friend's father."

"The answer isn't here. You learned that much, didn't you?"

"I guess I did," I said. "But what about Naomi Brotman and her father? Isn't there something I can do to help them?"

"Liat will take care of everything. You can see she's quite capable."

"She sure is."

"Go home."

I knew what he said made sense.

Shakespeare left London and went back home to Stratford but that was at the end of his career as playwright and poet. He was successful, famous and rich. I was going home, but I had to admit the rest of the analogy didn't stand up too well.

Claudio in *Measure for Measure* said it:

> *The miserable have no other medicine*
> *But only hope.*

CHAPTER 58

I was in a quandary. There were still loose ends in Jerusalem. Brotman's problems were not resolved. His daughter, Naomi, was in a messy situation. How would she handle it if those she loved went to jail? I knew I was conning myself with those thoughts. Of course I cared about Brotman and his daughter, but my thinking about them was a device to avoid facing the real issue in front of me . . . Liat.

I knew I was very attracted to her. Beautiful female cops did something to my libido, I guessed. We'd flirted and we'd kissed, but that was all. Were my feelings for her as real as I'd thought? Maybe they were influenced by the excitement of our escaping from danger together. And what, if anything, did she feel for me? One thing was clear, Liat's career was very important to her. It was obvious in her excitement as she came into that room with the gun in her hand. There was triumph in her bearing and in her eyes as she marched the two goniffs out of the house in handcuffs. What did she need me for? I might have been a pleasant distraction for a moment but possibly nothing more.

It struck me that while I'd been in this foreign place I'd somehow managed for the most part to stop thinking about the people back home who were important to me. My friends, my father. Toby, of course. And there was Sienna Nolan, still waiting, perhaps.

Recognize the truth, dummy, I told myself.

And after not much more reflection, that is exactly what I did.

Liat had me file an affidavit detailing the abduction and all that occurred. I asked her to e-mail me anything she might learn about Brotman's dealings with Blather, said my thank you's and farewells to her, to Herb Warshavsky, and to the Brotmans, confirmed a seat on El Al, and with an assortment of mixed feelings and still plenty of aches and pains in my once super-fit body, flew back to New York.

CHAPTER 59

Roger Bouvie, the ambassador's secretary, had kept his word. Landis knew almost to the minute when Jake Wanderman would arrive at JFK and that he was flying with El Al. Landis had been fully informed about everything in Jerusalem that had to do with Jake Wanderman ever since his arrival. What Landis did not know was what Wanderman had learned over there, if anything, and what his future plans were in regard to the inquiry of Blather's murder. He had already decided that if Wanderman continued to poke around, more than a distinct possibility, he would have to be eliminated.

He did not see that as too difficult a task since it had become clear that he himself was not under suspicion. Wanderman's murder could easily be made to look like a random crime, possibly resulting from a burglary. Just as he had staged Blather's demise, so he would do the same with Wanderman.

He drove to Wanderman's house to see what it looked like in regard to access and egress. He also needed to locate a place where he could park in order to observe the premises. He wanted to get another look at the man. He'd seen him once, when he'd first waited to have a talk with McCleod. Wanderman had come out of the house and gotten into his car too quickly for Landis to see much more than that the man was tall and fit.

There was a cross street a short distance from Wanderman's driveway. He found that he could see the driveway entrance if he parked at the end of the street. The house next to him was set far back and the trees where he was parked had full leaves hanging quite low so that his car was almost hidden in the darkness. He turned off the ignition, slouched low in the driver's seat, and waited.

There was very little traffic at this hour on Noyac Road. Occasionally he heard the sound of an approaching car. Lights would brighten the road in front of him then disappear, the road becoming dark and silent again. After a while his thoughts drifted back to his childhood, as they often did, and to his parents. He remembered them vividly, even though he'd been taken from them when he was barely nine years old. They'd been decent parents. They had little money, but even without luxuries the house he grew up in was not a bad one. His parents drank too much and there were bouts of yelling and screaming but nobody had taken it out on him. It had all changed dramatically when his father had gone to jail. He remembered the lack of food and heat in the house. The electric had been turned off at one point. They were eating beans and potato soup, drinking tea to keep warm. Somehow there was enough money for gin when the men began to appear. Rough-speaking men, most of whom paid no attention to him but sometimes there was a kindness. He remembered one man with a nose so red it was almost purple, who'd put some coins in his hand. *Get yourself a treat, laddie,* he'd said.

But, of course, it had all gone to pieces when his father came out of jail a broken man, and not long after hanged himself.

Blather had caused all this, and paid the price. Now there was Blather's friend who had become a dangerous threat. What right did Wanderman have to involve himself and investigate him? He ought to go back to what he'd been before, a miserable nothing of a high school teacher. Wanderman would soon learn that he ought to stay away from what did not concern him.

He looked at his watch and saw that he'd been waiting almost an hour. According to his information, the man should have arrived long ago. Then again, there were plane delays, traffic, perhaps security problems because of 9/11, all kinds of things. He would give him ten more minutes and if he didn't show up, come back another time.

He saw movement and looked out the window. A cat was walking by. It was barely noticeable because its coloring was dark, almost black, and quite small, not much more than a kitten. He opened the door, not worried about the overhead light coming on because he'd removed the bulb. He made kissing noises with his lips. The cat approached him slowly.

"Come here, little kitty. Don't be afraid. Come on, now." He held out one hand and reached into his pocket with the other.

The cat came closer and stopped, but was now close enough for him to reach it. He petted the cat's head and stroked its neck. "Isn't that nice? Don't you like that?"

The cat remained next to the open door of the car, allowing him to stroke it.

"Yes, you do like that, don't you?"

He pulled the knife out of his pocket with the other hand and pressed the button to allow the blade to spring open and lock into place with a click. The hand that had been petting the cat now grabbed it by its neck. The cat struggled to get free but he did not give it a chance. He pushed the blade into its stomach and pulled upwards at the same time so that the stroke gutted the animal in an instant. Even though it was dark he saw blood spurt onto his pants leg.

Instantly, he let go of the animal. It dropped into the street, its legs twitched once, then it was still. He carefully closed the door, reached into the glove box for a tissue and wiped the blade. He started the car and drove away, intending to see what

301

he could do about the blood on his pants when he returned home.

CHAPTER 60

After landing I had to go through passport control. That took a while because getting to the immigration and customs area required a walk through the terminal that seemed like a couple of miles. But the line moved smoothly, the official said, "Welcome home, Mr. Wanderman," and handed me my passport with a smile. The customs guy waved me through and I went out into the main part of the terminal past the crowds waiting for loved ones. Nobody was waiting for me.

By the time I got home it was well after nine o'clock. I hadn't made any arrangements so I was forced to use a commercial van which took hours because it dropped people off all over the Island. At first I was surprised by how dark the night was in Sag Harbor, nothing like night in a big city like Jerusalem, then I remembered having the same feeling on the nights I came back late from the brightness of New York.

I walked into the house, dropped my suitcase, and immediately felt something strange. I knew what it was . . . Rosalind. Her presence and her absence combined and closed in on me. The feeling of total emptiness was a surprise, even though I knew no one would be there. And the shock to my system surprised me even more. I heard a sound like a cry come out of my mouth. Tears filled my eyes. I knew why I was crying. I missed her immeasurably and stilled mourned for her. But what did that make me? What kind of a yutz was I that I was still lusting after other women? It took only another moment's thought and then I was able to smile, because I knew what Rosalind would have said: *Don't be a jerk. Go for it. There's only one time around.*

I guessed that jet lag had something to do with my reaction, too. My legs were suddenly made of rubber and my brain wanted to shut down. I wobbled into the bedroom and threw myself across the bed fully dressed. I was asleep in an instant.

I was wide awake again at four in the morning, aware of my ribs hurting and other assorted aches, but it still felt good to be back in familiar surroundings. My own house, my own kitchen, my book-lined den, and my bed, especially my bed. Unable to go back to sleep I had no choice but to wait for daylight.

My first priority was phone calls. I had to get in touch with Toby, with Sienna, with my buddy Morty, and of course, my father. He was the guy who'd inspired me to go to Jerusalem in the first place. And after all that had happened there I wanted . . . no, I *needed* . . . to hear a friendly voice.

So much had happened but what had I learned from it all? I'd gone there to help find Cormac's murderer but the only thing of value I'd really found was that Aren Brotman had been the one who'd sold the ossuary to Blather. I was pretty sure that Semontoya and Palkovich were telling the truth when they said they'd had nothing to do with the murder. What would it have done for them? Blather was not in their way. The opposite in fact: he'd disposed of the ossuary and everybody had made money.

I needed a fix. At first light I made myself a New York breakfast. Real food, not that Middle Eastern hummus, falafel, lamb. Would you believe I never saw bagels and lox in Jerusalem? But I had a freezer full of them. I saw that I even had cream cheese in the fridge. I opened the container with great anticipation but found blue and green mold all over it. Never mind. I had eggs. I had onions that were still edible because I always stored them in a brown bag in a dark corner of the pantry. I chopped and sautéed the onions, added pepper and sage and thyme. Then came the lox in chunks and the beaten eggs. I ate my eggs loose with a toasted bagel slathered with butter and thought I was in food heaven.

I unpacked, put away the few things that didn't need cleaning or washing and tossed the other stuff in the hamper. I'd brought home the Jerusalem version of brass knuckles I'd taken off the gorillas who'd tried to beat us up. I put it out on one of the small tables in the den as a souvenir. The metal looked like pewter and managed to have a nice gleam.

I noticed the answering machine was blinking at me. There were seventeen messages. I pressed the play button and listened. The phone company wanted me to buy a new long distance program. The cable company wanted to sell me all kinds of expensive ways to watch mostly garbage. There were a few calls from those who didn't know I was away: Morty twice, my father once. Not one from Sienna Nolan whom I also hadn't told. I was disappointed in her. I'd hoped she'd at least want to talk to me after what we'd had together. True, it wasn't a bell-ringing event, but it wasn't a nothing, either. At least, I'd thought so. There was also a call from Rabbi Benvenuti. All he had to say was that he'd call back.

I went back to the kitchen, poured myself another mug of coffee and even though it was only eight o'clock, dialed Toby. I knew it was too early to call anyone but I couldn't hold out.

"Omigod!" she said, sounding very unlike the ultra cool Toby Welch TV personality the world knew. "How come you're back? Did something happen to you? Tell me everything."

"Okay, okay. Everything's fine. I'm fine. Nothing to worry about."

"Then why are you here without a word of warning? Something must have happened."

"A lot happened."

"Then tell me."

I swallowed some coffee and proceeded to tell her the whole story (leaving out Liat) and concluded with, "I'm sorry to say that I'm no closer to solving your father's murder than I was before I went to Jerusalem."

"I'm glad you're safe. That's more important than anything."

"I'm safe. I'm healthy. And I'm here. And I'm not about to let this thing drop. I'm going to follow up with Detective Nolan to see where she is on the investigation. Maybe she's made some progress."

"Not much, I'm afraid."

"How do you know?"

"I spoke to her while you were away. I wanted her to know that I was not one of those people who would just go away if the police didn't do anything. I let her know I have a lot of friends."

I put the coffee mug down. "How did she react to that implied threat? Not well, I'd guess."

"You're right. She got really angry and said she didn't need to be pushed to do her job. She told me she wanted to find my father's murderer as much as I did. But so far, she has not gotten much further than before you left. I told her where you were, by the way."

That made me feel better about why she hadn't called me. "What did she have to say about that?"

"Something like, *good luck,* I hope he knows what he's doing."

"I think it's fair to say that she looks down on my abilities."

"Well I don't. I think you're wonderful. When can I see you? I'd like to hear the details in person."

"I'll be in touch as soon as I get everything done that I have to do."

"Don't let it be too long."

After hanging up I realized once more that Toby's feelings towards me were going to further complicate my life. Mainly because I wasn't sure how I felt about her. It's not as if she were someone I'd met recently. She and Rosalind had been extremely close. Rosalind had even gone to work for her as a personal assistant. When Rosalind died Toby had been kind and considerate. There'd been no romantic thoughts on either side. At least, that's what I thought at the time. But I saw that change. At first I was kind of put off by the whole idea of her wanting to get close to me. It was unseemly somehow. But working with her on her father's murder had brought about a change, subtle at first, then more distinct and obvious as time passed. Now I was definitely feeling something towards her, but still not sure exactly what it was.

I called Sienna at the police department. She'd never given me her cell number. As usual she wasn't there so I left a message asking her to call. I had to wonder about that relationship. Was she going to want to be with me again? I'd assumed I'd be hot to see her but now I wasn't sure. I was filled with all kinds of mixed feelings about everyone it seemed.

I called Morty. At least I knew where I stood with my best friend.

He wasn't home. Sherri answered the phone and told me Morty was in his office at work. "Not everybody is retired, Jake. You should know that."

"I don't even know what day of the week it is, so don't give me a hard time," I said, and hung up. Sherri was not on the list of my all-time favorite people.

There was no point calling Dr. Morty during office hours, although I knew he wouldn't mind taking a break from his patients to talk to me. I'd get to him later, maybe grab him for a quick lunch.

I was having more of that good American coffee and wondering what to do next when the phone rang.

"Jake, I'm so glad to find you home. This is Rabbi Benvenuti."

I'd forgotten that he'd left one of the phone messages.

"How are things, Rabbi? I hope you're not being bothered by another member of the congregation."

"Nothing like that. It has to do with Mr. Blather, though."

"In what way?" I was curious as to how the rabbi and Blather might have had any contact with each other.

"The day you came to my office there was a painting on my wall. I don't know if you noticed it."

"As a matter of fact, I did. It was a Chagall. I assumed it was a copy."

"I was led to believe it was an original. It was given to me as a gift."

"Incredible gift for a small synagogue."

"I thought so. I also thought the purpose of the gift was for tax purposes, you know, writing off a large sum of money."

"No doubt, Rabbi. But what does all this have to do with me?"

"The man who gave me that painting was Cormac Blather."

"That's odd, isn't it? Why would he give that to a synagogue? He wasn't a Jew."

"He told me the painting had come into his hands in such a way that he felt obligated to donate it to a synagogue. And since he'd heard such wonderful things about our little temple and the good work we've done, he felt it was the appropriate place for it."

"Pardon me, Rabbi, but that sounds like a load of bullshit."

"I didn't believe it for a minute, Jake, but I wasn't about to turn down the offer of a valuable painting. Of course, since the murder much has come out about fakes and all the rest of it."

"I don't see what this has to do with finding Blather's killer."

"Neither did I, which was why I'd never thought to mention it before. But there's something else. My office is being redecorated which meant taking everything off the walls. The painting was kind of dusty so I began cleaning it and that's when I discovered something. The back of the canvas was unusual in that it had an intricate series of leaves painted around the edge where it meets the frame. I'd never paid attention to it, but when I began running a rag over it to get the dust off I noticed what looked like initials cleverly worked into the pattern of the design. They were obviously meant to be hidden. Do you remember that artist, Hirschfeld, the one who drew famous people? He was known to hide his daughter's name in his drawings. This was the same kind of thing. I looked closer and made out that the initials were BJK. I assume they must be the initials of the artist who made the fake Chagall. Might that help you in some way?"

"BJK," I repeated the initials out loud. "Doesn't mean anything to me, but I'd like to come over and look at it, if that's okay with you?"

"Of course. When would you like to do that?"

"How about now?"

CHAPTER 61

I was out the door and on my way heading towards the village of Sag Harbor and Temple Adas Israel. I didn't know if this was anything but I was tingling just a little in the hope that somehow, in some way, this might open up a roadmap to the killer.

Traffic was light. There were even available parking spaces on Main Street, an unusual occurrence in modern times and the real estate boom. I drove onto Elizabeth Street, parked in the lot and went in through the side door of the synagogue to find Rabbi Benvenuti waiting for me. There were drop cloths on the floor along with ladders and pails and brushes.

"The painters are gone for the day," he said. He pointed. I looked where he was pointing and saw the Chagall leaning against the wall. "There it is."

The picture was similar to many that the artist was famous for. This one had a horse or a donkey kind of floating in the air. There were odd-shaped buildings and a few strange-looking people and a moon that might have been a sun. The colors were muted and to my untrained eye it looked authentic.

"Look at the back," he said.

I picked it up with both hands and turned it around. There was the pattern he had mentioned. It was a design in black that looked like a doodle with interlocking lines.

"Do you see the initials?" he asked.

I stared at the design and ran my eyes along it from one side to the other but saw nothing that suggested initials. "No. I don't see them."

He put one finger on a spot. "Here. You have to look at it from a certain angle, then it becomes clear."

I did as he said and then I saw them. He was right. I could make out a B J and K intertwined.

"What do you think?" he asked. "Could the initials BJK be anything but those of the artist?"

"I'd guess not. But I'm not sure if it means anything. We know from Cormac's history that he dealt in fakes. It looks like this was another. The question is, so what?"

"I can't help wondering why he gave this to us. It must mean something."

"Not necessarily," I said. "It could have been as you suggested, simply a tax dodge. At any rate, I'm going to do some research. There were a lot of things in Cormac's past that may connect. Who knows? I sure don't. But I thank you very much for telling me about this and showing it to me."

"I hope it helps," said the rabbi.

"If it does, you'll be the first to know."

CHAPTER 62

My initial excitement about the rabbi's painting had gone away. It was a fake, but Cormac had been dealing with fakes forever. I didn't see how the initials of the artist could turn out to be meaningful. But since there were no other leads to follow I thought I might as well see where it took me. I was headed back towards my computer when my cell phone rang. It was Morty.

"Hey, you S.O.B.," he said. "I heard you called. How about lunch? I want to hear what you've been up to."

"Sure."

"It's unusually warm. Maybe the Dockside is doing lunch outdoors. Sound okay?"

"Sure. I'll meet you in five minutes."

It was October, but one of those amazing days with a bright blue sky, hot sun, and temperature in the seventies. Sure enough, the outdoor tables at the Dockside on Bay Street were busy. The food was good, and the location afforded a view of the docks and the water, and in the season, all sorts of boats, everything from a put-put dinghy to a fantastic two-hundred-foot oceangoing yacht that chartered out at a hundred thousand dollars a week. At this time of year only a few boats were tied up but the view was still a pleasant one.

Luckily, there were a few empty tables. I picked up the menu and before looking at it glanced around to see if I recognized anyone. My eyes locked onto the eyes of the last person on earth I expected to see there. Sienna Nolan was more beautiful than I'd remembered. Her green eyes met mine with a kind of defiant look. I immediately knew why. She was with a man, a guy about her age, wearing a suit and tie, something you didn't see much of in Sag Harbor.

"Excuse me," I said to Morty. "I'll be right back."

I went over to her table. I felt comfortable with myself because I had a Jerusalem tan and was freshly shaved. I was wearing a navy polo and chinos, a more normal way to dress in these surroundings than this jerk with a suit. I held my hand out to him. "Hi, I'm Jake Wanderman, a friend of Detective Nolan."

He didn't get up. He put his knife and fork down and tentatively put his hand out as if I might be a transmitter of AIDS. He managed to shake my hand and let go of it at the same time. I hated him instantly.

"Jeff Vanderveer," he said.

"Glad to meet you." I turned to Sienna but did not offer to shake her hand. "And how are you? I called and left a message."

"I've been out all day," she said. "I haven't had a chance to check my voice mail."

I waited a few beats to see if she would say anything else, like tell me who this guy was. She didn't and I could see she was not happy to have me standing over her. They had stopped eating when I introduced myself so the remains of half-eaten salads were still on their plates. I waited a few seconds more hoping it would increase their discomfort. "Well, nice seeing you again," I said. "Enjoy your lunch." I began to leave and stopped. "I'd appreciate a call when you have the time."

I went back to rejoin Morty without giving her a chance to reply.

"Who's that?" Morty asked.

"That's the detective in charge of the Blather case."

"Good-looking lady."

"She is. And smart, too." I didn't say anything more. Neither Morty nor anyone else knew of my thing with her and as far as I was concerned, nobody was going to.

"What's the matter? You look upset," Morty said.

"Do I? I don't know why you'd think that."

"Don't try to hand me any crap. I can read you like a book, always could."

"Okay. I'm pissed because I left a message on her machine and she didn't call me back. And furthermore, she told Toby Welch that nothing new had developed in the case."

"What do you expect, miracles? Most murder cases never get solved anyhow."

"And how would you know that, my expert friend?"

"I read it in *USA Today,* or I heard in on CNN, or some patient told me. What's the difference? I still say you can't expect things to always go your way."

"I'm not asking for miracles. But I was working with her before I went to Jerusalem and I expected she'd at least have something to tell me when I got back. Instead, she doesn't even call."

"Jerusalem? That's where you were? What the hell were you doing there?"

I spent the rest of the time with Morty telling him about my sojourn. I didn't get the pleasure from the telling as much as I would have if I hadn't run across Sienna. I didn't even enjoy the usually great lobster salad.

CHAPTER 63

Mergenthaler, Landis's employer, had become involved with a new woman and for the time being had less need for Landis. This had given him the time to be able to keep track of Wanderman since his return from Jerusalem.

Last night he'd waited in vain for Wanderman to get home from the airport. This morning he'd driven to the man's house early, followed him to the synagogue and waited there for what seemed a very long time. He wondered about what might be going on in there but did not have any ideas. He could do nothing but wait. He was bored, exasperated, but felt it important to follow Wanderman and to observe his movements. It would help him make a decision as to when and how he would do what had to be done.

After Wanderman left the synagogue it was quite simple to follow him to the restaurant. Landis parked across the street and observed him through binoculars. Wanderman was with a man whom he did not recognize. They seemed to be friends rather than business acquaintances but that was just a guess. Landis was quite surprised to see Wanderman suddenly stand up and go over to another table. He followed him with his binoculars and saw none other than that female detective who had interviewed Mr. Mergenthaler and him after the murder. Nolan, he remembered. Detective Sienna Nolan.

He didn't like that. If she was back in Sag Harbor again then he had to presume she was still actively working on the case. He felt he knew enough about Wanderman's personality to recognize that he would not stop investigating Blather's murder. Having him meet the female detective in this venue only reinforced that conclusion.

He sat there watching Wanderman eat his lunch. He put down his binoculars and rubbed his eyes. Once again thoughts of his father and mother returned. They had suffered and he had suffered along with them. Nobody would ever know how their lives had been destroyed. Cormac Blather had shattered his family and ruined his life and now this man, a friend of Blather, was intent on doing the same thing. He felt heat generating in him, flooding his body, rising into his skull. His eyes burned, his temples began to throb. He hoped he would not have another of the headaches that seemed to have recently become a frequent occurrence.

He put his hand in his pocket and reached for the handle of the Beretta knife. He fondled it, enjoying the feel of the bone handle against the palm of his hand. He thought of the cat that had wandered by the other night. It had not been the only cat he'd ever killed. The first one was when he was ten years old, not long after he'd been sent to live with foster parents. They had two other children, two girls both several years older than him who greeted him on his first day with: "You're a creep. Your mother was a tramp and your father was a drunk."

The head of the house worked in a paper-goods factory. At home the wife and both daughters manipulated the father at will. He wasn't able to deal with them and took out his frustrations on the new boy. Landis became the scullery maid, the whipping boy who was assigned every household chore, from washing dishes, putting out the garbage, running errands, and anything else the master could think of.

They lived in a small town some fifty miles northeast of London. There were fields Landis would wander in when he was left alone. One day, he'd come across a stray cat and picked it up to pet it, but the cat squirmed and tried to get away. "Where are you going?" he said, angry that the cat wanted to leave him. He squeezed its neck to make it stop squirming and didn't let go until it was still. When he realized the cat was dead he felt a surge of power. It made him smile. He took the cat further into the woods and covered it with leaves.

After that incident he went out in search of strays. Sometimes, instead of strangling them, he would douse them with lighter fluid and then light a match. But his preference was strangulation. Their necks were so small and soft. His hands would go around them and snuff out their lives in an instant.

No one had ever suspected him. He had always been the perfect foster child, obeying every order, doing every chore, studying hard, and addressing his foster parents and their daughters and his teachers with respect. He'd always been careful to say *Please,* and *Thank you,* for everything, to hold the door for his mother and to do every chore, without complaint, knowing that one day his time would come.

He left them one night when he was sixteen. As a farewell gift, he'd poured gasoline in a corner of the basement and left a long piece of string as a fuse with one end in the pool of gasoline. When he lit the other end he calculated that it would reach the gasoline about an hour after he'd gone. He read about the fire in a newspaper a few days later. It seems the house had burned to the ground and all its occupants killed, except for one that was missing and unaccounted for. The fire was suspicious but no evidence of arson had been found.

He'd been involved with Wanderman for some time now. How long was he going to allow this situation to continue? He rubbed both temples with the tips of his fingers in order to ease the throbbing. It wouldn't be long now. He was quite sure of that.

CHAPTER 64

Cormac Blather had once told me a story about buying fake paintings from an artist back in the days when he lived in London. The artist had gone to jail. Cormac had not. Could this BJK be that artist? If so, what would it tell me? I didn't know but the rule said a lead was meant to be followed. Who made that rule, I also didn't know, but somebody must have so I got on my computer and began Googling.

BJK artist turned up a lot of material, more than two million listings. I had to narrow it down. I tried *BJK artist Great Britain.* Two and a half million. *BJK artist Great Britain forgery.* I tried all kinds of searches and couldn't find anything that connected. There were listings on listings and all over the place. I was at it for hours, following one site to another site and on to another. I took a break, had some coffee and went back to it again. I didn't give up mostly because I was irritated that I hadn't found anything. I knew it was there, it was only a matter of locating the key that would unlock the safe.

I finally found something when I used the phrase, *Art Fraud Great Britain.* The numbers were half a million but the items looked promising. There were sites relating to art forgers, and of police work in art forgery. As usual, there were also hundreds of sites that did nothing for me but waste my time. I was really about to give up when I finally got a hit that paid off. I found an artist that matched the initials. Bennett John Klopf. He apparently had made some impression as an art forger because there was more than one site concerning this guy. Klopf was born in 1934 and died in 1971. The time frame was right in regard to a possible connection with Blather because Cormac had been in London during those years.

The guy's background was rough. He was beaten by his mother. There was a quote from him about her: *She was a big woman and had a powerful punch. She loved to box my ears. After some minutes of this fun she'd tell me that if I did not stop howlin' she'd give me something to really howl about.*

He grew up getting into all sorts of trouble. From minor infractions he eventually hit the big time by setting fire to his school. For that he was sent to the Borstal Reformatory. That turned out to be lucky for him. He showed a talent for art and was encouraged by the teachers to pursue that career when he got out. It seems that he followed the advice and became connected to an art club where he had an exhibition at the age of sixteen.

He went to work for an art restorer named Henry Maslow. Maslow taught him that restoration could mean more than cleaning and retouching. He learned how to improve landscapes by adding to them, perhaps additional shrubbery, or more clouds, or augmenting the color of the sky. From there it was but a step to change signatures on the paintings. He saw Maslow take an old undistinguished painting that he had *improved,* put it into a gold frame, and have a gallery sell it for ten times what it had been worth before.

While at that job he produced original paintings which he entered in art shows. He won several awards and began to make somewhat of a reputation. He married and had a child, a son.

Up to this point it seemed clear that Klopf was not a forger on his own, that he was working under the guidance of Maslow and probably not making as much money as he should have been. Having the responsibilities of a wife and child apparently was all the motivation he needed to produce his own forgeries.

The rest of his biography showed that he became quite successful until at one point a gallery owner noticed something that caused him to decide what Klopf had sold him was a forgery. He was arrested, tried, sent to prison, and died, a suicide, in 1971.

I found another site that connected all the dots. One of the dealers named at the trial was Cormac Blather. When Klopf was arrested he claimed that Cormac Blather had been the mastermind. He had only done the dealer's bidding in his need for money. He didn't deny his guilt but felt that he should not be the only one to pay.

The site gave few details of the trial. Only the essential points were mentioned: Klopf was found guilty and sentenced to three years in prison. There was no indictment of Blather. While in prison his wife had no income and apparently turned to drink and prostitution. When he was released he came home a broken man and in a short time killed himself. The wife was situated in an institution and the child placed in foster care.

BJK. All those years ago, the man Cormac had told me about. When Cormac had originally told me the story I'd felt there was a twinge of guilt in the telling. And now the same artist had turned up on a painting that Cormac had held on to and then for whatever reason, given to the synagogue.

Could any of this tie in with his murder?

While I was pondering this question, the phone rang.

"Hey," Sienna said.

"Hey yourself."

"We need to talk."

"I'd like that. Where and when?"

"No. Not in person. I'd rather talk to you now. On the phone."

The tone of her voice was brittle. She was obviously not comfortable with this but I didn't feel I could do anything but agree. "Sure. Whatever works for you."

"I was surprised to see you today," she said. "Last I heard, you were supposed to be in Jerusalem."

"I came back."

She gave a brief laugh. "So you have."

There was a moment of dead air with neither of us saying anything. Finally, I said, "I thought I might find some connection in Jerusalem with the ossuary and the murder."

"And did you?"

"Not really. But I did find the men Cormac dealt with. The only thing was that it seemed pretty obvious they had nothing to do with his getting killed."

"What makes you so sure?"

"Motivation. There wasn't any. They had nothing to gain from his death. The murderer had to be local and it had to be for a different reason. I'm convinced of that. What about you? Anything happening at your end?"

"Nada," she said. "I wish it were otherwise, but that's the truth of it."

"I'm sorry to hear that."

"No more than I am to tell you."

Again there was a pause, the space between us empty. This time I let it go on. Hey, she was the one who'd initiated the call.

She broke the silence. "The man at the table . . ."

"What man?"

She disregarded my remark. "His name is Jeff Vanderveer. He was the one I told you about when we first met."

"I remember. You broke up because he had so many things wrong with him you couldn't stand to be with him anymore. Isn't that right?"

"This is no good," she said. "I shouldn't have tried to do this on the phone."

"Why not? It's as good a place as any."

"It's not. You're hurt. And you have a right to be. I owe you a real explanation. And in person. Face to face. Is it all right if I come over?"

"I don't think that would be a good idea."

"Why not?"

"I don't know. It's already a *fait accompli*, isn't it? What's the point?"

"Please," she said.

"I don't see what good it would do. You made your choices. First him. Then me. Now him again. Maybe it'll stick this time. You're like Cleopatra: *It is great To do that thing that ends all other deeds.*"

I heard a click. She'd hung up on me.

CHAPTER 65

I went back to the computer but couldn't concentrate. My body was all but twitching, never mind my brain. I needed a change of direction.

I got into my biking clothes, pumped air into the tires of my bike, adjusted my helmet, put on gloves and took off, pedaling as hard as I could. After a couple of miles of hard riding and working up a good sweat I began to feel better.

I tried to figure out why I was so upset about Sienna getting back together with her former boyfriend. It wasn't that I was in love with her. I knew I wasn't. Just as I hadn't been in love with Liat. Unlike Liat, whom I'd managed to kiss just once, I'd been to bed with Sienna. That was a *just once,* as well, and though it had been good, I'd have to say even *very* good, it had only happened because she'd wanted it. It had been *her* move from the get-go, not mine.

So what was bothering me?

I was pedaling along Sagg Road heading toward the beach while I was doing all this thinking, not paying attention to the weather or the scenery or the cars passing me by. All of a sudden I felt a jolt and suddenly the bike was rolling along by itself and I was flying through the air. I was only airborne a brief moment. Then one shoulder hit the ground. I let my body go slack and rolled over a few times before I came to rest. I was on grass at the side of the road and on my back looking up at the sky but not really seeing it.

I knew what had happened. A car had sideswiped me. Car drivers were notoriously unmindful of those of us on bikes, but I still had to wonder if it was deliberate. Maybe one of those Russian guys was still after me. When my eyes were able to focus I looked at the road to see if the car that hit me was there or if anyone had witnessed the accident and stopped to help, but there was nobody. I was alone. If it had been deliberate the driver would have been long gone. If it had been an accident, the person who'd hit me either didn't know about what he or she had done, or didn't care.

I tried to figure out if I was hurt. Happily, I never rode my bike without a helmet securely strapped over my vulnerable skull. I was able to move my right arm without too much pain. My body hurt all over but I could tell my arm wasn't broken, neither was my shoulder. My left arm and shoulder tested out okay as well. Then I checked my legs. Also okay. I sat up slowly. I was bruised, and a little dizzy. I put my head down between my knees and stayed where I was.

After a while I got to my feet and went over to examine my bike. The wheels were not bent. It seemed to be useable. There were some scratches on the paint but nothing to prevent it from working. But my ride to the beach was done. I got back in the saddle and rode slowly and carefully home.

CHAPTER 66

After I put the bike away and came into the house I realized how lucky I was not to have broken anything. I took a long hot shower, stretched out on my bed, and had no trouble falling asleep.

When I woke up it was dark. I wasn't hungry but thought I ought to eat something. I put on a pair of jeans and a shirt, and went down to the kitchen. I poked around in the fridge but found nothing that appealed to me. Instead of eating it seemed like a good idea to go back to the computer and see what mail I might have gotten.

Sure enough, there was a slew of e-mails. I was pleased to see one from Liat.

My dear Jake Wanderman, Surprise to say I miss your presence here. You were most pleasant to be with and I enjoyed so much the time we spent together. I thought you would be interested to know some of the facts I have learned since your departure from Jerusalem. In debriefing Mr. Palkovich and Mr. Semontoya, one of the items that came to light related to the ossuary in which you were interested. It seems they had heard they were being investigated. Because the ossuary had been sold for many dollars to an internationally known businessman they were concerned about the consequences if the forgery were to be discovered. They therefore hired someone to steal it from this individual and then to destroy it. In that way they felt safe.

You might also be interested to know that in spite of Herb Warshavsky's efforts, as well as all of mine, to help Naomi, she has returned to the side of Mr. Semontoya and is doing everything she can to assist him while he remains in custody. It is disappointing to her father and to me, her friend, but I do understand that where love is concerned, there is no logic.

I hope this finds you well and happy.

With all best wishes for you,
Liat

Liat. I said her name out loud to hear the sound of it. I tried visualizing her and remembered the time we were alone in her car. The lights from the hotel had come in through the windows illuminating her face and I'd kissed her. I could all but feel again the sensation of her lips pressing against mine.

It now seemed a long time ago, almost another era. Jerusalem was far away, and my time there had come and gone.

There was much more mail, some from friends, from drug companies, from the Democratic party, from moveon.org, printer ink supply, Travelocity. None from Sienna.

I began to go through it, reading, skipping, deleting ones I knew were of no interest, or possibly spam. I was in the middle of this boring exercise when I heard the front doorbell ring. I was glad to have an excuse to stop.

I left the den/library where I kept my computer and went to the front of the house. I looked out the window and saw someone I didn't know. He was a man in his forties, neatly dressed in a suit and tie. I checked to see if he was holding a briefcase or a bunch of pamphlets, assuming he was either a door-to-door salesman or a Jehovah's Witness, but his hands were empty. This was Sag Harbor. My door was hardly ever locked anyway. I opened the door.

"Mr. Wanderman?" he said. "My name is Landis Kalem. I believe you know who I am. May I come in?"

It took me a moment to recognize the name. When I realized who it was I was somewhat startled but stepped back to allow him to enter. "Of course." He came in and I closed the door. "This is quite a surprise," I said.

He stood stiffly, almost as if he were at attention. He didn't smile. "I beg your pardon for coming at this late hour. But my duties are such that I do not have much time for extracurricular activities."

"You're here on your own then, not at the bequest of your boss?"

"Definitely not at the bequest of Mr. Mergenthaler. He would be quite opposed to my having anything to do with you."

"All right then. Why don't you come with me where we can be more comfortable? Then you can tell me what this is all about." I led him back through the house and into the den where I pointed him to a comfortable chair. "Can I get you anything? A cold drink, or a hard one, if you prefer?"

"Nothing, thank you." He settled into the chair and crossed his legs. His shoes gleamed with polish. His suit was dark gray with a subdued blue stripe in it. It looked expensive. His face was smooth, no moustache, the sideburns cut short, hair neatly trimmed. He placed the palms of his hands together before he spoke. "You're wondering why I'm here, of course." He didn't give me a chance to respond. "Quite simply, it comes down to my sense of responsibility. You informed me that you were investigating Mr. Blather's murder and that you wanted Mr. Mergenthaler to answer some questions pertaining to his acquisition of the ossuary from Mr. Blather, as well as several other items. Mr. Mergenthaler is a very private individual and did not wish to answer any questions regarding his affairs. I asked him several times but he made it quite clear that it wasn't anybody's business but his own and that he had already given the police everything they had asked for. As far as he was

Boris Riskin

concerned, that was the end of it."

He re-crossed his legs and put his hands on his lap. He spoke in such a deliberate manner that I couldn't help feeling he had rehearsed it all before coming here. I was also curious about the slight accent I detected in his speech.

"You've been to Jerusalem, I understand," he said, suddenly changing the subject. "Was it a successful undertaking?"

"Mr. Kalem, I'd love to tell you all about Jerusalem and what a great city it is, but if you don't mind, I'd prefer that you finish telling me why you're here."

"Did you think I was prying? I apologize. That wasn't my intention. I shall continue. I began to think about the murder. I had personally dealt with Mr. Blather for quite a while and also knew a great deal about him. That came about because before Mr. Mergenthaler does business with anyone, he requires a lengthy investigation into the person's background. It is my responsibility to vet everyone with whom he comes in contact.

"My investigation showed that Mr. Blather had an unsavory reputation as a dealer. In spite of that, I recommended to Mr. Mergenthaler that he do business with him because I felt we were really in control of the situation. The fact that we knew of his past gave us an edge in dealing with him. Unfortunately, it is possible that he was still able to outwit us. I do believe the ossuary was not authentic, but since it was stolen, there was no way to prove it."

"Didn't he also sell you paintings that were forged?" I asked.

"I'm not aware of any. What makes you say that?"

How could he not know, or at least not suspect, that Blather had sold Mergenthaler forged paintings? I was about to tell him about Chase McCleod but decided against it. I had no idea how much this man knew and how much he didn't know. I also had a suspicion that he might be full of shit. I shrugged. "Just that he'd done it in the past. You said you'd researched his

328

background so you would know that. Wouldn't you be a little suspicious?"

He was not at all put out by my question. He leaned back in his chair and put the tips of his fingers together. "Of course I was aware of his having done this before. That was why Mr. Mergenthaler had everything inspected by dealers and other experts before he ever bought anything from Blather."

"What is it exactly that you came here to tell me?" I asked.

"Mr. Wanderman, I believe you misunderstood me. I did not have anything specific in mind in coming here. I came to answer any questions you still might have that may possibly assist you in finding the murderer. I felt I had an obligation to do this."

"That's very kind of you, and I appreciate it . . ." I wasn't sure what to say to him. The questions I'd had about the ossuary had all been answered. But still I hesitated to let the guy go without trying to get some kind of information out of him. The question was, what was the question? I followed my instincts.

"Does the name Chase McCleod mean anything to you?"

He thought for a moment, his expression serene, eyes unblinking. "No."

"He was an artist. He forged paintings for Cormac Blather."

"You used the verb, *was*. Does that mean he is no longer with us?"

"Correct. He was stabbed to death in his studio in a somewhat similar manner to the way Cormac was killed."

"How unfortunate. He might have had some vital information about the murderer."

"Exactly. The police thought so, too. He survived the attack and for a while we were hopeful he would give us some information, but he didn't make it. He never was able to talk."

"You say he forged paintings for Mr. Blather. Are you suggesting that one or more of those paintings may have been sold to Mr. Mergenthaler?"

"I can't state it as fact, but I'd be willing to stake a few bucks on it."

"Hmm," he said. "If what you say is true, I'm afraid that places me in a rather delicate position."

"How so?"

"I have to think about whether or not to report this information to Mr. Mergenthaler. You can see what it might lead to . . . a rather unpleasant re-vetting of all the paintings that were previously examined by our experts. And what would that do to their reputations if something were found to be bogus? Of course, their reputations are not what concern me. Frankly, it's mine, because I, of course, chose those experts in the first place. This is most unpleasant news." He stood up. "I think I shall be going, unless you have something else you wish to ask me."

"Nothing at the moment. Would it be all right if I call you sometime if I think of anything else?"

"Of course." He handed me an embossed card. "Would you show me the way out?"

"This way," I said.

I led him out of the den through the living room towards the foyer at the front door. As we approached the door I thought I heard a faint click. I had no time to wonder about what it was because I felt a searing pain in my back. I stumbled and almost fell. As I righted myself I partially turned and saw Kalem with a knife in his hand, bright blood on the blade. *My* blood. He jabbed the knife at me again and this time got me in my right shoulder.

I'd never had any reason to suspect this guy. The only thought I'd ever had about him before this was that he was a smug little prick. My mistake.

The expression on his face was no longer that of a serene gentleman in control of his emotions. He was grinning, but it was not a happy grin. His teeth looked like fangs, his eyes shining like small marbles.

I now understood that this was the guy who'd murdered Cormac Blather and Chase McCleod and was about to complete a hat trick by finishing off Jake Wanderman. While these thoughts were sprinting through my brain with the speed of light I was also able to understand that unless I did something immediately I was going to die.

I was taller and heavier. My only hope was to knock him down and then do what I could to get the knife out of his hand. In desperation I launched myself at him. He was wiry and quick and easily got out of my way. We faced each other, circling. Instinctively, I had my left hand across my body trying to hold the wound in my right shoulder. The wound in my back was bad. I could feel blood already soaking my shirt. He thrust the knife at me, feinting an attack. This caused me to shift backwards to get away from him. As I did my foot caught on the rug and I stumbled. He rushed towards me and thrust the knife into my side, then moved out of range. He stood there, watching me bleed. We both knew it was only a matter of time until I got too weak from the loss of blood to prevent him from doing what he had come to my house to do.

"Why?" I asked. "What did I ever do to you?"

"You're a snoop and you don't stop. Without you I'm in the clear. The police don't have anything."

I closed my eyes in an attempt to recover. I needed to get him to talk. I knew it was hopeless, but I had no ability to use logic any longer. I was just trying to do anything to keep myself alive. "As long as I'm going to die," I managed to say, "at least tell me why you killed Cormac."

The bared teeth had gone. He was still breathing heavily but he had calmed down, apparently because he knew he was in control. "You are trying to stall for time but it won't do you any good."

I was bent over, trying to keep myself from falling down. "You don't have to tell me everything, just why you killed him."

He didn't answer at first, apparently deciding whether or not he wanted to bother. "All right," he said. "My father was an artist with wonderful talent. Blather ruined his life, my mother's life, and because of that he ruined my life as well. Now turn around."

I had no choice. I moved my feet slowly, aware of the blood oozing out of my wounds. I turned so that my back was to him. I heard him take a step towards me. I held my breath and waited for the inevitable.

Suddenly I was falling. He had pushed me. I fell to the floor, my hands breaking the fall and rolled as quickly as I could onto my side so that I could see him. I was as powerless and vulnerable as a baby.

He stood over me, knife held firmly in front of him. "My mother went mad. My father hanged himself with a bedsheet. As the saying goes, *revenge is a dish best served cold*. I hunted him for years and when I finally tracked him down, I set him up to be killed at a time of my choosing."

My brain was working enough to make the connection. "So your father was BJK, Bennett John Klopf."

Kalem took a step and leaned over me, the knife poised to strike. "I was right that you were a danger to me. You know altogether too much."

He thrust the knife towards my heart. I turned aside in a desperate attempt to stay alive. The blade struck at the top of my chest but did not slide in. It must have hit bone. He pulled it back and struck again. This time he went for my stomach. The pain was intense. I could feel blood pouring out of me. I couldn't see anymore. It felt as if a flame was burning inside me.

There was a sound like an explosion but it seemed far away. Then I heard a voice that wasn't Kalem's. It was familiar but I couldn't identify it. By that time I'd lost so much blood I was no longer functioning. Before I drowned in blackness I heard the voice say something like, "Hang on, Jake . . . please . . . don't give up now."

CHAPTER 67

Almost eight weeks had passed since Landis Kalem had done his best to shuffle me off this mortal coil. It was late in December, the first night of Hanukkah and only a week before Christmas. I'd been in the hospital and all but unconscious through Rosh Hashanah and Yom Kippur, holidays that were important to Rosalind. Now I understood that this would be the first Hanukkah without her.

But my friends were going to be with me later: Morty, his wife, Sherri, and Toby and Sienna. Sienna was not bringing her boyfriend, although if she'd asked I would have said it was okay. One or the other of these wonderful friends, along with an aide I'd hired, had been taking care of me since I'd come out of the hospital. Even Rabbi Benvenuti had paid a few visits. My father would also be present, and Zeena, his twenty-seven-year-old companion. They were still not married. Knowing my father, the odds were not favorable for her.

Kalem's knife had missed my spine and heart but had pierced a lung. It had also caused deep cuts as well as minor ones all over my back, sides, and my head. My hands were even badly cut. I hadn't realized I'd instinctively held them in front of me trying to ward off his attack. This, on top of my still unhealed ribs and bruises from the beating I'd had not that long before, and the bike accident, had left me in a sorry and unfamiliar state. But I wasn't complaining. I knew I was lucky to be alive.

The doctors at Southampton Hospital had done a masterful

job. I felt the pain in my body but I was fine with it. They explained it was all part of the healing process. The pain was partially offset by the pleasure of reading about Shakespeare and his times and having philosophical thoughts about the peculiarities of life. In *All's Well That Ends Well* a French lord says, *The web of our life is of a mingled yarn, good and ill together.* Not the greatest thing Shakespeare ever had one of his characters say, but not so bad either.

There was no snow but the air had turned chilly and damp. It didn't matter to me because the only connection I had with the outdoors was to open the door and sniff the air. I still couldn't walk more than a few steps at a time.

I'd certainly misjudged Sienna. During my last phone conversation with her she'd told me she wanted to explain in person why she had gone back to her boyfriend, and what had I done? Insulted her enough so that she'd hung up on me. Fortunately, she still decided to come over. She arrived in time to find Kalem trying to finish the job on me he'd already started. When she ordered him to stop he made a threatening motion. Her response was to shoot him dead.

I was sleeping a lot and eating very little. I knew there would be some sort of special dinner for Hanukkah, hoping to get my appetite stirred. Food still didn't have much appeal for me. Breakfast, lunch, dinner, it was all the same. I was content with cereal, a scrambled egg, or a slice of whole wheat toast. But I was pleased they were coming. That was much more important to me than any food they might bring.

The front door was now locked. Talk about the barn door. I'd given keys to Morty, Toby, and Sienna, allowing me the luxury of being able to lean back in my recliner without having to worry about letting anyone in. I was getting sleepy again and closed my eyes. I imagined that I could hear Rosalind asking me to do something for her but I wasn't sure what it was she wanted, and then I thought I must be dreaming, and then I was asleep.

Murmuring voices woke me up. I heard my father shout, "The boy's awake, everybody. Let's get the party going."

I blinked a few times to get my eyes in focus, and straightened the recliner. My father leaned over and kissed me on both cheeks. "Good job, son. Good job. I'm really proud of you."

"I didn't do a thing. It was Sienna. She saved my life." I noticed there was no one else in the room. "Where is everybody?"

"They're in the kitchen and dining room setting up for dinner." He was holding a glass and raised it to his mouth. "Happy Hanukkah and *Cin-cin*. Can I get you something to drink?"

"No alcohol yet, Dad. But some ice water would be good."

He shuddered and made a face. "Ice water, ugh! That's what sunk the *Titanic*."

I wasn't about to tell him W.C. Fields said it first, but he might have known that already.

They came into the den: Morty, Sherri, Toby, Sienna, Zeena. They kissed me one at a time, saying with straight faces that I looked really good.

"I have some news for you," Sienna said. "They did a DNA check on the skin that was under McCleod's fingernails and it was Landis Kalem's. Not a surprise, but it's nice to have additional confirmation that he was the murderer."

"The only confirmation I want is to know he's actually dead."

"I can vouch for it," Sienna said.

"*Dear God I pray, that I may live and say, the dog is dead!* That's from *Richard the Third*. Act four, scene four. I think it was Queen Margaret but I'm not sure. My head isn't quite right yet."

"Nobody cares who said it," my father said. "But it's an apt quotation." He turned to Zeena. "The boy wants ice water. Would you get him some?"

Zeena looked as if she were going to say *Why don't you get it yourself?* then decided against it. She went out of the room.

Toby, regal and beautiful in an off-white pants outfit, said, "We're going to have a scrumptious dinner. All the classic ingredients for Hanukkah. Chicken soup, chopped liver, brisket, applesauce and potato pancakes. How does that sound?"

"Filling," I said.

"Silly. You don't have to eat all of it. A taste of this and that, just so you know you had a celebratory dinner."

"I agree about the celebratory. I have everything to celebrate: my life and my friends."

Morty snarled, "Don't go getting sentimental on us. If you keep it up I'm going to puke."

Zeena came back with a glass of ice water. We had our drinks for a while and then went in to dinner. The little I tasted was every bit as good as Toby'd said it would be. I didn't ask who'd catered it.

Afterwards, we were back in the den having coffee. I was feeling satisfied and content although tired and sleepy again.

Toby said, "I have a surprise for all of you." She pulled a small notebook out of her purse. "You'll never guess what this is."

"You're right," my father said. "So tell us."

Toby ignored him. She had a strange look on her face. I couldn't tell if it was pride or something else. "I found journals my father kept. They're years and years old. Around the time of World War Two and shortly thereafter. There's a lot of fascinating material about what it was like to be in London during the years of the bombings and the rockets, but that's for those interested in history. For us, here and now, I discovered writings about Mr. B. J. Klopf."

"Who's that?" came from Morty.

Of course he didn't know what she was talking about and

with the exception of Sienna, neither did any of the others.

"He was Landis Kalem's father," Toby said. "An artist my father did business with. Unfortunately it was illegal business. Klopf forged masterpieces and my father sold them. Let me read you something I think is very important." She had the notebook already open to the page she wanted. *"Wednesday, July fourteenth. They've arrested B.J. The poor soul called me from jail, begging for my help. Of course, I went to see him immediately. He was beside himself, all but incoherent, raving about what was going to happen to his wife and son. After much calming talk on my part I was able to discern why he had been arrested. He had made a lovely Pisarro landscape which I had managed to sell for the considerable sum of thirty thousand pounds. What he hadn't told me was that he was so pleased by his work he decided to make another one, identical to the first, and sell it on his own. Unfortunately, the dealer he sold it to happened to visit the gallery where the first one was. Putting two and two together, he called the police. 'I'm sorry, so sorry,' B.J. cried. 'You've been so good to me. Why did I have to become greedy? Look where it's gotten me. What am I going to do?'*

"I assured him I would do everything in my power to keep him out of jail but emphasized that in no way must he ever mention my name as being in any way associated with his endeavors. He assured me that he would follow my instructions. I hired a solicitor, through the auspices of John G., so that the solicitor had no way of connecting me to the case. He did his best but was unsuccessful in preventing jail. I was also quite disappointed to learn that B.J. did, in the course of the trial, give my name to the authorities. Luckily for me, I had been careful to pay in cash and to keep no records that could tie me to him. After he went to jail I sent money to his wife, but later heard that she had had a breakdown and had been put into an institution and her son transferred to a foster family. When B.J. was released from jail, I sent him a large amount of cash anonymously but he was apparently too far gone to make good use of it. I was terribly sad-

dened to hear of his suicide."

Toby stopped reading and looked up.

"Landis killed Cormac because he thought he was responsible for ruining his mother and father's life, as well as his own," I said.

"It was all a mistake," Toby said. "He killed my father for no good reason. It was *his* father's fault that he went to jail, not my father's!"

"What a bummer," my dad said.

Understatement of the year, I thought.

They cleaned up, put everything back in place, and went their separate ways, leaving me alone once more. I got into bed but was no longer ready for sleep. I stared into blackness, thinking about how life is filled with the unexpected. Kalem seeking revenge in error. Chase McCleod dead for no good reason. My death all but certain if not for Sienna.

I realized I was alive due to the assistance of women. Ah, the other sex, with qualities of compassion that escaped most men. They were sensitive to the vagaries of life and had more strength to deal with them than any guy with so-called balls. Now I had even more reason to love and admire them. If it weren't for Liat and Sienna, I'd probably be side by side with Rosalind, except that Rosalind had been cremated and her ashes scattered in Noyac Bay, so that was hardly possible. Oh well, maybe my ashes would commingle with hers some day.

The important thing to remember was that it was fantastic to be alive.

And of course, there was always Shakespeare:

Cleopatra's servant, Charmian, is talking to a soothsayer. He says, *I love long life better than figs.*

Couldn't have said it better myself.

ABOUT THE AUTHOR

Robert Boris Riskin has been writing fiction most of his adult life. He went to the University of Michigan where he studied playwriting with Kenneth Rowe, but switched to fiction shortly thereafter. He did the usual stint at helping his writing career by working at a variety of jobs from dishwasher to busboy to factory worker to selling discounted clothes to high-fashion women. He has published short stories in *The New Yorker* and a variety of literary magazines. A lover of mystery-thrillers, he decided to try writing one. It was called *Scrambled Eggs,* and featured Jake Wanderman, retired English teacher and Shakespeare maven, who is also the hero of his second mystery-thriller, *Deadly Bones.*

A Brooklyn native, he has traveled the world. He lived in France for a few years. One of those years was spent studying at the Sorbonne. The other was on a honeymoon. But New York is where his heart is, as well as the food, family, friends, and the ocean.

He now lives in Sag Harbor at the eastern end of Long Island where the bay and ocean are nearby and the air is filled with creativity.

Please visit his Web site: www.robertborisriskin.com.